HANNAH'S WAR

HANNAH'S WAR

A Novel

JAN ELIASBERG

Little, Brown and Company

New York Boston London

Little, Brown and Company
Hachette Book Group
1290 Avenue of the Americas, New York, NY 10104
littlebrown.com

First Edition: March 2020

Little, Brown and Company is a division of Hachette Book Group, Inc. The Little, Brown name and logo are trademarks of Hachette Book Group, Inc.

The publisher is not responsible for websites (or their content) that are not owned by the publisher.

The Hachette Speakers Bureau provides a wide range of authors for speaking events. To find out more, go to hachettespeakersbureau.com or call (866) 376-6591.

ISBN 978-0-316-53744-5 (paperback) / 978-0-316-53746-9 (hardcover, library edition)
LCCN 2019944145

10 9 8 7 6 5 4 3 2 1

LSC-C

Printed in the United States of America

For Ross, who taught me how to love

"Those blessed with a brilliant mind and a gift for science have a higher duty that comes before discovery, a duty to humanity. Science can be used for good or evil; so it's incumbent upon scientists to ensure that their work makes the world a better place."

—Dr. Lise Meitner

1

They come for me at dawn, as I knew they would. I've slept in my clothes, and I ask if I may step into my shoes. They allow that, but nothing else. He tells me to go outside, and I do. Parked on the dirt road between my barracks and the laboratory is a vehicle the Americans quaintly call a "paddy wagon," an absurdly chipper term for the dank iron trolley that will transport me from Los Alamos to the prison at Fort Leavenworth, where I will wait again (not for long, I fear) for my perfunctory trial and inevitable execution.

The chain reaction leading to my death has been accelerated by my own divided heart. I see that now in a way I never could when all was theory, white chalk on blackboard, equations like pale bones scattered across scorched earth. The man I shouldn't have trusted latches the manacle around my wrist and fixes it to a hasp welded hard to the bench.

"I'll protect you," he says, with such earnestness it makes me smile.

"You're lying again."

He glances over his shoulder. Sufficiently assured that no one can see us, he takes my face between his hands. "I will protect you, Hannah. If I can."

I think he might kiss me, but that would be a danger to both of us. He is a meticulous and cautious man by nature, skilled at the art of keeping secrets. Most lovers are. I have limited empirical evidence to support this hypothesis, having loved only two men, but both of them held truth at a safe distance. Safe for them, not for me. His promise of protection—however well intended—doesn't comfort me. So I comfort myself with equations.

The distance from the laboratories in Los Alamos, New Mexico, to the prison compound in Fort Leavenworth, Kansas, is 874 miles. We left when dawn was still a wishful glow behind dark mountains. We are traveling, I estimate, at an average speed of forty-two miles per hour, allowing for stops—

Oh God. Will they stop? Will they allow me that simple comfort?

No. I won't think about that. The equations. Stay with them. I drum the fingers of my free hand, playing an invisible keyboard, on the metal beside my legs. This is my habit when I run numbers, drumming my fingers on hard surfaces, desks, and tables. A distance of 874 miles at an average speed of 42 miles per hour creates a probability of 20.8095 hours of actual travel time, plus the approximately 27 minutes it would take for the MPs to force the paddy wagon to the side of the road, slide a bag over my head, and—

Stay with the equations.

"I will protect you, Hannah," he said. "If I can."

A distance of 874 miles, leaving at dawn, allowing for the variable *If I can*.

2

The sun burned a hole in the haze; blistering sand sizzled against the electric-blue sky in a crackle of pure white. The machine-gun *WHU-pa-WHU-pa-WHU-pa* of the rotor blades clattered overhead, and as the helicopter banked to land, Major Jack Delaney could see its shadow on the flat sand below. It was a vertigo-inducing view, but Jack scanned the terrain with an unflappable, predatory gaze.

As they descended between mountains carved out of the earth in striated gashes of red, a dust storm rolled slowly forward, obscuring the horizon. The copter approached a primitive landing strip, two crossed lines etched into the parched earth, and the pilot danced on the pedals to correct for crosswinds, hovering for a long moment, then settling. As the rotors ground to a slow stop, he checked his watch and said, "You can step out now, sir." He handed Jack his regulation army duffel and a black umbrella. "For shade, sir."

The pilot flashed a cowboy grin, and less than a minute later, with a brash clamor, the R-4 was gone, leaving Jack in a whirling cloud of dust. A trickle of sweat and impatience teased the back of his neck. No matter the high security of the mission, it struck Jack that they were going overboard with the cloak-and-dagger secrecy of this place. Raising a hand to shade his eyes, he squinted at what looked like a long, shimmering rattlesnake on the far horizon: a string of army supply trucks crossing the desert, making for the distant hills. The head of the rattler—a long black Buick flanked by two light utility vehicles—peeled away from its body and rolled down the mountain toward the airstrip where Jack stood with his duffel and open Mary Poppins umbrella, an odd accessory given the obdurate dryness of the place. The Buick barreled toward him through the heat waves, a tiny black nucleus in the highly thermal middle of nowhere. When the cars reached his position, the escort vehicles waited at a respectful distance as the driver of the Buick rolled down the window.

"Major Delaney?"

Jack nodded. The driver got out and extended his hand.

"Collier. First sergeant. I'll be working alongside you. Orders of General Groves. He'll meet us at the base."

Collier deposited Jack's duffel with the umbrella in the trunk. By the time the sergeant was back behind the wheel, Jack had accurately sized him up: a high-energy Midwestern bootlicker eager to do his master's bidding.

"I was expecting my assistant," said Jack.

"Jewish fella?"

"Lieutenant Epstein."

"Came in by train last night," said Collier. "Said he wanted to avoid the heat."

"Smart man, Epstein."

"Aren't they all," Collier huffed. "Jew number-crunchers. Kraut scientists. Feels like I died and woke up in New York City."

Jack laughed, crookedly tickled by this. After rolling up his window against the acrid stink of diesel fuel, he settled into the back seat and perused the orders commanding him to report to this location, specifying where and when but neglecting to mention why. Whatever the military were doing in New Mexico, they were determined to keep it highly classified, but Jack didn't need his own role spelled out—he was here to catch a spy.

The war had laid bare the limitations of the FBI when it came to the larger scope of international intelligence. The Office of Strategic Services was the purview of William Donovan, and Donovan had handpicked a pungent collection of thugs, post-debutantes, millionaires, professors, military professionals, and corporation lawyers, all of whom operated under high tension and in whispers.

When Donovan turned his discerning eye toward corner offices, he found men like Jack Delaney making better-than-good livings as they took turns outwitting each other in courtrooms, boardrooms, and back rooms.

"Maybe your talents could be put to better use," Donovan had suggested to Jack as they cooled down after a game of squash.

"Doing what?" Jack asked.

"What you do now. Only with higher stakes."

"And what is it that you think I do?"

"I think you ask the right questions," said Donovan, "and you know when you're not getting the right answers. That's a marketable skill when there's a war on."

He was right. It turned out that Jack had an unusual talent for sussing out the stories people didn't want to tell. Even the smoothest lie snagged his ear like a slightly out-of-tune piano key. Within two years, he'd proven himself a savvy interrogator and a rising star in the intelligence world. After Jack was wounded, Donovan had pulled him out of the European theater and consoled him with the assurance that an even brighter future awaited Jack if he succeeded at this particularly sensitive mission. Was that a carrot or a stick? Jack still wasn't sure and his uncertainty buzzed, an insistent, low-frequency thrumming under every conversation and every silence.

"You're wasting your time here, Major," Collier opined from the front seat with just enough artful politesse to conceal the extent of his disdain. "Me and Groves—we got this place tight as a tick."

The ambitious verbal alliance of "me and Groves" caused a twitch at the corner of Jack's mouth. "Hardly tight," Jack commented. "Seventy-two concerned scientists have signed a petition demanding ethics oversight of—"

Collier cut in, throwing Jack a dismissive glance in the rearview mirror. "Some of the longhairs got their panties in a knot, felt the need to voice opinions about how their work is going to be used. Got it off their chests; now they're back at it. That's all that matters to General Groves."

The Buick bounced and fishtailed up the mountain road, Collier hauling on the wheel in a desperate tug-of-war with each hairpin turn and switchback. The road was under construction as far as the eye could see. The air reverberated with the sound of jackhammers. The half-finished roadway was crowded with backhoes and bulldozers perched at the edge of the perilous drop-off. For a top secret mission, it seemed absurdly random and improvised. As the Buick, all kinetic energy, crested the final peak, Jack was overcome by a sudden alertness, a combination of the altitude and the stinging blue of a cloudless sky. Encircled by tiers of cyclone fencing, a bizarre encampment of barracks and jerry-built structures sprawled across the flat mesa like a poorly thrown hand of jacks. Collier presented the proper documentation at the well-guarded sentry gate and pulled into the compound.

"There's your office over there." Collier pointed to a Quonset hut on the corner of an unpaved intersection. Lieutenant Aaron Epstein stood on the stoop, his high forehead glistening with sweat above his thick, military-issue acetate spectacles. Collier pulled to the side of the rutted road, got out, and popped the trunk. "Your quarters are up the street there on the right."

"I think I'll pay a visit to the lab first," Jack said, getting out of the car.

"Actually, sir, General Groves would like to see you as soon as—"

"Certainly. Right after I visit the lab."

"Sir, yes, sir. You'll have the use of this car during your stay." He lobbed the keys to Jack, who grabbed them on the fly and tossed them to Epstein.

"Good to see you, Lieutenant. Anything new?"

They fell into an easy lope, heading to the makeshift office.

"There is," said Epstein. "Censors snagged this."

He handed Jack a Western Union telegram. Jack fingered it, troubled. He recognized the name of the intended recipient from a list of Swiss scientists who did a lot of coming and going across neutral borders. TO: GREGOR STERN. LET ME KNOW SABINE'S ALL RIGHT. STOP.

Uninvited, Collier slipped into the office with them, the door bouncing, then slamming shut behind him.

"I interviewed the Western Union operator who reported it," said Epstein. "She insists a twelve-year-old boy brought it in."

"Makes sense," Collier said. "If there is a spy here, he's no dummy." He laughed at his joke and glanced over at Jack like a puppy expecting a treat. Seeing Jack's stony expression, he fell silent.

"Sergeant Collier," said Jack, "this telegram suggests that one of your people might be in covert communication with our foreign adversaries."

"*My* people? I can assure you, sir, they are not." Collier's tone was clipped tightly within the bounds of deference to rank.

"We'll start the questioning with the European scientists who've signed the ethics-oversight petition."

"There's four thousand scientists on the Hill, sir. Two-thirds of them are European."

"Then we'll start with the German-speakers who've signed the petition and are working directly on the bomb."

"Gadget," said Collier. "Orders are we call it the gadget, sir."

Epstein pushed his glasses up on the bridge of his nose. *"Oishe geveine lech."*

"Yeah, you'll get along with the eggheads." Collier grunted something between a snort and a snicker.

"Allergies, Sergeant?" said Jack, but Epstein took the barb without flinching. He was used to it, Jack figured.

Epstein indicated a substantial stack of files on Jack's desk. "I've pulled personnel files for all the scientists who've signed the petition. There's Reichl; he's the one who initiated it—"

"The shit disturber who thinks a bunch of eggheads know more than top brass," Collier interjected.

"And Weiss—"

"German as knockwurst and sauerkraut."

"Austrian, actually," Epstein corrected him.

"Were there any Americans present the day they taught nuclear physics?" Jack wondered.

"Well, Oppenheimer," said Epstein.

"Pink as a stuck pig," said Collier. "General Groves wants to see you as soon as you get settled."

"Certainly," said Jack. "I'll check in with him after I visit the lab."

"Sir, yes, sir."

"Don't worry, Sergeant, I'm not here to step on any toes," said Jack. "Dismissed."

"I'm dismissed," Collier said, wincing. "You'll miss me when I'm gone."

"I'll take my chances."

He dug into the first file and found J. Robert Oppenheimer staring up from a photograph paper-clipped to a regulation personnel form, eyes gleaming with preternatural focus, a cobra about to strike. Jack saw in his gaze the arrogance of a spoiled child whose sullen depression might swing toward the erratic if he didn't get his way.

He skimmed Oppenheimer's curriculum vitae: Born in New York in 1904, the pampered, precocious son of wealthy Jewish parents. A Phi Beta Kappa wunderkind at Harvard, speeding through in three years, then on to Cambridge, where he confessed to putting a poisoned apple on his tutor's desk. While teaching at Berkeley and Caltech simultaneously, he had earned the respect of the world's most eminent physicists as well as a coterie of admiring students who imitated his elegant gestures, their ever-present cigarettes dangling from their lips at rakish angles and porkpie hats slicing dark shadows across their foreheads.

Anecdotal reports described him as "brilliant but aloof," "lost in abstractions," pretentiously injecting among his equations quotes from Hindu scripture and the Bhagavad Gita. One thing seemed certain: He was an odd duck. Hardly the man one would trust to lure the world's greatest scientists up to this lonely plateau for a quixotic mission rife with intense personalities and unpredictable circumstances.

Jack gathered the files into his satchel, and he and Epstein walked a few hundred yards up the street to the Tech Area. The place looked more like a prison than a laboratory. Surrounded by armed guards and spirals of razor wire, tall, artless structures stood in harsh contrast to the red shale and pink sandstone cliffs behind them. In the space between, whorled piñon trees grew up from the fallen boulders and gently eroded slopes.

Jack's gaze traveled up the wall, tracing each window, drawn inexorably to a shadow on the second floor. A woman stood behind the glass like a modern-day Rapunzel surveying the world from her unassailable tower. The elegant lines of her head and neck opposed the restraint of her high collar and the severe cut of her lab coat. In the brief moment before she noticed Jack and moved away, she seemed to be exactly where she belonged, framed in the window like a portrait.

3

D r. Hannah Weiss pushed a dark curl from her forehead, studying the arid landscape through coils of concertina wire. Beyond the hodgepodge of rustic cabins, Quonset huts, and guard towers, the desert teemed with unseen life and ancient secrets. There was no place like it in Europe. No place like it anywhere else on Earth, perhaps. Its parched singularity offered her the hope that its purpose, too, was singular, never to be repeated, no matter how history would be rewritten by their work here. She and her colleagues held tight to the belief that the war would end, this ad hoc community would disband, and Roosevelt's promises—his belief in divine justice and essential human freedoms, his commitment to preserve civility and human kindness, everything that made for a good State of the Union address—would usher in an era of peace and progressive thought.

The compound known as Site Y had previously functioned as a ranch school for boys. Now the old classrooms were crowded with laboratory equipment rather than wooden desks. Instead of faculty dinners and alumni mixers, the stately timber-built Fuller Lodge hosted rowdy parties that lasted into the early morning. Los Alamos had left the rest of the world behind and all the rules of engagement with it. Few had known what they were signing up for when they came, but no one talked about giving up on the difficult work at hand. They were creating the Weapon to End All Wars, placing a feat of unspeakable genius between a madman and the world he intended to destroy. Tensions had to be vented. Steam released. What was the occasional indiscretion compared to the impending possibility of world peace on the one hand or mass extinction on the other?

The gravity of the task was never far from Hannah's thoughts. It kept her from caring about the lack of creature comforts. When climbing up and down the ladder at the tall chalkboard left her calves aching, she imagined her uncle Joshua at *Appell,* compelled to labor in all weather and for hours on end. She gave thanks for his easy humor and deep faith, which would surely stand him in good stead no matter what horrors he endured. When the dry wind made her hands cracked and raw, she thought about Sabine, wherever she might be—finishing her studies in New York, perhaps, walking up Broadway with tears in her eyes from the wind. And knowing that walking in the bitter cold was the least terrifying scenario facing Sabine, Hannah forced herself to focus on her own task, ignoring whatever gossiping or trysting was going on around her.

Her life at Los Alamos was simple and isolated. She was a woman working among men. They were afforded freedoms not available to her. In the black-market shack, she bargained for lipstick—that was a necessity—but stockings were a thing of the past, far down the list of items that mattered. She hoarded her sugar and flour coupons to trade for notebook paper and no. 2 pencils.

The wives of the other scientists had things sent to them from home, and a few of them made dresses to sell, but Hannah carefully mended the clothes she'd had with her when she arrived: three straight skirts (black, gray, and dark red), two blouses (one white, one pale rose), a modest peplum suit (navy blue with fine black piping), a pair of oxblood pumps that worked with any combination of the above, and a small treasury of undergarments purchased the last time she was in Vienna. She slept in a camisole, having traded her nightgown for a dog-eared copy of Einstein's *Science and Religion*. Hannah kept her thick dark hair swept back neatly from her face and tucked into a tight roll secured by an intricately jeweled comb, her only concession to femininity, the only artifact of a life in which she—for a moment, at least—had been made to feel precious. Hannah traced the hard edges of the comb with the tip of her finger as she studied the world beyond the familiar window.

On the road below, she saw two men closing in on the lab area with the subtlety of sharks scenting blood. Sergeant Collier had dropped them off. She knew Collier—they all did; he was General Groves's lackey. Hannah had noticed the bespectacled man in the cafeteria the night before, wearing khakis, dining alone in a corner, nearsightedly perusing the contents of a manila file folder that he held too close to his face. The other man, the cut of his suit too dapper for wartime with its vest and wide notched lapels, was a stranger, but Hannah had seen his kind before and immediately knew what he was. She recognized the set of his jaw, that "lean and hungry look," the narrowing of his eyes as his gaze crawled up the wall like a click beetle. His kind usually entered the encampment in the haze of late evening. They were typically gone by dawn the following day, and Hannah was never surprised to discover that one of her colleagues had disappeared as well.

"So what's the problem this time?" Oppenheimer rapped a bony knuckle on the chalkboard behind her. "We can't fold up our tents now. Hitler knows the Allies are on his doorstep. If the Germans have the bomb…well, I don't have to spell it out."

As Hannah turned away from the window, squinting against a cataract of sun, she was reminded again of the contrast between their grand mission and their improbable surroundings. The small Critical Assemblies Team, of which she was a part, had been corralled into Technical Area 18, a cheap wooden structure dangling perilously off the rocky outcropping at the top of Omega Canyon. Her colleagues looked as if they were in the giddy first weeks of adventure camp. On nights when it snowed, they would bang on doors before sunrise saying, "Wake up! Let's go skiing!" Missing breakfast, they would stagger into work, thumping their hiking boots together until small chunks of snow and ice drizzled to the floor.

Peter Reichl, his ample stomach bulging prominently beneath a hand-knit woolen vest, spoke up. "We've gone as far as we can go without actually creating an atomic explosion. How can we prove our theories without—without…" He made an expansive gesture with his hands, unable to articulate the magnitude of the problem.

"Without igniting Earth's atmosphere?" Hannah volunteered.

"Roosevelt would probably frown on that," said Oppenheimer. He lifted his cigarette to his mouth with a fluid, feline elegance, took a deep, theatrical drag, and slid Hannah the off-kilter smile that made him the center of attention with the ladies. "How does our lovely Cassandra think we should test the untestable?"

Hannah was unmoved. "Stick to the lab assistants, Oppie. It's been a long time since a man managed to charm me into doing what he wanted."

This prompted a bubbled giggle from Alice Rivers, the only other woman in the room. Where Hannah was self-contained, Alice seemed always in need of rearranging—her mended stockings springing new ladders, cardigan unbuttoned to show a bit too much cleavage, unruly curls escaping the constraints of her bandanna. Alice spent her days waiting patiently for the scientists to say something brilliant while dutifully jotting down everything they said—brilliant or not—in a notebook, each quote tagged with the initials of whoever was speaking. She was quick to emit an infectious giggle, something that kept her in her post when other stenographers, all dour faces and chunky brogues, might have done a better job. Oppenheimer echoed Alice's laugh, but Hannah observed that his eyes appeared more darkly sunken than they used to be, more wary, less ready to spar.

Because Hannah was always quiet unless she had something consequential to offer, her colleagues came to full attention when she approached the chalkboard, slid the ladder to one end, and climbed a few rungs. As she scrawled the first few figures of a lengthy equation, she posited the question tormenting them: "Why exactly would an atomic explosion blow us to bits?"

Peter Reichl wearily repeated what they already knew: "Uranium two thirty-five reacts so quickly, there's no way to control it. The metal housing will be instantly converted to a fireball."

"Do we have to use metal?" asked Hannah.

"You want us to build a bomb out of Lincoln Logs?"

Hannah glanced over her shoulder and smiled. "I was thinking of gingerbread."

Reichl looked abashed; he hadn't meant to be so snappish.

"But here—oh, wait—" Otto Frisch, as was his habit, had been pacing, a contrail plume of cigarette smoke following him around the room. His western shirt was a size too small, so his neck, wrists, and hands extended out like a scarecrow's. He pressed his palms together as if to contain his idea. "What if we mix the uranium with hydride? That would slow the reaction time."

"Only by an exponent of ten," said Hannah. "Still too fast to control it."

"But what if we exposed it for only a split second?"

"How?" Oppenheimer leaned forward as if he could will the idea into being. The scientists listed forward as well, Oppenheimer the choreographer and they his dancers.

"By dropping the core through a hole in hydride blocks." Frisch motioned to Alice, who nodded and initialed and jotted furiously.

Hannah pondered the possibility for a moment and then began

another equation. "And that leads us to the inexorable question—how do we trigger it?"

"That's what you're here to figure out," said Oppenheimer, rising from his chair with loose-limbed ease and striding with long, decisive steps toward the door. "How to tickle the dragon without waking him. And how to do it before the Germans blow England to smithereens."

4

FIELD NOTE

CONFIDENTIAL

HEADQUARTERS

U.S. ARMY AND EASTERN MILITARY DISTRICT

303 Counter Intelligence Corps

APO 403

April 3, 1945

SUBJECT: SITE Y SECURITY CONCERNS

To: Donovan

From: Delaney

SUMMARY: (1) On March 13, 1945, it came to our attention that a petition calling for ETHICS OVERSIGHT of gadget implementation was circulating among scientific community. (2) On April 3, 1945, agents of this detachment arrived to find Site Y as expected—security tight as a bug's ass, climate dryer than dog biscuits, pedants roaming unobstructed—and learned that censors had intercepted a telegram addressed to STERN, Gregor, a Swiss person of interest.

RECOMMENDATION: Personnel who signed petition have been identified for enhanced background checks; they include Critical Assemblies Team members REICHL, who initiated the petition, FRISCH, WEISS, SZILARD.

5

Jack shifted a Ping-Pong paddle from hand to hand, casually studying Peter Reichl across the broad green table. Reichl seemed a pugnacious, competitive sort, so Jack had let him score the first few points, but not without making him break a sweat. The Ping-Pong table in the rec room at Fuller Lodge had seen a lot of action when the place was a school for boys, but it was still in decent shape. The same could not be said for Peter Reichl. Countless late nights, an affinity for rich Austrian schnitzel and Sacher torte, and an abundance of alcohol manifested themselves in his spare tire and extra chins. Rivulets of sweat dribbled down his brow and behind his ears, leaving damp spots on his collar. Sparse silver tufts of hair sprouted at his temples, and his skittish movements made him look a bit like a jack-in-the-box. Playing the good-natured loser, Jack shucked off his jacket, loosened his tie, cuffed his shirtsleeves, and let Reichl score a few more. As far as Reichl knew, he was winning a friendly game over which two gentlemen were having a friendly conversation. They were on the same side, after all. Weren't they?

As he slammed down on the ball to return Reichl's errant high shot, Jack felt a familiar throbbing deep in the tangle of nerves and arteries of his brachial plexus and quickly shifted the paddle to his left hand. He spiked his next return, compensating for any noticeable weakness. Jack confined the scope of his questions to an affable survey of who was who in the world of nuclear physics but listened with interest when Reichl went off on a tangent about a particularly illustrious conference at the Kaiser Wilhelm Institute in Berlin. Jack didn't have to look over his shoulder to know that Epstein was taking notes just in case the constant *ka-chunk, ka-chunk* of the Ping-Pong ball impeded the microphone under the table.

"Who attends an event like that?" Jack asked.

"Everyone attends."

"Define *everyone*. Just for kicks."

"Faculty, students, alumni, scientists."

"What about Kurt Diebner?"

"Of course. He was an adviser to the Reichswehrministerium at the time."

"The Reich ministry of defense," Jack clarified for whoever might be monitoring the hidden recorders.

"Diebner." Reichl expelled a disgusted puff of air at the recollection, and his expression went dour. "Oh, yes. He was there. Practically wearing his Nobel around his neck. He and Stefan Frei were holding court in front of all the luminaries, fairly tripping over each other pushing Albert Speer to fund their research."

"Stefan Frei?"

"Goldenes kind." Reichl let the ball go by and stood panting. Sweat stains now soaked the armpits of his white shirt. "The charmed Adonis with blond hair, a profile etched like a sculpture of ice, born with—*ach,* what is the expression?"

"Silver spoon?"

"In horse's mouth, *ja.* Privilege of privilege." Reichl nodded, setting up a sullen volley. "A brilliant theoretical physicist. No one could deny this. I only suggest that, had his father been anyone other than the director of the Kaiser Wilhelm, perhaps he would have had to work a bit harder to maintain his position—and his success with the ladies."

"I see." Jack caught the ball in the palm of his hand and placed it in his pocket. Huffing a little and wiping his brow for effect, he gestured to a couple of cracked leather easy chairs a bit closer to a microphone he knew was tucked under the lip of the coffee table. In case things got interesting.

"Dr. Reichl, you didn't leave Germany until…"

"'Forty-one."

The men sat. Jack opened a file and began placing equations, lab reports, and photographs on the coffee table in front of them. One photo captured a group of scientists, black-coated and bespectacled, standing on the steps outside the Kaiser Wilhelm Institute in Berlin. There were four Nobel Prize winners in the group, and Jack knew Reichl wasn't one of them.

"I'm afraid my Jewish colleagues saw the writing on the wall long before I did." Reichl sighed. "Most of them had emigrated by '36. They were smarter than I, and not just at science."

Jack took the Gregor Stern telegram from his breast pocket and smoothed it out on the table. Reichl seemed mildly surprised.

"The telegram? That's what this is all about?" he said. "I assumed it was about my petition."

Jack held his gaze steady, listening to the silence and Reichl's still slightly labored breathing. Jack understood that people abhor silence the way nature abhors a vacuum; they rush to fill it with the same uneasy alacrity. In his experience, the power of silence had provoked many an anxious confession.

"You'd think I was agitating to take over the government, not safeguarding the bomb's possible use," sputtered Reichl. "All my petition does is present a necessary warning: Any nation using these newly liberated forces of nature for purposes of destruction must be prepared to bear responsibility for opening the door to an era of devastation on an unimaginable scale."

"Yes," Jack said with a calculated edge in his tone. "But we're talking about the telegram."

Reichl shrugged. "It's a telegram."

"You admit to trying to send it to Gregor Stern?"

"I admit to giving a Mexican boy a quarter to take it to Western Union."

"Why not take it in yourself?"

"The petition hasn't exactly made me the teacher's pet." Reichl folded his arms across his ample belly. Defensive, Jack observed, but not about to offer up much.

"The Swiss-Soviet trade deal remains in place, as I'm sure you know; a scientist based in Switzerland could be a valuable liaison to the Russians."

Reichl barked a quick, nervous cough. "You G-twos imagine Bolshies in every corner; you're reading too much into it. Gregor Stern is a close friend. I've been concerned about his wife, Sabine. She's been in poor health."

Jack let him wallow in that for a moment before he said, "It must be hard for a physicist in Switzerland. Here you are, working with the greatest minds in modern science. Stern must feel left out of it all."

"Gregor has plenty to do," Reichl said sharply. "There's more to physics than building weapons, you know."

Jack took this in without comment; he waited precisely five seconds before he said, "And, of course, he has Sabine to care for."

"Of course." Reichl nodded emphatically.

Jack folded the telegram back into his breast pocket and began gathering the array of evidence on the table; he carefully tucked each item back into the manila folder.

"That's it?" said Reichl.

"For now."

Taken aback, Reichl struggled up from the easy chair and left with a curt "Good day, Major."

Jack took a long look at the photo of the scientists lined up on the steps of the Kaiser Wilhelm as he absently batted the Ping-Pong ball against the wall. It had been easy to miss the only woman in the picture. She stood at the far end of the group, petite and serious, edged out of the hierarchy. There was much he didn't understand about the Reich's scientific pecking order, but it was clear that Diebner and Frei—right in the center of the frame and accustomed to taking up space—were at the top of it.

"Next," Jack called, suspecting that Collier was eavesdropping right outside the door.

Sergeant Collier barreled in before Epstein had even risen from his seat. Jack's expression remained unchanged, but the batting of the little white ball ratcheted up to a tense *ka-TACK ka-TACK ka-TACK.*

"Reichl admitted to trying to send the telegram," said Collier. "That's what we're after."

Again with that ambitious "we," Jack observed. Jack gave the ball a decisive whack, sending it caroming off the wall and into a wastebasket.

Epstein cleared his throat softly. "Sergeant, did you know Gregor Stern is a mechanical engineer, not a physicist?"

Collier looked at him, not understanding.

"Neither did his 'close friend' Peter Reichl. And who the hell is Sabine?" said Jack. "So who's next?"

"Weiss."

"Bring him in."

Jack didn't miss the smug expression on Collier's face. Collier was that guy who calculated the bar tab to the last penny, never wanting to pay for more than his own share, a small man who relished the instant between realizing he knew something you didn't and letting you know it.

Collier opened the door and said, "Dr. Weiss." And then savored Jack's reaction as Hannah Weiss stepped into the room.

Jack rose from his chair, brushed his shirtsleeves back into place, and fumbled briefly with the buttons at the cuff before he offered his hand.

"I'm Major Delaney," he said. "This is Lieutenant Epstein. And you know Sergeant Collier."

"We've met. More often than I care to think about," said Hannah.

"Please, have a seat." Jack indicated the chair by the bugged coffee table, but Hannah remained standing. Her eyes were a startling pale blue, piercing, with an otherworldly glow, a contrast to her glossy brown hair swirled into a French twist at the nape of her neck.

"May I ask what this is about?"

"Simple background check. We'd like to get to know you, hear about any concerns you may have."

Hannah smiled wryly. "Is that what you told Peter?"

"Is he a friend of yours?"

"We're both Viennese. We work together," she said. "The poor man is constantly hounded by you intelligence people."

"Why do you assume I'm—"

"You didn't even stop at your barracks before you started interrogating us." She glanced at Jack's duffel in the corner. "I notice things."

"Fair enough." So much for pretense, Jack figured, and he opted to go straight to work rather than making nice. It was clear that Dr. Hannah Weiss—a beautiful woman working in a world of lonely men—had experienced her share of come-ons, overtures, and seemingly idle but predictably charged conversations.

"Please." He indicated the chair again, and this time she sat down, perching with her back straight, hands folded in her lap. Jack placed the photo of the scientists on the coffee table in front of her. "You were at the Kaiser Wilhelm Institute from 1931 to 1938?"

"That's correct."

"Tell me about your colleagues there."

"They didn't consider themselves to be colleagues of mine."

"But I'm sure you noticed things," said Jack.

"I noticed that the more important our work became, the more military uniforms I saw." Her pointed gaze slid from Jack's starched collar to Epstein's khakis.

Epstein bristled. "Surely you're not comparing us to the Gestapo."

"Not at all," said Hannah. "I'm simply saying notice with whom you work."

"And with whom were you working, Doctor?" Jack asked.

"The institute had hundreds of scientists."

"Let's start with Gregor Stern, then."

"Why on earth would you care about him?"

Her gaze was challenging. Jack returned it without comment.

"I see," she said. "You're not willing to answer questions, only ask them."

Hannah adjusted the jeweled comb in her hair, a gesture that struck Jack as being a bit too graceful and practiced. He tapped the photograph where Gregor Stern stood next to Hannah and said, "Seems as if you and Stern knew each other fairly well."

"Gregor is a lovely man."

"That's an interesting way to describe a colleague."

"Is it?" she said. "How would your colleagues describe you, Major Delaney?"

"Tenacious."

"Ah. Well. Try not to take it personally."

She seemed to be enjoying this, and that didn't sit well with Jack, but then she raised her hand in that same graceful gesture to tweak the jeweled comb in her hair again, and he knew. It was her tell. Now he had to discover the lies it served to keep hidden. He knew enough to do that gently. He settled back in his chair, posture open, hands relaxed in his lap.

"Tell me, Dr. Weiss," he said, "what's a nice girl like you doing in a place like this?"

6

"M ajor?" Collier appeared at the door. "It's General Groves."
"Time to kiss the ring?" Jack said dryly.

"A simple salute will do." Brigadier General Leslie Groves
pushed past Collier, bringing with him a blustery air of cigar
smoke and imposing authority. For such a corpulent man, he
moved with surprising grace, clearly relishing the power of being
the largest man in the room. Epstein bolted up from his chair and
snapped to attention. Jack peeled the wrapper off a pack of Camels
and placed the cigarettes on the table before he stood to salute.

Hannah sat, hands folded in her lap, until Groves tipped his
chin toward the door and said brusquely, "Thank you for your
time, Dr. Weiss."

Collier began to usher Hannah out, but Jack stepped between
them before she reached the door.

"One more question, Dr. Weiss."

"Yes, Major?" Her expression was neither guarded nor overly innocent.

"What's the first name of Gregor Stern's wife?"

"His private life was no business of mine," said Hannah. "And we both know you already have it in your files."

"Humor me."

"Annalise."

Jack exchanged a brief glance with Epstein, then offered his hand. "Good evening, Dr. Weiss."

Hannah left without returning the pleasantry. Observing Jack's lingering gaze as she walked down the hall, Groves uttered a guttural laugh.

"Every hose on this base has tried to water her petunias. And failed. So will you, Major."

Jack shrugged, neither confirming nor denying the implication.

Groves stepped in front of Epstein. "Lieutenant, have you been to Ashley Pond since you arrived?"

Startled, Epstein said, "No, sir."

"You definitely want to see that."

"Absolutely, sir."

"Now, Lieutenant."

"Oh! Yes. Yes, sir." Epstein snapped a quick salute and hightailed it out, gladly leaving Jack in the hot seat. The moment the door closed, Groves bore down on him.

"Major Delaney, I thought I made it clear to your superiors that I don't want you up here disrupting my scientists."

"I took that as more of a suggestion, sir."

"This is the army," Groves growled. "We don't wear short pants, we don't play tiddlywinks, and we don't give suggestions."

"Yes, sir."

"Where the hell did you do your training anyway?"

"Harvard Law, sir."

Groves shrugged one beefy shoulder. "Am I supposed to be impressed?"

"I wouldn't presume to say, General."

"Oppenheimer has the fate of the world in his hands, Major Delaney. I have enough trouble keeping a lid on his Commie tendencies without you poking his nuts and questioning the loyalty of his colleagues."

"If he's not going to question their loyalty, someone else needs to." Jack handed Groves the telegram.

Groves read it aloud, parsing the syllables skeptically. "'Let me know Sabine's all right. Stop.' Oh, yeah, I can see how that's cause for deep concern there."

"Gregor Stern is a person of interest."

"Sir," said Collier, "we already determined it was Peter Reichl who tried to send the telegram."

"And that Reichl lied about it," said Jack.

"We wired his barracks as soon as he started organizing meetings and passing that petition around," Collier said. "He's no spy. He hardly has the balls to cross the street."

"He's covering for someone, General. I'd like an opportunity to find out whom. And why."

Groves mulled this over, strolling a broad circle around the room. He reminded Jack of nothing so much as a bulldog with his short, well-muscled legs on which was perched an out-of-scale body. Jack had read that bulldogs were bred for a barbaric sport; a trained dog would latch onto a tethered bull's nose and not let go until it had pulled the bull to the ground. Groves struck him as a smug bulldog, ready to toy with any unlucky animal that crossed his path.

"When I first took over here, J. Edgar Hoover came to see me. Brought three of his fancy G-men with him. Supposed to scare me, I guess. All they did was make him look shorter." Groves didn't bother to suppress a smirk. "Anyway, the ol' Jew-baiter's got his tit in a wringer 'cause Oppenheimer's running the show. Hoover shows me all these secret files—how Oppenheimer's brother is a card-carrying Commie, how Oppie's mistress has gone down on half the Red Brigade. He wants me to cut Oppenheimer loose, replace all the scientists with Republicans, for Christ's sake. So I promise him that when I'm through, I'll serve Oppie up to the Feebs on a silver platter. Until then, that SOB Hoover and his thugs better leave me the fuck alone."

"General, with all due respect—"

"Major Delaney," Groves said as if he were scolding a child, "every minute you're questioning my scientists is a minute they're not focused on the mission. Do you really think some G-two know-it-all with a fancy telegram's gonna keep me from building my bomb?" Groves held the Gregor Stern telegram between his thumb and index finger and wafted it briefly in front of Jack's nose before he allowed it to drift slowly to the floor between them. "You've got seventy-two hours. Find your spy or hit the bricks."

"Seventy-two hours is hardly—"

"Seventy-two hours, Major, and if you distract my scientists, you'll live to regret it." Groves checked his watch and then, as if he had marked his territory, waddled out of the room, leaving the stink of hubris in his wake.

7

FIELD NOTE

SUBJECT: SITE Y SECURITY BREACH
To: Donovan
From: Delaney
SUMMARY: (1) Telegram sent by REICHL, possible cover for WEISS. (2) Telegram puts TARGET in covert communication with person of interest STERN, G.
RECOMMENDATIONS: (1) Search WEISS and REICHL quarters. (2) Petition Swiss government for right to interrogate STERN.

8

When Jack met Collier and Epstein at Hannah's modest room in the Sundt units, he was wielding the master key; she had waived her right to privacy when she came here as a scientist instead of a wife—not that the wives were exempt from the eavesdropping that modern technology made possible. Collier opened the door, and Epstein began a methodical search of the room. Jack wandered in a less predictable pattern, taking in the details, fascinated by the meticulous order and delicate placement of Hannah's small cache of essential but pretty things. He could feel her presence in the room like a haunting. The air carried a faint scent, a soft powdery smell with a hint of jasmine. On her dressing table, a brush, a comb, and a hand mirror were set straight and even with a tube of dark red lipstick and a jar of inexpensive cold cream. One item caused Jack to pause—a silver case engraved with ornate, distinctly German script: *Vertraue dir selbst.*

"'Trust yourself.'"

Jack didn't realize he'd said the words out loud until Epstein glanced up and said, "Excuse me, sir?"

"Nothing. Carry on, Lieutenant."

Jack opened the silver box and studied the dark velvet lining, which bore the distinct impression of the unusual ornament he'd noticed in Hannah's hair. It wasn't the utilitarian sort of barrette worn by the clerical workers or wives around the encampment; the finely wrought gold comb extended its tines from the open wings of what looked to be two moths, the wings of which were studded with small pink diamonds and scaled with tiny cobalt-blue sapphires. Jack balanced the empty box in the palm of his hand. A single strand of Hannah's hair had been snagged by the hinge, and it caught the light, a glowing, gossamer thread.

Epstein knelt beside a gunmetal-gray footlocker at the end of Hannah's bed and cracked his knuckles uncomfortably before he opened it. He glanced impatiently toward the door where Collier stood, a stiff nonparticipant in the invasion.

"Waiting for an invitation, Sergeant?"

"Looks like you've got it under control," said Collier. "Wouldn't want to step on any toes."

Jack cut in with quiet authority before Epstein could respond: "Lieutenant Epstein, I asked you to coordinate the search," he said. "Coordinate the search."

"Yes, sir." Epstein stood up, fixed Collier with the hard gaze of a man mindful of his rank. "Start with the footlocker, Sergeant."

Collier uttered a grudging "Yes, sir," and went to it.

Jack moved on to Hannah's bookshelves, a depth of culture remembered: Thomas Mann, Kant's *Kritik der reinen Vernunft*, Newton's *Principia Mathematica*. On her nightstand, next to a standard army-issue study lamp, he observed a well-thumbed German volume: Goethe's *Faust*. He picked up the book, allowed the pages to fall open as they would, and took note of a few passages underlined in pencil. One in particular caught his attention: *Sobald du dir vertraust, sobald weißt du zu leben*. "When you trust yourself," says Mephistopheles, "you know how to live." One couldn't argue with the sentiment, but it took on an ironic tinge in the context of a story about selling one's soul to the devil.

Tucked between the pages of the book was a yellowing, dog-eared newspaper clipping; it showed a photograph of a peroxide-blond film star boarding a ship, blowing a kiss to her fans on the dock below. Jack vaguely recognized the actress, her painted eyebrows arching to the heavens, from some B movie in which she'd played second fiddle to Luise Rainer. The headline over the photograph read "Diva Lotte Scheer Bids Fond Farewell to Germany." Jack also found a folded and creased article from the *Journal of the Royal Society of Physics:* "Thermal Neutrons and Transuranium Elements," by Dr. Stefan Frei and Dr. Anthas Winik Sanheiser.

Next to the book was an ornate pewter frame that held a grainy photograph of a lovely, spirited young woman next to an older, somewhat paunchy fellow with a full beard and a broad smile. They stood on a snowy hillside, frosted pines sloping away into the distance behind them, cross-country skis strapped to their boots, poles looped to their wrists. A soft cloud of breath smudged the air next to the girl's mouth as if she had been saying something at the moment the photo was taken. What was it Hannah heard this girl whisper when she turned out the light?

Also on the nightstand was a photograph of Hannah and her colleagues in front of the University of Chicago Library.

"How long was she in Chicago?" Jack asked.

"Arrived in '38," said Epstein.

"In America for six years," Jack observed, "yet everything she owns is German."

"Maybe her life stopped when she left."

"Or maybe her life is still there."

Jack passed by the drop-leaf table near the rudimentary kitchenette and settled his attention on Hannah's dresser. A single white candle sat in an antique silver holder engraved with the Tree of Life.

"On the run from the Nazis, and she brings a Shabbat candle holder," he pondered aloud. "But only one."

Epstein appeared pleasantly surprised. "How did you know what it is?"

"You and I have been working together for three years," said Jack. "I've picked up a few things."

Jack eased the top dresser drawer open and drifted his hand through Hannah's small supply of silk and lace, his mind flowing almost inevitably to the lines of the body of the woman who wore them. The faint smell of jasmine enveloped him in a quiet intimacy until his fingers came in contact with something solid. He moved a neatly rolled slip aside and withdrew a bundle of postcards, tinted German vistas—Burg Rheinstein, Oberwesel,

Grindelwald, München Continental Hotel—tied with a length of delicate grosgrain ribbon. Rather than pull the end of the ribbon to untie the bundle, Jack tucked the neatly bound packet into his coat pocket and said to Epstein, "Let's go."

Back at the office, Collier made coffee and served up a stack of Hannah's files. He and Epstein began sorting them, prioritizing the highly classified matters. Before long, papers and file folders covered every inch of desk and floor space, and the two of them navigated the maze, trying to make sense of the hieroglyphics of higher mathematics with its incomprehensible numbers, slashes, and squiggles. Jack, meanwhile, sat at his desk examining the front and back of each postcard, parsing the German syllables, translating out loud for Epstein.

"'How often at this desk I sat into the depth of night and looked for you. Love, Sabine.'"

He organized the cards by date, placing them in careful rows and columns.

"'What good is easy'…*Vollendung*." Jack struggled to put his finger on the right word. "*Consummation,* maybe? 'What good is easy consummation? The pleasure is not half so keen as when you first must clear your way through thickets.'"

"Thickets." Collier snorted a giggle, applying a lewd spin to the couplet. Jack was reminded of another of Goethe's observations: "Nothing shows a man's character more than what he laughs at."

"There are dozens of postcards here, all quoting Goethe and all signed 'Love, Sabine,'" said Jack.

"They sound like love poems," Collier said. "I had a feeling she might be a muff-diver."

"Actually, the quotes are from *Faust*. It's the story of a man who sells his soul to the devil in exchange for all the knowledge in the world."

Collier shrugged with lumpen indifference and continued digging through the documents. "So obviously she asked Reichl to send that telegram. She was worried that something had happened to her pussy-pal."

Jack drew the delicate circle of grosgrain ribbon through his fingers in a thoughtful game of cat's cradle, flicking his gaze over the files in front of him.

"In December 1939," he said, "Gregor Stern gets a visa to attend a conference on low-temperature physics. Guess where it's held."

"The University of Chicago?" Epstein guessed correctly. "But Stern's a mechanical engineer—"

"Get a dispatch to Colonel Pash," said Jack. "Have they rounded up Stern?"

"The secretary won't clear an operation in Switzerland," said Epstein. "It'll jeopardize their neutrality."

"I don't care if Stern is holed up in the Vatican. We need to know what he knows."

Jack stood abruptly and slipped the postcards back in his pocket on his way out the door. A pleasant tingle of cat-and-mouse raised a self-assured smile on his face as he strolled out into the evening air.

9

Hannah Weiss sat on a park bench, focused on a thick tome in German by Walter Benjamin.

"*Guten Abend,* Fräulein Weiss."

Without looking up, Hannah said, "Careful, Major. People might think you're a spy."

Jack laughed, disarmed for a moment.

"You speak German quite well," she said. "Most Americans get lost in the glottal consonants."

"I figured it would come in handy if I ever bought a Mercedes."

"Rumor has it Daimler-Benz is using Jewish slave labor. But I'm sure it'll drive like a dream." Hannah closed her book with a sharp clap and stood up to go.

"Come on," said Jack. "Give me the tour. I've been told I must see the petroglyphs on the Tsankawi Trail."

He watched Hannah weigh the request carefully before she took his arm, and for a while they walked without talking. To the casual observer, they might have appeared as comfortably paired as any of a dozen couples who wandered hand in hand or picnicked along the scenic trail. But neither of them was a casual observer; this was the one thing each of them knew about the other.

"May I ask you a question?" Jack said.

"Now you're asking permission?"

"Not a question for them," he hastened to clarify. "For me."

"Go ahead."

"How do you know you've split something you can't even see?"

Hannah picked up a smooth stone the size of an apple, handed it to him, and pointed to a juniper tree twenty feet away. "Throw it. Like a baseball."

"Tennis is more my style. Or crew."

"The noble sports," she observed. "Next you'll tell me you like riding to hounds."

A crackle of pain fired from beneath Jack's right shoulder blade and sizzled down his arm when he hurled the stone into the dense branches, sending up a flurry of tanagers that flashed yellow, orange, and black as they scattered.

"Where did those birds come from?" she said.

"The tree."

"But you didn't see them there."

"Ah." Jack nodded, understanding.

"When atoms split, they release a tremendous amount of energy," said Hannah. "That's what we measure."

Evening shadows stretched between the excavated trail and the unexplored ruins around them. It was a relief to feel the heat of the day ease off into pine-scented dusk. The farther they hiked, the more solitude they encountered, and other noises fell away until there was only the sound of their shoes scuffing companionably along the trail.

They reached a rocky passage with a steep wooden ladder that leaned against the jagged cliff. Instead of suggesting they turn back, Hannah took off her pumps and carried them in her hand as she scrambled up the worn rungs toward the ancient pueblos with their etched geometric patterns, anthropomorphic designs, and caves, haunted by echoes, that sank into the rock face.

"It's easier this way," she called over her shoulder.

It impressed Jack that she was game to go on, and it stirred something in him to hear her breath, their breath, twinned and slightly ragged in the emptiness around them. He was aware of her skin and the arch of her bare foot. The perfectly straight seam of her stocking was actually a trompe l'oeil, painted on the back of her bare leg with henna ink that curved over her calf and disappeared under her skirt. Jack steeled himself against the unbidden image of that henna line teasing up the pale skin of her elegant thigh.

"Pretty rustic surroundings," Jack said. "Compared to Kaiser Wilhelm, I mean."

"I feel privileged to be here," said Hannah.

"Why? You're as qualified as any other egghead, far as I can tell."

"I'm a woman. There are those who would prefer I stay in what they perceive as my place."

"Aren't scientists immune to that sort of antiquated prejudice?"

"Scientists are human, like anyone else," said Hannah. "The work is paramount. It requires a cooperative effort. Vanity has no place in the laboratory."

"Has anyone told Oppenheimer that?"

"Oppie is a prince compared to some others."

"Such as…"

Hannah declined to comment. "What difference does it make in the grand scheme of things?" she said. "Does anyone know the name of the man who invented fire?"

"No, but they assume it was a man. Doesn't that bother you?"

"A lot of things bother me, Major. But my feelings have no effect on the laws of physics, and that's where my interest lies…" She trailed off and looked around, seeming, for the briefest of moments, unsure of herself. She stepped up onto a boulder, hoping for a better view, maybe needing to reorient herself. The light of the day was gone, replaced by the afterglow of a fiery sun and elongated purple shadows.

"What do you think it means?" Jack asked as he studied the faint etchings that scored the tuff-stone surface.

"You're the one who solves puzzles," she said.

"Perhaps some things are better left as a mystery."

"I'm certain of that." Hannah ran her hand over the tuff stone, then traced the cryptic spiral design with the tip of one finger. Jack could feel her working its arcane geometry.

"Where did you spend your childhood?" Hannah asked.

"Lower Manhattan." Jack offered this small truth because he

suspected a lie would ping her radar and silence would pique her curiosity. He watched her evaluate the risks and benefits of further small talk.

"We should go back," she said. "It'll be dark soon."

Jack offered his hand, and Hannah allowed him to help her down. He wondered briefly if she had calculated the precise duration and weight of her grasp. She held his hand and touched his arm just long enough to step safely onto the path. A fraction of a second longer and he might have imagined, hoped, that she was flirting with him. A fraction of an ounce lighter and he might not have felt the pleasant discomfort of attraction.

As they made their way back to the trailhead, her arm looped comfortably through his, Jack asked her the sort of questions an eager student might ask. What's the difference between kinetic and thermal energy? How is energy contained? How did Einstein arrive at the theory of relativity and what did it mean?

"When you consider it's been less than forty years since the existence of the atom was confirmed," Hannah said, "Einstein's use of statistical fluctuations—"

She paused for a breath and glanced up at him to see whether he was listening or his face had taken on the blank expression that he imagined must come over most men's faces. He smiled at the thought of those fools who invited her to stroll, patronizingly smiling and nodding until they realized that they couldn't begin to understand what she was saying and had to abandon the pretense.

"Go on," Jack offered, "I won't pretend to understand, but I do find it fascinating."

He was listening intently, his expression engaged, and slightly bemused.

"What made you want to join the OSS?" she asked.

"What made you take up physics?"

"I like to solve puzzles too," said Hannah. "I'm good at it. I knew this when I was a very little girl in Austria."

10

Her childhood in Josefstadt had been filled with secrets and mysteries. Why did her father not take the Communion wafer? Why was she an only child when every other student in her class at school had multiple siblings? Why did Hannah feel comfortable in her father's lab or going on rounds with him in the hospital but gawky and uncertain when her mother took her shopping? Once, for Christmas, at the height of the trend for rural-chic, her mother had bought them matching dirndls. Hannah refused to wear hers because it was too tight.

After her father explained Landsteiner's classification of blood types, Hannah decided that her parents must be incompatible, with a toxic immunological reaction to each other. She'd inherited her mother's blue eyes—a prized color called *das blaue vom himmel*—but nothing else. She had her father's dark, wavy hair and angular features, so she must have inherited her father's antibodies as well. Knowing that was a relief; it meant that she could stop trying to win her mother's approval and instead bask in the complex harmonies of her father's world.

Abraham Weiss impressed upon his beloved daughter the rigorous certainty of the scientific method and the higher wisdom of mathematics. He taught her to play the piano, relating form, rhythm, and meter, the tempo and pitch of Mozart's concertos, to the elegant angles of geometry. She grew comfortable in a world where melodies resolved, questions had answers, and hypotheses were proven or disproven.

Her father volunteered to tend the soldiers in what was naively called "the War to End All Wars," and after he left, Hannah set everything out for his return: their favorite concerto, with all his markings and careful notations, on the music stand; his lab, which she kept dusted and cleaned while he was away, ready for the next experiment. Piled high on his desk were exams with the highest marks that she'd brought home from school so he could look them over, double-check the equations, and tell her how proud of her he was.

He didn't come home.

When inhaled, mustard gas causes bleeding and blistering in the throat and lungs. Its cruel effects don't take hold right away, so her father was, for twelve hours, a walking corpse. No matter how thoroughly Hannah mastered the properties of sulfur mustard, no matter how desperately she tried to discover an antidote, she couldn't bring him back.

After a socially acceptable season in black lace, her mother remarried. Her stepfather, Gunther, was devoted to the Heim ins Reich movement; he was a wealthy dealer in art and artifacts, so moving among aristocratic circles was essential to his business. He was willing to overlook beautiful, fair-haired Renate's sullied past, as long as the evidence of it remained out of sight. Her child, a *mischling* of the first degree, was a visible stain on the tabula rasa of her mother's newly imagined life. It was easier for Hannah to be an orphan at the University in Berlin than a shameful secret in Austria's genteel society.

Hannah's uncle Joshua, whose full beard and belly laugh were identical to his late brother's, moved mountains to secure her a place at the university where he was a professor of literature. He needed help with his daughter, Sabine, who was twelve years old, impossibly spirited, and without a mother because of tuberculosis. The three of them made quite a pleasant life in their spacious apartment on Leichhardtstraße. Though born out of great loss, the little family was gifted with music, lively conversation, and an even livelier sense of humor.

Upon graduation, Hannah sent her mother a letter announcing that she had achieved a doctorate in applied physics, summa cum laude. The card Renate sent in return contained a cordial message of congratulations that began "Dear Friend." She also sent a package that held a bracelet of diamond baguettes, which Hannah sold to finance a ski trip, new skis for Sabine, and new lab equipment for her research fellowship at the Kaiser Wilhelm Institute. That established the pattern—on birthdays and Christian holidays, Renate would send an extravagant but impersonal gift. The pangs of her mother's conscience were thereby allayed, and Hannah's orderly world was restored. She heard the sound of her father's laughter every morning at breakfast. The neighborhood gossips clucked as she happily passed through her twenties without marrying. She was busy raising Sabine and solving the entrancing riddles of radiographic mathematics and physics.

She was stunned when she looked up from her all-engrossing equations and discovered that, once again, the axis of the universe had tilted in a terrifying direction.

11

At the trailhead, Hannah leaned against the wooden gate, brushed the sand from the soles of her feet, and stepped into her shoes. Jack stood still for a long moment, his eyes fixed on the horizon and then on Hannah.

"Where is Sabine now?"

"We haven't been afforded the luxury of knowing the fate of our loved ones," Hannah said. "Some days I have hope. Other days…"

"'Es gibt nichts auf der Welt das beschamter ist als sich selbstauf Lügen und Fabeln zu gründen,'" Jack said. "'There is nothing in the world more shameful than establishing one's self on lies and fables.'"

She looked up at him with surprise. "You know Goethe."

"So does your cousin, apparently."

Jack removed one of the postcards from his breast pocket and thrust it toward her; Hannah's eyes turned glacial. She steeled herself against the unbidden thought that the little privacy she had had been invaded by his roving hands and calculating eyes.

"The next time you interrogate me," she said, "have the decency to call it that."

"I'm just looking for the truth, Fräulein Weiss."

"Really? Are you looking for the truth, Major? Or are you looking for what you want the truth to be? *'Man sieht nur das, was man weiß,'*" she quoted Goethe back at him. "'You see only what you know.'"

Hannah walked off alone, willing herself not to look back, and when she finally did, Jack Delaney had disappeared into the falling gloom.

The silhouettes of the surrounding mountains were traced with an outline of electric yellow, the last dregs of a sunset that had asserted its saffrons and scarlets through the perpetual scrim of dust. In the compound, darkness had already fallen; the paths between barracks snaked toward the inevitable periphery of chain-link fence, illuminated by floodlights, that separated the camp from the blackness that surrounded it. As Hannah strode through toward her unit, she crossed her arms against an undeniable chill. The encampment was bathed in moonlight now. It softened the faces of the soldiers and scientists who smiled and nodded as she passed by. Hannah smiled and nodded back, but her face felt like a hardened mask. Instead of taking the planked walkway to her barracks, she continued up the street, feeling lonelier than she'd felt sitting by herself on the park bench.

Foolishly, she'd let her guard down. For a moment, she'd mistaken Jack's company for something that felt personal. She'd misinterpreted his machinations as respect for her opinion. It was an easy mistake to make because his loneliness was so palpable, as it was for the vast majority of the men who worked in Los Alamos, even those who were there with their families. Perhaps more so for the family men, because they were required to keep their wives in the dark and never speak of the work that consumed their waking thoughts. Left behind by their husbands, the wives bonded and kibitzed, but their community left Hannah somewhere in between. It was like being seated at the center of a long table at a dinner party; she was never really included in either the professional conversation to her right or the political debate to her left.

The men who approached Hannah for anything other than work were invariably seeking a swift, silent assignation—something to be hastily walked away from the moment a fly was zipped, a skirt resettled—and there were times when Hannah ached for that sort of relief, although never enough to allow it. Her singular focus made it possible for her to lie alone in the dark willing herself to sleep in preparation for another day of work. She recognized the same sort of isolation in Major Jack Delaney. She felt her own loneliness resonating with his, like parallel strings on a violin. But he was not to be trusted, and Hannah would never again make the mistake of thinking that he trusted her.

The windows of the laboratory were dark, but the lamp was still lit in Jack's office, and Lieutenant Epstein could be seen laboring away over a stack of files at a desk next to the window. Hannah rapped sharply on the glass, making him almost jump out of his skin with a startled yelp. He opened the door and gestured her in, dabbing spilled coffee from his shirt.

"May I help you, Dr. Weiss?"

"No, just letting you know that I'll be out of my barracks for a while," said Hannah, "in case you and your commanding officer want to rifle through my underthings."

"We have a job to do," said Epstein.

"And you do it thoroughly."

"I'm brewing coffee," he said, and Hannah watched him struggle with the proper upbringing that required him to offer her a cup. "Would you care for some?"

"Isn't it a little late?" she said.

"Yes, but you know how it is. 'Miles to go before I sleep.'"

"Your New England farmer-poet."

"You know Robert Frost?"

"You'll find I'm full of surprises," Hannah said, observing the careful way he assembled his cup and saucer with two cubes of sugar and a precise pour from a little ceramic creamer. He did it without even looking at his hands. His eyes were fixed on a framed photo of a woman on the rocky shoal of a winter beach. Her bobbed hair had the expanded volume that came with salt air. Hannah was all too familiar with that humid tangle of dark Ashkenazi curls. She and Sabine had both grown up trying to wrestle theirs into submission. No hairdresser's chemical bath could make it straight. No heated instruments of torture could tame it.

The woman was holding a toddler, who had his father's dark eyebrows and whose thick glasses were secured by a strap around his head. Hannah smiled and asked, "How old is he?"

"Two when that was taken," said Epstein. "Five now."

"A long time to be away from home."

"They've given me a short leave for Christmas."

"How thoughtful."

"Dr. Weiss, if there's nothing else—"

"Perhaps I will have some coffee. It's so kind of you to offer." Hannah took a seat at the empty desk she assumed to be Jack's, trying not to enjoy the fresh crease between Epstein's ample eyebrows. "One lump, please."

Epstein brought her a cup of black coffee with one little American sugar cube on the saucer beside it. Hannah had been away from Europe for years and had still not gotten used to the vaguely acrid aftertaste of those sad sugar cubes or the weakness of the coffee for which they sacrificed their boxy little lives.

"I've made a play for some Scandinavian coffee on the black market," she said. "I'll bring you some if I manage it."

"I stick with the Maxwell House," he said.

"Ah. You keep kosher, then? Even here?"

Epstein made a temporizing seesaw motion with his hand. "I try."

"It's difficult," she said, "when those around you are… unfamiliar."

"Major Delaney is pretty in the know," said Epstein. "About a lot of things."

"Delaney," Hannah said, musing. "What sort of name is that, do you suppose?"

He shrugged. "A surname."

She nodded toward Jack's blank workspace, devoid of any

personal effects, in contrast to Epstein's ceramic tea set and family photos. "He doesn't seem to have any attachments. Somehow that doesn't surprise me."

"Not really my business." Epstein sipped his coffee, eyeing Hannah over the rim of his cup.

"Does he have a family?"

"Why are you poking into his personal life?"

"Why did you poke into mine?"

"I told you," he said crisply, "we have a job to do."

"Ah, the eternal excuse."

"We don't need an excuse, Dr. Weiss. You knew what you were signing up for when you came here."

"Did you?"

"Yes!"

"To save the Jews?" said Hannah. "So we could all go home for Christmas?"

Flustered, Epstein rose abruptly from his chair, opened the door, and said, "Good evening, Dr. Weiss."

Hannah carefully placed her cup and saucer on a tray below the makeshift tea cart.

"Lieutenant Epstein," she said, "perhaps if you and Major Delaney could see past your preconceptions about—"

"With all due respect," Epstein said, cutting her off, "you don't know a damn thing about what Major Delaney and I have seen."

"That's true," she said, studying the strange expression on his face.

"Good evening, Dr. Weiss," he said again. "Watch your step on the way out."

"Good evening, Lieutenant Epstein."

As Hannah walked past him into the quiet street, his gaze remained fixed on the framed photo of his wife, but in his eyes, Hannah detected a shadow of something she knew he would never be able to share with this woman he clearly loved. Hannah recognized that familiar shadow. It was the isolating burden of a terrible secret.

12

"You forgot to touch the mezuzah," Sabine scolded. She was only twelve and Hannah was almost twenty, but Sabine's mother had taught her to observe that sort of tradition with pride, while Renate had conditioned Hannah to remain discreet and unnoticed. The mezuzah fixed to the right side of the doorway was about eight centimeters long, delicately crafted from pewter with blue enamel inlays and what seemed to be a bending calla lily made of tiny white pearls.

"It does look like a lily, now that you mention it," Uncle Joshua said, "but it's the Hebrew letter *shin*. For *shalom,* Shadai, Shema."

"Our mezuzah is the prettiest one in the building," said Sabine. "It was a wedding gift from my mother's cousin."

"Her cousin must have loved her very much," Hannah said, tugging the pink bow that bound Sabine's unruly brown hair.

Sabine had never seen the *klaf*—the tiny scroll inside the mezuzah—but she knew the words by heart. As she proudly recited Devarim, chapter 6, the phrase "houses full of all good things" stung Hannah's heart. She had come to a house full of all good things. Here was faith, love, and listening. Here was quiet for study and music for dancing. It was a tribute to Sabine's mother in so many ways far beyond the lace curtains, wedding china, and tasteful furnishings. Hannah understood why it was so hard for her uncle to contemplate leaving this place. He'd carried the love of his life over this threshold when they were married and he'd carried her to the coroner's van after she died.

When Hannah came to live on Leichhardtstraße, most of the doorways featured ornate little mezuzahs made of pewter, like theirs, or porcelain or, in one particularly avant-garde residence, Bakelite. The National Socialist Party was always trying to gin up seemingly urgent fears—of Jews, of immigrants, of Communists, of homosexuals, of "deviant artists"—but it was easy to dismiss these people and their ridiculous little leader as an annoyance, the lunatic fringe that had to be indulged in a society where all should be free to speak and believe as they like. But in 1933, a few weeks after the Reichstag fire consumed the parliament buildings, the Nazis managed a stunning 43.9 percent of the vote in the March elections, and not long after that, Adolf Hitler—this warthog of a man with his ludicrous lies and conspiracy theories—was awarded total dictatorial powers.

Then, one by one, the mezuzahs vanished from the hallways in the building. Some were taken down by Jewish families who feared being identified. Others were removed by the new tenants after the old tenants had mysteriously disappeared. By 1935, all that remained of them on most of the doorways in the building were small scars where slender nails had been pried out of the wood. Neighbors the three of them had regarded as friends— the parents of Sabine's schoolmates, the lady who gave her piano lessons—now averted their eyes when they passed.

"They don't hate us," Uncle Joshua said. "They're afraid of who might be watching."

"Oh, well, then," Sabine said tartly, "by all means, award them a gold star." She wasn't as forgiving as her father and had developed a teenager's knack for sarcasm.

"We must look for the good in people, Sabine. If we allow hatred to consume us, how will we all live with each other when this is over?"

"Over? How will this ever end?" Hannah wondered.

"'Those he commands, move only in command, / Nothing in love: now does he feel his title / Hang loose about him, like a giant's robe / Upon a dwarfish thief,'" he said. "Shakespeare's *Macbeth*. Evil men inevitably turn on each other. A tyrant always dies on the point of the same dagger that put him in power. So it will be with Hitler." Joshua refused to give up his faith in the neighbors he'd known for twenty-five years, and there were those who came to him privately and offered things they thought he might need: fresh flowers in 1933, new mittens in 1934, milk in 1935, and, in 1936, a place to hide. Those were the good neighbors. A few others approached in a less generous spirit and offered to buy the apartment, art, and furnishings for a fraction of their value.

Uncle Joshua never spoke about money, but Hannah noticed

precious things missing. Money became an issue after Jewish professors were forced out of the universities. Uncle Joshua referred to it as his "sabbatical" and insisted that he was happy to have time to work on translating German literature into English, but it wounded his pride that his niece's job at Kaiser Wilhelm was the family's sole source of income. His magnanimity sorely tested, he began looking for a way out for himself and Sabine, but by 1937, even if you had money, the waiting list for proper papers had burgeoned several years out into an uncertain future. He gently suggested that Hannah should apply for a position at Cambridge.

"No," she told him. "I won't leave you."

"We'll be all right," he said. "We'll get the papers. I have my wife's jewelry. She would have wanted me to sell it to find a way for Sabine."

Joshua never knew the luxury of a true turning point, a moment when his path was made excruciatingly clear. No, his hope and faith were wrung out of him gradually, over a period of years.

Hannah's inflection point was less ambiguous. Her eyes were wide open. She knew the facts as readily and clearly as she knew the elements of the periodic table.

But there was something she'd forgotten or perhaps had never learned—knowledge and wisdom aren't the same. Wisdom grows in the deep recesses of the soul and is governed, not by the head, but by the heart.

13

The night-chilled metal sheeting of the Quonset hut was absorbing the sun's heat to form condensation, drops of water that fell inside in a regular, even pattern like Chinese water torture. Jack was counting on this humid discomfort to give him the upper hand, but so far Hannah had remained preternaturally calm, watching him with a wary stillness.

Jack nudged the microphone across the table toward her.

"Just to let you know," he said, "you're being interrogated."

Hannah didn't laugh, but she seemed slightly less irritated than she had when he'd invited her to leave the breakfast line in the mess hall and accompany him to his office.

"How long will we be?" she asked now. "Oppie will be wondering where I am."

"Lieutenant Epstein, would you please let Dr. Oppenheimer know that Dr. Weiss is having breakfast with me?"

"Yes, sir." Epstein checked the reel-to-reel before he went out, leaving Jack and Hannah alone.

"Before I dive into questions," said Jack, "is there anything you'd like to tell me?"

"Several things," said Hannah, "but decency suggests I should keep them to myself."

Jack cleared his throat and leafed through his notes, trying to find the best place to start. "This won't take long."

"What makes you think someone on the Hill is spying?"

"Gut feeling." Jack shrugged before realizing that he'd never actually revealed the reason for his presence. "Are you a spy, Dr. Weiss? Smuggling secrets in picturesque postcards?"

"What is it they say—when one is a hammer, everything resembles a nail?"

"They do say that," said Jack. "Sometimes they're right."

She pursed her dark red lips and chose to ignore the insinuation. "I was calculating the energy of fast neutrons when Oppie recruited me in Chicago. If you could've seen him then, so full of hope…we all were, so certain what we were doing was right, so sure we owed it to science—to mankind—to find the heart of the atom."

"What changed?"

"Everything."

"Perhaps you could be more specific?"

"Oppie had a mistress. Her name was Jean Tatlock; she was a card-carrying member of the party, the only one he refused to renounce when he came here. He took extraordinary risks to be with her—he was followed, his phone was tapped, as was hers. One day, they came and told him she'd committed suicide the night before. Took so much codeine and pentobarbital, so many barbiturates and sleeping pills, that she drowned in her own bathtub, bathwater in her lungs and stomach. They wouldn't even give Oppie the day off to go to her funeral. He kept working—harder than before—but he knew the work wasn't ours anymore. It belonged to the generals. And the thing I realized then—something few others seem to see—is that the truth in the wrong hands will destroy us all."

"Are all the scientists as single-minded as you and Oppie?"

"It is not the hypnotic single-mindedness that enthralls compulsive problem solvers. It's the dual aphrodisiac of danger and discovery." Hannah propped her elbow on the table and rested her chin on her hand. Her long, tapered fingers were devoid of ornamentation, not even a tiny band of white skin exposed by the removal of a ring.

"We are loath to admit that we do what we do because of a deep-seated thrill that follows a familiar path from awakened inkling to assiduous pursuit to compulsive repetition, repetition, repetition, to final fruition, an instant of overtaking that engulfs all conscious thought and spiritual capacity, the mental equivalent of physical climax."

As he listened, Jack found himself thinking of the way she'd looked in the gathering shadows of Tsankawi, holding her ground with the pale, immovable grace of the jagged cliffs around her.

"Inverse to this," she said, "is the potency and pleasure of being discovered. To be the focus of such puzzling until one is solved—this requires a terrifying nakedness, the sacrifice of whatever secrets lurk below the radar of polite observance, forsaking the comforting cover of darkness. And therein lies the danger."

He felt her piercing eyes on him as if the heat of her gaze could burn away layers of secrets to reveal his nakedness beneath. The reel-to-reel rolled with a soft, rhythmic squeak, and the drip, drip of condensation echoed with a dissonant plink. He thought Hannah might fidget or ask for water, but she didn't.

"Dr. Reichl was telling me about a conference at Kaiser Wilhelm," he said. "I'd like to hear about that from your perspective."

Hannah shrugged one slender shoulder. "The perspective of a wallflower."

"I doubt that," said Jack. "But please, go on."

Hannah's blue eyes never wavered from his as she told him about a sumptuous ballroom filled with Germany's scientific crème de la crème and the aristocratic elites with the resources to fund cutting-edge discovery. Jack listened, waiting to hear that soft cloud of memory or the stiffened resolve of a skillful lie. But he heard something else—something unreadable—as she quietly, consciously crafted an account that might or might not be pure fiction. Her voice was tempered with an unhurried, melodic grace. The details rang true enough, but there was something she was deliberately omitting. Jack felt it lurking below the surface like an eel lying at the bottom of a placid lake.

14

The opulent ballroom at the Kaiser Wilhelm Institute was awash with reflected light and an iridescent array of silk gowns of lavender, apricot, and amber, all in perpetual motion as couples sailed by to a waltz by the Henschel string quartet. Hannah stood uneasily on the sidelines. This aspect of her job always left her feeling off balance and behind the times. She detested the frantic political jockeying, men incessantly angling to dominate the conversation, flagrantly interrupting and always, but always, insisting that they were right. And then there was the female equivalent—the posing and preening for attention. Her mother had set a fine example of style and bearing, and Hannah had an innate sense of the difference between fashion and fad, but the rest of the world didn't always share her aesthetic. Some saleswoman was constantly prodding her to accentuate her small waist or show more décolletage than she was comfortable showing. Even here and now, in Berlin's remarkably progressive environs, Hannah walked a tightrope that required her to be indefatigably feminine while functioning in a professional world that automatically dismissed her for not being male. It was exhausting, keeping up this façade, and Hannah would have preferred to spend these hours in the lab, where she knew herself and had confidence in the unalterable style of scientific principle.

Gregor Stern, a Swiss engineer in Berlin on a research grant, emerged from the carousel of the dance floor to stand beside her, and Hannah was glad to see him. He kissed her on one cheek and then the other. "You look as nervous as I was at my debut."

"Is it that obvious?" Hannah straightened self-consciously.

"Don't worry," Gregor said kindly. "We outsiders will stick together." He was a handsome fellow with a ready smile and a thick mass of curly hair, closely shaved at the nape of his neck, that fell in a tangle across his forehead. In his breast pocket, he carried a little bag of Swiss candies shaped like fruits, sweet and slightly tart. Now he popped one in his mouth and offered her a piece of secret sweetness. Aside from Max Frei, the director of the institute, Gregor was the only scientist who had bothered to engage Hannah in an actual conversation since her arrival. She never had to wonder if it was her or her ideas that drew him to her. He always met her eyes when she was speaking, never a furtive glance toward the clock on the wall or a drifting of his gaze from her mouth to her clavicle to the front of her blouse.

"Ah, voilà!" said Gregor. "The golden boy of Kaiser Wilhelm."

Hannah glanced anxiously toward the floor, where Stefan Frei swept his dance partner along in time to the crescendo of violins. He moved with a dashing lack of inhibition, a bon vivant blessed with the magical amalgam of physical beauty, social status, an unfettered income, and a lack of scruples that freed him to enjoy it all to the fullest. Stefan Frei was adored, and he made whomever he was with, in whatever ballroom, laboratory, or lecture hall, feel aglow in the spotlight of his presence.

"Would you like me to introduce you?" asked Gregor.

Hannah shook her head. "He seems to be otherwise occupied."

Stefan's *Tanzkarte* was full; this particular quadrille had been claimed by Ulrike, the younger sister of renowned Nobel Prize winner Kurt Diebner. Her brother's meteoric rise within both the scientific community and the Reich made her an ideal playmate for Stefan, the alabaster better half of a quintessential power couple. And she wore it beautifully. Ulrike's corona of stylish curls formed a blond halo; her luminous porcelain skin seemed lit from within, a natural habitat for diamonds and finely wrought platinum. Her bias-cut white satin gown hugged the slim lines of her figure, making the other women with ruffled gowns in garish pastels look dowdy in comparison; next to Ulrike's iridescence, Hannah felt like a dark shadow. She didn't want to be caught staring, so when Ulrike's eyes met hers, Hannah quickly looked down. When she looked up again, she realized that Ulrike was glaring at Stefan, whose frankly amused smile was firmly focused on Hannah's blushing discomfort. The lace collar around her neck had begun to feel like a pearl-buttoned garrote. Hannah pressed one cool hand against her burning cheek and tried to back away and disappear, grateful that Gregor stayed close, a proprietary arm around her waist.

"Like it or not, the alliances forged in the social world steer the scientific opportunities," he reminded her.

"I know," said Hannah. "Nothing happens without money, and money doesn't happen without the occasional fox-trot."

"Ulrike is every bit as intelligent as her brother, and she has a far greater understanding of the social graces. She supports the advancement of women. It would be good for you to get to know her."

"Ulrike chooses not to know 'non-Aryan' women like me," said Hannah. "You are aware of this, Gregor."

"This antiquated prejudice against Jewish Physics is nonsense. More to the point, it's impractical. The institute has already lost some of its best scientists—Hans Bethe immigrating to America, Peierls to England—and with them patents and funding. When prejudice is no longer financially advantageous to the institute, Hannah, it will pass. It must pass. Meanwhile…" Gregor gestured toward a corner sitting area where Kurt Diebner, his shock of silver hair slicked down and pomaded, held court in front of a rapt cadre of scientists and sycophants. "Shall we?"

"I've never met a Nobel winner," Hannah admitted.

"They're human," he said, "contrary to what they'd like you to believe."

Gregor took Hannah's arm and led her into the inner sanctum. Diebner was mid-argument, holding forth on one of the intensely debated topics of the moment: nuclear magnetic resonance.

"When heavy nuclei are bombarded by neutrons," he said, "the fragments should be lighter elements farther down the periodic table, so the results are absurd. Unless you put your faith in Jewish Physics," he added.

There was an awkward silence. The name *Einstein* hung palpably in the air, but no one dared invoke it. Hannah was horrified when Gregor piped up. "Kurt, Dr. Weiss has been working on gamma excitation with boron."

"How ambitious," Diebner said without looking at her.

Hannah could feel the cold disdain of Diebner and his devotees, but Gregor nudged her forward with a gentle hand at the small of her back. "Dr. Weiss, perhaps you could share the results of your experiments with beryllium?"

A tic in Diebner's eyebrow registered his annoyance. "Such an extremely rarefied and complex process," he said.

Hannah felt a warm breath tickle her neck as someone said softly in her ear, "Don't pay any attention to Kurt. He's still claiming Einstein stole his ideas."

Hannah turned, startled. "Dr. Frei."

"Dr. Weiss. I'm pleased to finally meet you," said Stefan. "Gregor has been singing your praises since you arrived. I'm told you're twice as brilliant and half as much trouble as any man on our faculty."

"No trouble, I hope."

"Not even a little? What fun is that?" Stefan teased with the confidence of someone who knows exactly how charming he is and exactly how much his charm will allow him to get away with. Hannah knew she was blushing, but she willed herself to maintain frank eye contact with him.

"I'm less interested in fun than I am in fission," she said.

"Then we must find the opportunity for a long, private tête-à-tête." Stefan leaned in, and she inhaled the bergamot scent of his expensive cologne. "There may be some interesting opportunities arising."

His tone was less playful this time, and Hannah saw nothing dismissive or patronizing in his face.

"Mein Schatz," said Ulrike, tugging at his arm.

It wasn't until they whirled away that Hannah realized she had been holding her breath. She'd been standing her tallest, a natural response as she strained to hear Stefan's mellow tenor voice through the ballroom din, and she felt herself diminish slightly as he departed. It made her aware of the protective posture she and so many of her Jewish colleagues had recently adopted, a defensive hunching of the shoulders, a deferential lowering of the head, a desire to simply go about one's business without being noticed. It was the antithesis of Ulrike Diebner's impressively statuesque carriage. Admiring eyes followed her around the ballroom. Hannah said to Gregor what everyone else seemed to be thinking: "She's very beautiful, isn't she?"

Gregor took Hannah's elbow and steered her toward the dance floor. "It doesn't take a nuclear physicist to see who's the real beauty at this party," he said. He bowed slightly and offered his hand in an invitation to dance.

"I'm sorry. I don't—"

"Of course you do."

Before Hannah could voice a meaningful objection, Gregor had his arm locked around her and they were off, sailing to the Strauss waltz. Hannah felt the scour of eyes on her, and not in the admiring spirit that Ulrike enjoyed. A murmur rippled across the dance floor, trailing them like the wake of a ship. A gentile dancing with a Jew? And this Jew in particular—this woman who fancied herself a scientist? When Gregor waltzed her past the corner settee, Hannah was aware of Kurt Diebner's steely glare.

"They're all staring," she whispered nervously.

"Because they're envious," said Gregor.

Hannah raised her eyes as Stefan Frei crossed their path. Ulrike's bejeweled arms were draped around his neck, but his cool, appraising gaze remained firmly fixed on her.

15

FIELD NOTE

SUBJECT: SITE Y SECURITY BREACH

To: Donovan

From: Delaney

SUMMARY: Black-bag job in WEISS quarters yielded postcards of a cryptic nature.

RECOMMENDATIONS: (1) Remove WEISS from Critical Assemblies Team. (2) Continue HUMINT into WEISS with all speed and delicacy. (3) Where the FUCK is GREGOR STERN?

16

The log-and-timber Fuller Lodge was the hub from which all of Los Alamos' spokes extended: Ashley Pond and the post office to the south; the all-important Technical Area to the southwest; the hospital to the west. To the north sat "Bathtub Row," cottages for Oppenheimer and his elite colleagues, so called because they had actual bathtubs instead of the leaky, jerry-rigged showers with which the lower-IQ folks had to make do. By day, the lodge was a massive dining hall, open fires ablaze in huge stone fireplaces, enormous elk heads peering down imperiously at the goings-on. By night, with tables and chairs cleared to the side, it became a grand dance hall.

Jack could see slats of light angling out of the open doors, across the porch, and onto the grass lawn in front of the lodge. He heard the high-pitched rippling of women's laughter and music, the irresistible buoyancy of a swing piano, and the throbbing punctuation of bass, drums, and brass. A couple of women from the steno pool were giving dance lessons under the eaves, and the air was filled with the smell of wood smoke and pine, of tobacco and women's perfume.

The army had encircled these brilliant minds with concertina wire to keep the rest of the world out, and somehow, so far, it had worked. Despite censored letters, rutted roads, and the inconveniences of army barracks, hideous food, and the constant monitoring for security, these giddy scientists seemed to live in a state of constant exhilaration, throwing themselves into lab work and the Lindy hop with equal zeal.

Jack waded through thick wafts of smoke and into the din of partygoers competing to be heard over the music. He wandered over to the punch bowl, thinking he'd allow himself one drink before heading to bed. The altitude had made him light-headed, and he was conscious of Groves's watch ticking away his time. He searched the crowd for Hannah, perhaps hidden in a corner, veiled from view by a shroud of smoke.

He spotted Peter Reichl on the dance floor. Determined to be a good sport, Reichl stumbled through the paces of Count Basie's "Splanky." One of the younger scientists, in cowboy boots and a turquoise bolo, executed the steps with the concentrated precision of someone conducting an experiment, always a beat or two off. Dance moves that should have looked suave resembled the herky-jerky spasms of a marionette. The more intricate the maneuver, the more inevitable his missteps and the louder the hoots of encouragement and enjoyment from the sidelines.

The whole gathering seemed slightly ludicrous—the jazz combo on stage might be composed of a quantum mathematician, a metallurgist, and an analytical chemist; the young man with the cowboy boots and bolo, shirt now drenched in sweat, might be the world's leading expert in tube alloys.

"Good evening, Major. I was hoping we might have a word."

Jack turned to find J. Robert Oppenheimer looming behind him, a martini glass in one hand, a cigarette in the other.

Oppenheimer was skeletal, almost frail; his hollowed skull and paper-thin skin offered no distraction from his gaze. Jack had expected the probing stare but not the weariness so profound that his eyes' glassy sheen was almost feverish. The hum of the room seemed to contract around him, weaving a complicated cocoon of complicity.

"Don't let this shindig alarm you," said Oppenheimer. "We'll be back at work at seven a.m. none the worse for wear. Nothing a couple of cups of coffee can't cure."

Oppenheimer's voice was low and musical, so soft and whispery that Jack had to lean close to hear him. This created a conspiratorial intimacy, the feeling of a shared bond. His intense focus made Jack feel that he was the only person in the room, or at least the only one who mattered. Now Jack understood how much of Oppenheimer's vaunted charm lay in exclusion. There were always others waiting to speak to Oppenheimer, to ask him a question, command a bit of his precious time, but his careful scrutiny told you that he had no interest in anyone else. What could be more flattering than this intoxicating searchlight of attention from one of the world's greatest minds?

Oppenheimer tilted his head in an ironic oriental gesture and moved toward the door. Jack followed him to a fairly quiet space at the end of the porch where they sat in wooden Adirondack chairs that offered an unobstructed view of the human-computer girls Lindy-hopping with each other on the gravel patch of driveway. Anonymous couples at the outer edges of the circle of light entwined their limbs, hands clinging to backs, frantic fingers groping at fabric.

"You've created an unusual work environment," Jack observed.

"We play almost as hard as we work. It's like riding a bicycle— to keep our balance, we must keep moving. We work as if we're running out of time. Do you know how far along the Germans are with their nuclear research project?"

"No," Jack said, a bit surprised by the question.

"You were with the Alsos team in Europe, were you not?"

"I was," Jack said, "but I got only as far as Paris before I was wounded and returned stateside."

"A year ago, Allied intelligence predicted that London would not be bombed again. Then von Braun made fools of us all by launching his V-two rocket. We must never, never underestimate them."

"Dr. Oppenheimer, if you don't mind my saying—"

"Or even if I do," said Oppie. "But by all means, have at it."

"Is this about Dr. Weiss?"

"It brings out the mother hen in me when someone comes along to make our job more difficult." Oppie's sudden smile, a flash of teeth, was disarming, then it was dropped with the finality of a lowered curtain. "I can't have you monopolizing her time as you

79

did this morning. And now Collier tells me you're lobbying to have her security clearance revoked. That's not acceptable, Major. She's a key member of my team."

"That's a problem, Dr. Oppenheimer."

"You're determined to paint Dr. Weiss as a femme fatale out of a Raymond Chandler novel, and believe me, I understand exactly why she is pleasant to focus on, but scientists don't work on hunches. We work on facts."

"I thought you worked on theories."

"I won't work on anything if you rob me of my key team members." Oppenheimer scrutinized him for a long moment as if his gaze could penetrate the polished surface of Jack's armor, glimpse a bit of fraudulence beneath his perfectly tailored suit.

"Doctor, do you have any idea what Dr. Weiss might be up to?"

"'Up to'? That's a bit cloak-and-dagger, Major, don't you think? Not the subtlety I'd expect from a Harvard man."

"Do you consider her a friend?"

"I need physics more than I need friends," said Oppenheimer. "I know Dr. Weiss well enough to understand that she and I have that in common."

"Why is she so important to the project?"

"It wasn't until we were able to sustain a chain reaction that we could be certain Einstein's theories were true." Oppenheimer's gaze moved past the dancers to the dark-mirror windows of the laboratory. "The work she did in Berlin, the work she brought to Chicago—that's the discovery that made the gadget feasible."

Oppenheimer's expression betrayed not a scintilla of doubt or discomfort, but Jack could see the man's pulse fluttering in a vessel under the skin stretched taut over his Adam's apple.

"The science, you see, that's the easy part…keeping the team focused is what consumes me. Groves ordered the scientists to wear army uniforms—Bethe refused. He'd build the bomb, he said, but only as a professor, not as a colonel. Robert Serber's wife, Charlotte, used the word *proletariat* in one of her letters. All of a sudden, the Serbers are fellow travelers, and I had to trade five of my best PhDs to keep them here. And Edward Teller—standing over there by the door, waiting to accost me…"

Jack glanced toward the lodge and noticed a short, truculent man, his bulk encased in a shiny, double-breasted suit, with dark, luxuriant eyebrows that set his face in a perpetual scowl.

"Teller thinks the work he's doing is beneath him. Complains there's no beauty or elegance in his equations."

Oppenheimer rubbed the bridge of his nose between his thumb and forefinger, closing his eyes for a moment to ease the strain. He stretched one lanky leg and then the other.

"If you must find a spy on the Hill, Major, go after Teller. But leave Dr. Weiss alone. Now, if you'll pardon me, I'm said to be the life of the party, and they'll be wondering where I've gone." Oppenheimer stood and made his way into the crowd. At the door, Teller stopped and harangued him, as predicted, dark eyebrows pinched, fingers like sausages gesticulating wildly in Oppenheimer's face.

Jack was feeling as frustrated as Teller, but his frustration collapsed inward, curling resentfully around the dull, impacted pain of the bullet near his spine. It was clear that Dr. Weiss had lied to him; he suspected that she'd lied more times than he knew, and yet Groves and now Oppenheimer seemed intent on safeguarding her. Perhaps she'd even charmed Oppie into making a special plea on her behalf.

Two can play at that game, he thought. With a burst of rebellious energy, Jack pushed himself out of the low-slung Adirondack chair, ignoring the twinge in his back. Better to lose a chess match than have it end in a stalemate. After giving Oppenheimer a crisp civilian salute, he marched back into Fuller Lodge to continue his pursuit.

17

In the five years since Hitler had been appointed Reich chancellor, more than a hundred of Hannah's colleagues had disappeared from the ornate hallways and pristine labs of the Kaiser Wilhelm Institute. The Law for the Restoration of the Professional Civil Service declared that all non-Aryan scientists should be dismissed. The most famous of the banished scientists were lured away by offers of fellowships at great universities—Cambridge, Princeton, the Sorbonne. The less renowned, fearing the direction the country was taking, fled to resettle abroad and so spent what might have been their most productive years sweeping floors and stocking shelves. Others, too old and tired to relocate, went home to live out their years as unobtrusively as possible. Those who spoke out against the new policy were quickly and quietly removed with their families to Jewish ghettos and then the camps or made to labor as slaves in Nazi factories. Hannah was given an unexpected exemption due to a hasty amendment that allowed those who'd lost a father, brother, or son in the Great War to remain in their positions. When Hannah announced the news, Uncle Joshua put his hands together and said, "Your father died so you could live and do the work you love."

"Papa!" Sabine slapped his arm. "How could you say such a thing?"

"I would gladly give my life for you, Sabine, and my brother would gladly have given his life for Hannah. And it would seem now that he did. I take comfort in that."

"Well, fine for you," said Sabine, placing a protective arm around her cousin's shoulders, "but you have no right to put that burden on Hannah."

But Joshua was adamant. "Don't you see, Hannah? This gives his death some meaning."

Hannah shook her head, sickened by the irony.

"There is no meaning in the death of innocent people," said Sabine. "I refuse to accept that we're meant to be marched out and murdered for the sake of some greater good—for God's grand and mysterious plan. You might as well say it's for the good of the fatherland."

"That's not the same thing." Joshua's tone was gentle but uncompromising. "And I'll remind you about speaking to me in that manner, my dear."

"Oh, yes, we mustn't raise our voices," Sabine said. "If we were heard, the whole world might crack in half."

Hannah, nostrils filled with the scent of yeast, pinched together the three strands of dough and tucked them neatly under the braided loaf. "I need to go back to the laboratory," she said, untying the strings of her apron.

"Hannah, don't go," said Sabine. "He's sorry. Papa, say you're sorry."

Uncle Joshua didn't need to tell Hannah for the hundredth time that he disapproved of her working on the Sabbath. "At the very least, stay while we light the candles," he said.

"I can't." Hannah fetched her things from a coat tree in the hall. "If I hurry, I can get there before curfew."

"But how will you get home?"

"Carefully," said Hannah and kissed his cheek. Then she kissed Sabine's cheek and said, "I'd better find you safe in your bed when I get back."

Making her way to the laboratory, Hannah hugged a patterned shawl close around her body and kept her eyes down, counting each crack in the pavement. The strange supper conversation replayed itself in her mind. If her work was to mean anything, it must, like her father's, save lives, and what she was doing now had that potential. In her lifetime, she might see an end to all wars. Black-lunged miners might be emancipated from the coal mines. A new era of peace and prosperity might be set in motion. World travel in vehicles not yet dreamed of would become as unremarkable as driving down the street in automobiles; when she was a child, they were startling and new, but now they were as common as a daily milk trolley.

Hannah's own curiosity and ambition resonated with Germany's well-funded hunger for innovation. Pride and gratitude lifted her heart when she saw the copper spires of the Kaiser Wilhelm Institute. Tonight, when Hannah arrived, she saw most of the other scientists—dapper men in tailored suits with leather briefcases and wire-rimmed glasses—leaving for the day. Hannah nodded without meeting their eyes, making sure her long hair fell across the gold star sewn to her coat. She had been grateful for this job every day of the past five years, even after she was relegated to a tiny makeshift lab in the basement. It was more like a storage facility and doubled as a woodworking shop for the maintenance men, but Hannah kept it sanitary and well organized.

Whenever she was alone there at night, she kept the blinds drawn and the lighting to the essential minimum, but tonight, before she put on her lab coat, she took out her grandmother's two silver candle holders and placed them at the center of her worktable. She took the spark lighter from a drawer beneath her Bunsen burner, clicked the trigger, and whispered, *"Baruch atah, Adonai Eloheinu, Melech haolam, asher kid'shanu b'mitzvotav, v'tzivanu l'hadlik ner shel Shabbat."*

When Hannah touched the tiny flame of the lighter to the first candle, it flared, casting a sudden light on the looming silhouette of the man standing in the doorway. Startled, Hannah stumbled back, upsetting a metal stool that tipped and clanged against the tile floor. "Who's there?"

"Dr. Weiss, it's Stefan Frei." He stepped into the warm circle of candlelight. "I'm so sorry. I didn't mean to frighten you."

"No need to apologize."

"I didn't expect you to be here so late."

Hannah righted the metal stool, feeling profoundly foolish and freshly conscious of her humble surroundings. Dr. Frei was dressed for an evening out, wearing the sort of silky ascot and perfectly cut tails Fred Astaire might dance in. A glimmer of light caught the chain of his gold watch fob. The glow in his eyes seemed to be part amusement, part predation.

"Candlelight becomes you," he said, "but you're allowed to turn on a lamp or two, you know, even after hours."

"It's Friday," said Hannah. "Time to stop work and honor the Sabbath with one's family."

"Ah." Stefan nodded. "So why aren't you at home doing that?"

"My work is the way I honor God."

Hannah lit the second candle, expecting him to make some jaunty remark in response, but he didn't. He pushed his hands in his pockets and looked down at the tile floor.

"Don't worry," said Hannah. "Despite what your führer says, it's not contagious."

Stefan waved the idea aside. "I don't engage in politics. And I leave contagion to our biomedical division."

"Where it belongs."

"I am curious to know, Dr. Weiss, how a scientist—one who's dedicated her life to empirical proof—reconciles her work with a belief in God."

"I'm not trying to prove there is a God. I just want to know how He works."

"In mysterious ways, they say."

"No more mysterious than the ways of men."

Stefan took a silver cigarette case from his inner pocket. He patted his other pockets for a lighter, and when he didn't find one,

Hannah dug her nails into her palms, not knowing what she would do if he bent to light it from one of the candles. Instead, he took the cigarette from his lips and slid it carefully back into the case.

"I've heard so much about your work," he said. And there it was again in his eyes, amusement and…something else. "The beautiful and brilliant Dr. Weiss exiled to the basement by my father."

"I consider it a great privilege to be here," said Hannah, but the words sounded practiced, even to her own ear.

"I'm glad to hear it." Stefan smiled his broad bon vivant smile. "Still, it would never do to have you catch cold from the damp."

"Hardly my most pressing concern."

"No. I suppose not," he said, and the smile faded.

"If there's nothing else, Dr. Frei—"

"You should call me Stefan."

"No," said Hannah, "I don't think I should."

"May I call you Hannah?"

"I would prefer you didn't, but it's not my place to say." Hannah drummed her fingers impatiently on the lab table. "Is there something I can do for you, Dr. Frei? Before you leave?"

"There is, actually." He took a manila folder from the in-box on the wall outside Hannah's office door, flipped it open on the table, and thumbed through several pages. "I came down to leave this for you. A few equations had us stumped upstairs. We were standing around scratching our heads this afternoon, and I got to wondering…" He closed the file folder and slid it across the table with his long, elegant fingers; his nails, with their perfectly white lunules, were buffed and smooth. "Would you mind running these?"

"Certainly! I mean, no, I wouldn't mind. Not at all. I'd be happy to do it." She grasped the folder, hoping he wouldn't see in her face how proud and delighted she was to be asked, to be recognized and valued in this way.

"By Monday," he said.

The curt tone of his voice undercut his winning smile. Hannah was reminded of her place and became keenly aware of how easily he'd manipulated her, allowing her to imagine for a moment that he regarded her as a colleague or even a peer.

"Yes, Herr Doktor," she said. "Monday. Certainly."

"Good evening to you, Dr. Weiss."

She held the folder against her chest, expecting him to leave, but he stood there, his gaze fixed on her, until she pointedly said, "Good evening, Dr. Frei."

Hannah didn't move until he'd disappeared down the half-lit hallway. Then, still clutching the folder, she crossed the room and closed the door as quickly and quietly as she could manage. In the air where he'd been standing, she detected the faint scent of his rich cologne, the aromas of bergamot, cognac, and sandalwood.

She sat down at her desk, spread the folder open in front of her, and set to running the complex equations. The numbers played like a symphony. There was not a wrong note. Hannah went over the pages again. She got up to pace, clasping her hands behind her back to stretch her shoulders for a moment. There had to be a reason why they weren't getting a higher level of radioactivity. Between the lines and digits—some carefully written and rewritten, others scrawled in the heat of inspiration—Hannah sensed the elusive essence of a hypothesis toward which they were working. She was certain that if she were ever allowed to be part of the whirlwind of collective consciousness circling these ideas, she might see a glimmer of something she wasn't seeing now. If she could only be in that room...

But to dwell on that was a waste of an opportunity to prove herself. Hannah sat down and ran the numbers again. And again. And again. She didn't realize she'd fallen asleep until she was jarred awake by the rattle of the door. The moment between unconsciousness and consciousness felt like falling, like the flare of a guttering candle casting terrifying shadows. *They're here.* Hannah sat up, spine straight, heart hammering.

The door opened, and her assistant, Karin Hoenig, edged her way in. Karin was a tentative and slightly awkward graduate student, ginger-haired and with a sprinkling of freckles that were the only distinguishing characteristics on her long, plain face.

"Karin," Hannah breathed. "What are you doing here?"

"You're at work early," said Karin.

"What time is it?" Hannah asked, squeezing the back of her neck.

"You've been here all night again. What could possibly be that important?"

"Stefan Frei brought me these equations."

"He came down here?" Karin's eyes went as big as saucers.

Hannah tried not to smile. It was obvious that Karin, no doubt along with every other young woman in Berlin, had set her cap for Dr. Frei; he had exactly the kind of pure blood and breeding a young German girl would want. "Dr. Frei asked me to run some numbers."

"Is he coming back?"

"I don't know," said Hannah, realizing that she wasn't sure if the implication was that he would come back for the results or that she should deliver them to him. "I suppose I'll take the file to his lab."

"Or I could," said Karin. "I mean—I'd be happy to do that. If it's helpful to you."

When Karin was first assigned to her, Hannah had tried to be a mentor, going out of her way to explain things and demonstrate useful shortcuts. But she'd quickly come up against Karin's truculence, the girl's irritation that she had to work and her resentment that she hadn't yet found a husband. Hannah had sympathy for Karin's yearnings; she, too, saw the propaganda posters depicting young, breastfeeding mothers and their families in idyllic, soft-toned settings. She understood that Karin, who was young and impressionable, had been told that the only truly noble goal for a woman was to bring children into the world, and the more children the better. Karin's insufficiently masked rancor, however, did nothing to smooth the rough edges of their relationship.

"Thank you, Karin. That won't be necessary." Hannah gathered Stefan's papers back into the folder. The equations were correct. There was nothing more to be done with them, she realized, because all he'd asked was that she run the numbers, and the numbers were not the issue. She took a red pen from a cup on her desk and wrote on the front of the folder: *You're doing it wrong.* Not knowing how Dr. Frei would respond to this, she told Karin, "Perhaps it's best if I slip the file under his door and let him find it on Monday morning."

"Oh. Yes, I suppose." Karin seemed crestfallen.

"I'll be leaving now, Karin. You'll lock the door after me?" Hannah wanted to make some small gesture, gently touch Karin's arm, but she sensed it wouldn't be taken in the spirit intended, so she put on her coat and pulled her shawl around her shoulders.

"Of course. Have a nice weekend, Dr. Weiss."

Hannah went up the deserted stairs to the main floor and was surprised to see Dr. Frei's laboratory door standing open. The contrast between his workspace and hers was striking. She hardly dared to imagine what it would be like to spend her days in a spacious lab where long mahogany tables held state-of-the-art equipment and tall windows flooded the room with air and light. As Hannah approached the open door, she heard the tremolo strings of Bruckner's Fourth playing on a gramophone. And, over them, the lilt of a woman's laughter.

"Stefan! You're incorrigible."

It was Ulrike Diebner. Hannah shrank back into the shadows behind the door, not because she was afraid but because she was curious to hear what they might say.

"We're going to miss the presentation," Ulrike said. "Dr. Speer is sure to be there."

"Sorry, darling. Father's been after me to complete this, and the devil if I…"

His words were lost beneath Bruckner's tempestuous horns and the scratching of chalk on the blackboard. Hannah ached to see the numbers flying from his fingers, the equations taking shape, connecting the physical world to an unseen universe of ideas and possibilities.

"...before Monday," Dr. Frei was saying. "I need to work through these numbers once more."

"Isn't that what your Jewish slave is for?" said Ulrike.

Hannah gasped as if she'd been slapped. She flattened herself against the wall, torn between wanting to hear what he would say next and wanting to fling the equations in his face.

"She can be useful," he said. "She's a top radiographic mathematician."

"Well, that's what they're good at, I suppose." There was a *click-clack* of expensive heels as Ulrike crossed the room, apparently to turn up the gramophone, because Bruckner's triadic hunting calls rose up and overwhelmed whatever else was being said. Hannah slipped the file folder into the in-box on the wall and hurried down the hall, wanting nothing more than to go home and sleep.

Walking back to the apartment, she passed the bakery where, just a few months ago, she'd splurged to buy Sabine's favorite breakfast treat, raspberry custard kuchen. Now she stared into the lit windows of the shop. Everything looked the same—the girl in her white cap, the glossy loaves and pastries in their splendid glass case, the golden patina of the polished gas sconces. But now, in the window, was a placard, small but distinct, announcing that Jews were not welcome. Hannah yearned for the simple days when she'd enjoyed the long walk to her bus stop, passing the florist, with its displays of blue and yellow gentians, cornflowers, and fire lilies, and the *Apotheke,* where she could window-shop or get advice about herbal remedies from the pharmacist. Now she didn't know which stores she was allowed to enter on a Saturday morning, and she steeled herself for the even longer walk home because she was not sure which buses she was allowed to board. There were so many rules now; almost four hundred separate edicts had filtered down from national and regional powers, all of which shored up the *Verordnung zur Ausschaltung der Juden aus dem deutschen Wirtschaftsleben*—the Decree on the Elimination of the Jews from Economic Life.

There was a law that forbade Jews to purchase bread from non-Jews prior to 5:30 p.m., a law that forbade Jews to sell bread to non-Jews at any time, a law that forbade non-Jews to purchase bread on behalf of Jews, and a law that forbade the gifting of bread-baking ingredients from non-Jews to Jews, from Jews to non-Jews who might bake the bread for them, and from Jews to other Jews. There was a limit on the number of cigarettes that could be sold to Jews and an ancillary limit on lighters; limits on the days and hours during which Jews could purchase aspirin, shoes, postage stamps, butter, and wine; laws prohibiting Jews from buying luxury items; laws designed to prevent Jews from following kashruth dietary laws; and, of course, a law requiring every Jew to display the gold star so that no merchant could claim that he didn't realize he was measuring out two ounces of licorice bits for a Jewish child prior to 6:00 p.m. on a Thursday.

Deciding against even a perfunctory attempt at shopping, Hannah wearily made her way back to the pleasant neighborhood where she lived. It was an elegant, upper-middle-class enclave where rows of well-kept houses sat comfortably together on a quiet street. The bay windows, beveled glass, and elaborate moldings spoke of a time when Berlin was a younger, more civil place, its citizens concerned with art and architecture. The tall oak trees were past the peak of their fall colors. Dry leaves scattered down the sidewalk and drifted golden in the gutters. By the time Hannah reached her front stoop, she felt nearly normal again, almost as if she were living in a sane and stable world where she could still sit at her favorite lunch counter and indulge in a small bowl of ice cream.

18

Alice Rivers, wobbling slightly on her high-heeled pumps, called across the dance floor, "Jack! Major Delaney." She'd clearly already had a few generous servings of punch, and she slurped from a cup that dangled, precariously, from her forefinger. "I thought they never let you boys out to play."

"Hello, Miss Rivers." Jack smiled amiably but shook his head when she offered him her punch cup. "Still on duty. But thanks."

"Aw, c'mon," Alice purred, draping an arm around his neck. "It's spiked with lab alcohol. Two hundred proof."

"Maybe later."

Alice's giggle faded when she realized Jack was looking over her shoulder toward a leather armchair where Hannah Weiss sat with a cup of tea and the book she'd been reading earlier.

"She's not available," Alice whispered with an air of one in the know. "I think she's having an affair with one of the married men."

Jack leaned in and matched her conspiratorial tone. "Has she mentioned anyone in particular?"

"Once. Funny name. Starts with *G*, I think."

"Gregor?"

"Yeah, maybe. She says, 'Blah-blah Gregor,' and then she clams up. Not a very social sort."

"Unlike yourself."

"So unlike myself!" Alice drifted the tip of her fingernail along Jack's jaw. "I'm not a gossip. I just like to help the effort wherever I can."

"I appreciate your devotion, Miss Rivers. Maybe I'll find a place for you on my team."

"And maybe—if you're a good boy—I'll save a dance for you."

"Please do," Jack said as he gently but firmly disentangled himself from her embrace. "Another time."

Alice pushed her bottom lip forward in a faux pout. She was pretty in that wholesome, born-to-be-good way that sold war bonds, but Jack wasn't one to act on a passing attraction, and he certainly wasn't going to allow himself to be drawn into any romantic intrigue in the close quarters of Los Alamos. This place was a petri dish for the sort of trysts, forbidden flirtations, and rarefied indiscretions that occurred when folks were removed from the constraints of polite society. Jack was particularly cognizant of the fiery freedom embraced by a lot of the single working women. Some of them acted like sailors on shore leave, and when he considered the environment in which they'd been raised—post-Victorian conventionality with a dollop of Great Depression—he could see a lopsided logic to the way they celebrated their personal emancipation.

Hannah Weiss's starchy self-determination was something different. Her restraint awoke an unwanted curiosity in him, a desire to break through her shell to find the soft vulnerability underneath. Jack knew there was more to it than Groves and Oppenheimer had already concluded. There was no point in trying to be cagey or casual. This was a tennis match in which the combatants were so closely equaled, each had to hope that the other would slip for a second and allow a razor-thin stroke of strategy.

"I'm surprised to see you here," Jack said, drawing a wooden stool over to the table by her armchair. "Didn't think you were much for parties."

"It's less crowded here than in my own barracks."

"Now, don't tell me you're still mad about that."

Hannah folded her hands in front of her, resting her slender wrists on her open book. Jack examined the doodles and equations that filled the margins.

"Do you ever stop working?" he asked.

"Do you?"

"Nope." Jack sighed heavily. "I need to ask you about the postcards."

"Of course you do. You think they mean something they don't, so you're going to keep bringing them up."

"Tell me what they mean. Maybe I'll shut up about it."

Hannah sat quietly, her expression unreadable. Jack waited for the silence to draw the story out, and after a long moment, it did.

19

Early on the Monday morning following Stefan Frei's Sabbath visit, Hannah and Sabine pulled on their wool coats and made sure their gold stars were firmly fixed in the correct place. A girl at Sabine's school had been dragged into an alley and raped recently, and the assailants had gone free when they claimed they were teaching her a lesson because her star was not displayed where it should have been. To Hannah, this was a cautionary tale about not following the rules; to seventeen-year-old Sabine, it was a cautionary tale about the utter stupidity of adults and the unfairness of life in general. Joshua exhausted himself trying to mediate enough peace for them to enjoy their breakfast. The practical reality was that, in order for Sabine to board her bus and get to school, she had to wear the star, and that was all there was to say about it.

As they paused to touch the mezuzah, Hannah said, "Sabine, if you come home from school someday and find that the mezuzah has been broken—vandalized in any way—"

"I know, I know." Sabine groaned. "Run to Frau Wutke's as fast as I can. Secret door at the back of the wardrobe. You've told me a thousand times."

They chatted as they headed down the staircase, but when they came to a narrow window that looked out onto the street, Hannah grasped Sabine's arm. "Wait!"

Across the sidewalk from their front stoop was a black Mercedes, a rare sight in their neighborhood. A man sat on its rounded quarter-panel smoking a cigarette, one foot on the rear bumper. He wore a long black coat. His face was hidden by a smartly tilted fedora.

"What's wrong?" asked Sabine. "Who is that?"

Hannah gripped her cousin's hand. "When we get to the lobby, I'll go out first. Alone. You stay by the mailboxes and count to a hundred and then you come out and go to your bus stop and to school. Do not look at me, and do not look back, no matter what."

"No! Hannah, I'm staying with you."

"You'll do as I say! For once—please. We don't have time to argue." Hannah pulled Sabine into her arms and hugged her tight. "I'm sure it's nothing. All right? Everything will be all right."

"Stop saying that!" Sabine tried to push herself away, to put Hannah at arm's length.

"The smartest people I know, Sabine—they keep telling me it'll pass. This craziness. It'll be over soon, and we'll have proper elections again, and everything will go back to the way it was. They're certain of it. But right now—to be safe—please do as I tell you."

Sabine looked through the glass, swallowed hard, and nodded. Holding hands tightly, they went down to the bank of brass mailboxes at the bottom of the staircase.

"Be brave," Sabine said, but it was clear her own bravado had slipped a little.

"I'll see you at supper. Right?"

"Yes. Right." Sabine nodded emphatically. "Supper."

Hannah managed a smile as she turned away to cross the lobby. She pushed through the front door, glancing right and left to see if anyone else was on the street, and scanned her neighbors' windows, wondering how many of them were watching through the eyelet of their fine lace curtains. The man by the Mercedes dropped his cigarette on the sidewalk, tamped it out with the sole of his shoe, picked up the butt, and deposited it in his coat pocket. When he stood and Hannah saw his face, relief flooded through her, then caution and a tinge of fear at what his presence might mean.

"Dr. Frei…"

"If I'm doing it wrong," he said, "why did you even bother?"

"Because you were asking the right questions."

Hannah turned back to the door and fiddled with the lock while she gained control of her trembling fingers and let the wild pulsing of her heart slow to a steady, even beat. This was the second time in forty-eight hours that he'd wreaked havoc on her day, smiling as carelessly as if he'd come to escort her to a dinner party. Either he was oblivious to the tightrope reality of her life or he was uninterested in it—and it made no practical difference to Hannah whether it was one or the other. She

descended the stairs and headed toward her bus stop. Stefan Frei
fell in step beside her.

"Kurt thought it must be actinium," he said.

"Kurt's only looking for applications," said Hannah. "You
should be splitting atoms that have more than one neutron."

"But von Laue already tried that, and the resulting—"

Hannah cut him off. "His work was incomplete. I can't give you
a simple answer, Dr. Frei, particularly if I'm not allowed to partic-
ipate in the experiments. But that's what I'd have my Jewish slaves
working on, if I were you."

"Hannah…"

He stopped walking, and when Hannah looked back, he appeared genuinely abashed. Rather than attempt an apology, he
said, "Let me give you a ride."

"No, thank you."

"Don't be stubborn. It's starting to rain."

"You don't want to pull up to the institute with me in your car."

"Hannah."

This time she didn't look back. She strode to the bus stop, placing one foot deliberately in front of the other, and when her bus
came, she boarded it, showing the card that gave her a dispensa-
tion, as an Austrian citizen, to ride.

Over the next weeks, she received occasional files from Dr. Frei
in the in-box on the wall next to the door. It amused Hannah to
think of it as a mezuzah of sorts. Hannah ran the numbers, making notes and, occasionally, suggestions in the margins, and Karin
was more than willing to return the files to Dr. Frei's office. Finally, one morning in late autumn, Hannah received a summons

to attend an assembly in the teaching auditorium. She arrived early, took a seat toward the back, and observed the other audience members as they drifted in.

The scientists were grouped in organic cliques according to personal friendships and professional factions. Some angled to sit advantageously near Kurt Diebner and Stefan Frei in what Gregor Stern facetiously called the Nobel Ghetto. Max Frei entered last, accompanied by Commandant Gerhard Scholl in full Nazi military regalia. A collective unrest rippled through the room, silent but unmistakable. The assembled scientists had labored under what they imagined was a separation of science and state. There'd been whispers, of course, but it was a shock to see an armband and swastika so boldly positioned in the front row. It was the first time Hannah saw her colleagues stiffly raising their arms and saying, in unison, "Heil Hitler." Hannah had grown used to hearing it in the post office and delicatessen. Children said it on the street. The bus driver said "Heil Hitler" before he swung the lever that clapped the door shut. The waiter said "Heil Hitler" when he handed someone the bill. But somehow this, in her sacred place of work, carried a new chill of foreboding.

"Good morning, Hannah." Gregor dropped into the seat next to hers and offered her a sweet. Then he put his finger under his nose to simulate a mustache and said in a cartoon voice, "Heil Hitler!"

Hannah brushed his hand away from his face. "Don't be an idiot, Gregor."

"I was born in Zurich," he said. "They can kiss my Swiss ass."

"Please, don't draw attention."

"From what I hear, you're the one drawing attention these days."

Hannah kept her gaze forward. "I'm sure I don't know what you mean."

Gregor kept his voice low, but there was no more humor in it. "Don't miss this opportunity, Hannah." He tapped Hannah's temple with his index finger. "This right here, Fräulein, is your ticket."

"To where?"

"Wherever you might need to go," said Gregor. "I'm just saying—"

"What?" Hannah crossed her arms defensively. "Just saying what?"

"That you have something they need, and as long as you don't get too uppity about it, you and yours are safe."

"Gregor," said Hannah, "if I needed a hand with something personal—if someone required papers, for example—do you think I could get help circumventing the waiting list?"

"Possibly." He glanced over his shoulder at a small group of colleagues seated a row or two behind them. "Look. Keep your head down. Do as you're asked. I'll make some discreet inquiries into— oh. Here we go." Gregor squeezed her hand. "Fasten your seat belt, dear heart."

"Gentlemen, good morning." Stefan Frei stepped to the podium. "If you could all be seated, please. Yes, thank you. Thank you for being here."

He gestured to Kurt Diebner to join him on the stage as the room fell silent.

"Good morning, gentlemen," said Diebner. "I have some very exciting news to share. Dr. Frei and I have made a major breakthrough. The moment we realized that we should be splitting atoms that have more than one neutron, we took the work of von Laue to the next level."

There was a hearty round of applause, and then Diebner laid out in detail the work that was all too familiar to Hannah. She kept her eyes on Dr. Frei, who stood aside, hands clasped behind his back. She wondered if he would at least tip an appreciative glance in her direction, but he didn't.

"The X-ray photon collided with a series of electrons," Diebner finally concluded, "accounting for the higher measurements of radioactivity."

He gave a stilted little bow, and the auditorium erupted in another round of applause that lasted until Commandant Scholl got to his feet and raised his hand for quiet.

"Dr. Diebner," he said, "are there military applications for this work?"

Stefan Frei stepped forward. "Herr Commandant, we have not yet begun to consider—"

"If the increased energy can be harnessed," Diebner said, interrupting him, "the results will transform modern warfare. We plan to make that our focus."

For the first time since he entered the auditorium, Stefan Frei looked up and met Hannah's eyes. She was gathering her things to leave.

20

Sitting at a small table next to the window, looking out on the cold and damp cobblestones of Ku'damm, Hannah just wanted her cousin to be still, drink her hot chocolate, and for once—just once in her life—follow instructions without argument.

"I'm not a child," Sabine protested. "I'll be eighteen in a few months. You don't want me to grow up, Hannah, but I have, despite your best efforts to keep a pink bow on top of my head."

Hannah sighed in the long-suffering way she knew Sabine hated, but they'd walked sixteen blocks through the freezing drizzle before finding a café willing to serve them, and Hannah's patience was exhausted. "I do want you to grow up. That's why it's so important that you go live with your mother's cousin Miriam in Chicago."

"Without you? Without Papa?"

"We can't get visas for all three of us. There are other ways for your father. Yesterday, I heard of a program to bring Jewish professors to universities in the southern United States. He's an excellent candidate."

"What about you, Hannah?"

"I have a plan," Hannah told her. "You don't need to worry about me. There's something I have to do here before I go, but I'll join you as soon as I can. Or this will end soon and you'll come back to Berlin. Meanwhile, Miriam will take you in. You can finish school in Chicago. Or New York. Wouldn't you like to see the Statue of Liberty? The Grand Canyon?"

"No. I have no interest in either of those things."

"You'll be able to go to a store and buy a dress. Eat at any café you please. Go to the movies again. Walk into any movie theater and see *The Wizard of Oz*."

"That movie is for children." Incensed, Sabine rolled her eyes. "You've just proven my point."

"*Gone with the Wind,* then, or *Dark Victory* or *Wuthering Heights* or any of the movies we can only read about in magazines. Your father and I only want what's best for—"

There was a light rap on the window. A young man stood on the sidewalk. He looked to be about Sabine's age, maybe a little older, with dark eyes and curly hair and the intensely hopeless expression of a boy in love. Around his neck was a scarf Sabine had been knitting a few weeks earlier. Hannah tried very hard not to raise an eyebrow. Sabine didn't look at her at all.

"I'll be right back."

She ran to the brass-rimmed door at the front of the café and appeared a moment later out on the sidewalk; she and the young man held a brief, animated conversation, their excited breath forming puffs of white mist. She tugged his sleeve to lead him away from the window where Hannah sat. They stood beside a lamppost, chatting for another minute or two. He handed her a folded sheet of paper, then he leaned in to kiss her. Sabine glanced in Hannah's direction, allowing his lips to graze her cheek but avoiding his mouth. She gave the scarf a playful tug and waved as he walked away. When she returned to her seat inside the café, Sabine was flushed and smiling despite herself.

"What's this about?" Hannah teased, assuming he'd handed her a love letter. "Going over notes for exams?"

"Don't start," said Sabine.

"You won't even tell me his name?"

"Daniel," said Sabine, and the way she said it told Hannah everything she needed to know.

"He's cute. Did he write you a poem? Let me see."

"It's private."

Hannah recognized the big eyes and defiantly pursed lips, an expression she'd seen on Sabine's face a thousand times. She was hiding something. "Sabine?"

Sabine volunteered nothing, but she didn't try to stop her cousin from taking the paper from her hand and unfolding it. Beneath a grotesque caricature of Adolf Hitler were words in bold print: *Studenten! Du musst Dich entscheiden!*

Hannah shoved the leaflet into her purse. "Do you have any idea how dangerous this is?"

"Is it safer to bury yourself in your lab and do nothing?"

"Yes! I'm not a fighter like you."

"It's hard to fight with your eyes closed."

Stung, Hannah straightened her spine and swept a silent look around the room. A gentleman at a nearby table glanced at her over his newspaper.

"I try to solve problems," Hannah said. "Instead of flailing around in naive idealism. Instead of endangering myself and my family."

"Let's just shut up and drink our cocoa."

They sat in silence until Hannah said, "We should get home," then they walked in silence sixteen blocks back to the apartment. Pausing in the lobby to check for mail, Hannah saw, perched on top of the brass mailboxes, a small package with her name on it. It was wrapped in brown paper, tied with a pale blue ribbon.

"Who's it from?" Sabine asked.

"How do I know?" Hannah said irritably. She slid the ribbon aside, removed the paper, and opened the silver box. The interior was lined with velvet in which nestled an unusual hair ornament, a jeweled comb designed to incorporate two night moths of breath-taking beauty. Their bodies were delicately molded from pâte de verre, extended wings almost translucent, carved of onyx and rose gold and studded with tiny pink diamonds and sapphires. The moths were poised for flight. Their sensuality and dark elegance so startled Hannah that she quickly closed the box and shoved it in her bag. Sabine could not see her so exposed, possessed of such a forbidden gift.

21

D r. Frei knows I can't accept this."

Hannah placed the box with the velvet lining firmly in Gregor's hands.

"Why not?"

"He cannot buy my work, my ideas, for the price of a piece of jewelry, no matter how fancy."

Gregor cradled the box. "When I first met Annalise, I wanted to give her a gift. One of my professors said, 'Give her a hat. Women love hats.' So I bought her the most elegant hat I could afford, and she wore it everywhere until the day we were married. Then she confessed that she'd always hated it. She thought it made her look like an ostrich. But she'd worn it because she understood that it was the only way I knew to tell her how I felt. We men can't always express our feelings in words."

He offered her the box again, but Hannah shoved her hands deeper into the pockets of her lab coat.

"One must be practical, Hannah. There is a war on, after all."

"I will not be bought."

With a shrug and a sigh, Gregor dropped the box into his pocket. He kissed Hannah on one cheek and then the other. "I'm off, then. Go home before curfew."

"I will," Hannah promised. She had the best intentions, but when afternoon stretched into evening, she was still immersed in her work. When she realized curfew had passed, she rummaged in her desk for a little tin of nuts and dried berries and wandered with her feast to an out-of-the-way room where she sometimes went to think.

The lab where Einstein had discovered the field equations was tucked away in an old, all-but-forgotten part of the building. She turned on a brilliant gas arc lamp and lowered the prism assembly, projecting spectral lines onto the chalkboard. She wrote out the equation that had been perplexing her all afternoon. She contemplated it for a little while before she heard the soft shuffle of footsteps in the hallway. This time it was Stefan who was caught off guard.

"Hello," he said. "I wasn't aware anyone else knew about this place."

"Whenever I get stuck," said Hannah, "I come here hoping some of Einstein's genius is still in the air."

"My father invited him to our home for dinner after a lecture," said Stefan. "I was eight years old. He wore a morning coat, slippers, and a pair of striped trousers with one button missing. I thought it was the grandest way to dress."

"It is, isn't it?"

"After dinner, he read to me from his favorite children's book. 'And there's a dreadful law here—it was made by mistake, but there it is—that if anyone asks for machinery—'"

"'They have to have it and keep on using it,'" Hannah chimed in. *"The Magic City."*

"Yes! You know it?"

"My father—*alav hashalom*—used to read it to me. I worry now, in our search for the truth, that we're making dreadful machinery the world will have to have and keep on using."

Stefan wandered to the blackboard. "This is what you're stuck on?"

"It's nothing." Hannah took the felt-block eraser from a trough below the board, but he stopped her hand. The weight of his touch was firmer than she had expected, perhaps firmer than he'd intended, and his hand remained pressed against hers so long, she could feel his skin, soft, smooth, warm.

"Worried I might steal your idea?"

Hannah glared at him without answering.

"For what it's worth," said Stefan, "I'm truly sorry."

"And what about Kurt? Is he sorry too?"

"I wouldn't presume to speak on his behalf."

"A real scientist doesn't exploit," Hannah said, pulling her hand away. "He collaborates."

"Then let me be a real scientist." Stefan stepped back to take in the broad sweep of the equation. He picked up a stubby bit of chalk and rattled it in his palm as if he were about to roll a pair of dice. "Let's try x to the fifth and see what happens."

He dashed the chalk against the blackboard in a rapid-fire way, like striking a flint to create a spark. As the equation was transformed, Hannah inhaled sharply.

"Yes!" She clapped her hands together. "Yes, that's it."

"Maybe there's a bit of Einstein in the air after all," said Stefan. He flashed the cocky grin of a proud schoolboy, but it faded when he noticed the crestfallen look on Hannah's face. "What is it? Doesn't that solve your problem?"

"Forget it," Hannah said.

"Look, I apologized. There's nothing else I can—"

"It's not about that," said Hannah.

"Then what?"

"I've been struggling for three days over a problem you solved in less than three minutes between dinner and the theater." She copied the equation down in her lab notebook, relishing its elegance. "Whatever happened to the little boy who loved Einstein?"

"He's exactly who he always was," said Stefan. "Max Frei's callow, underachieving, immature son."

"Maybe it's time he grew up." Hannah snapped her notebook shut and pushed her pencil through the bun on the back of her head.

"That would be exceedingly dangerous," Stefan said, his eyes traveling across the equation on the board.

"What do you mean?"

"Nothing." He brushed his hands together, scuffing off the chalk dust. "Let's see if it works."

22

After ten long days in the lab working and reworking theorems, testing and retesting hypotheses, Stefan stood behind Hannah, his hands cupping hers with an easy affection that was starting to feel as natural as numbers falling together in an inevitable formula.

"It's time," he said, and Hannah turned on the atom smasher, and they observed as the crystal fluorescence glowed vibrant green. She glanced at the second hand on the wall clock and noted each tick as the color grew weaker, weaker, almost gone. The color died away. Stefan checked the data and entered the tweaked equation in his expensive leather-bound lab book.

"How about a proportional amplifier?" he asked.

"Fine, in theory," said Hannah. "We just have to make it work."

"Well, more accurately, *you* have to make it work. I just have to take credit for it."

"Hilarious." Hannah cuffed his arm with the back of her hand. "Anyway, you can rightly take whatever credit they give you. I couldn't have done this on my own."

"Neither could I," Stefan said. "I can't think as well as this up in my own lab."

"Perhaps it's the lower altitude."

"I've been meaning to ask you something—" Stefan started, but Hannah cleared her throat and nodded toward the door. The sharp *kleck-klock, kleck-klock* of expensive heels could be heard in the hallway.

"Stefan?" It was Ulrike. "Stefan Frei, are you down there?"

Hannah retreated behind the lab table. Stefan snapped to attention and called, "In here."

Ulrike appeared in the doorway wearing a black silk dress studded with copper beading. She turned slightly to reveal a daring drape of silk that plunged down her back and lean muscle under powdered white skin. Ulrike's hair was slicked close to her skull, emphasizing her angular cheekbones, her starkly handsome features. "Whatever are you doing down here in the dungeons?" She slid a fleeting, contemptuous look in Hannah's direction. "Funny, you've never been so committed to your work before."

"I've never been committed to anything before," said Stefan. "Isn't that what you love about me?"

Hannah detected a slight twitch in the corner of Ulrike's mouth at the word *love*.

"Did you forget? Tonight's the night we're to see *Die Walküre*.

Lotte is making her debut. We're already late, and now we have to stop off so you can change into proper evening attire."

"I haven't forgotten. I'm just not certain attending the opera is the best use of my time right now."

"I promised Lotte that we'd be there."

Hannah watched as Stefan ran his thumb along the edge of the worktable, feeling the old wood as if searching for runes or an ancient text carved into stone. He deliberately avoided looking at Hannah, and she felt the heat rise in her face, the irritation; he was behaving like a spoiled child who doesn't want to make a choice lest he have to take responsibility for his decision.

Ulrike moved toward him, plucked an imaginary thread from his lapel, and dropped her voice to a low murmur as she said, "Henry Ford and his wife are attending. He and his contingent are eager to meet you, Stefan; he has proposals to convert Ford's German production lines for military uses. They're expecting us for cocktails in twenty minutes. Kurt arranged a private suite at das Französische."

"Yes. Right." Stefan's tone was oddly flat. "Ford."

"Stefan. Darling. There is a great deal of money in play here. Perhaps that doesn't matter to your family, but it does to mine. Kurt is counting on you to be there. You have five minutes to meet me in the car. If you choose to remain here with *her,* I cannot predict the consequences." She turned on her heel and swept out the door.

Stefan swore softly. "We can pick this up tomorrow."

"Of course," said Hannah. "Mustn't forget what's truly important. There's a war on, after all."

She made no attempt to keep the tinge of acid from her tone, but she knew him well enough now to realize that, no matter how provocative she was, he would choose not to engage. That would require a level of principle, a commitment to doing something other than taking the path of least resistance, and Hannah suspected he wasn't capable of that.

"Why don't you go home and get some sleep?" he said as he shed his lab coat and retrieved his overcoat. "We've been at it for days. We're allowed to take a break."

"How would you know the difference? Your entire life has been a break," she said, turning away from him.

"And your entire life is in this basement."

"You say that as if I have a choice!"

"Hannah." He set his hands on her shoulders and turned her to face him. In his eyes, there was a strange combination of urgency and indecision. "Do you trust me?"

"What?"

"It's a simple question: Do you trust me? We've been in this laboratory together sixteen hours a day for ten days. We've shared progress and frustration, talked about science and ambition and our childhoods. Have I not earned your trust on any level?"

Hannah was baffled as to why he was asking her this question and unsure of the answer. "Good evening, Dr. Frei. Enjoy the opera."

He left her standing in the silence and solitude of the lab that was once her refuge. He'd taken that from her, she realized now. The blackboards were filled with his hieroglyphics, and that specific scent of cognac, bergamot, and tobacco hung in the air. Her shoulders felt tender even though his touch had been feather-light. Hannah was unsettled to recognize that she was no more immune to his charm than Karin was, and Karin, in these past days, had been making a fool of herself, arriving earlier and staying later, hanging on Stefan's every word. She'd brought him strudel baked by her mother and made sure his coffee maintained the proper heat and sweetness. At the end of each day, when Stefan praised her dedication and insisted that she must go home and rest, Karin glowed like a Roentgen ray. Hannah stiffened at the thought that he was manipulating her in the same manner, making her feel indispensable and brilliant, playing to her craving for professional respect, and injecting just enough personal conversation and physical affection to lead her to believe they were growing close.

So here was the answer to his question, clear enough: No, she did not trust him. But she liked him. There was no denying it. She was happy to see him arrive each morning, knowing that the work would ignite an electrical storm in her brain. Once silent, dank, and somber, the room now crackled with ideas, laughter, and moments of genius. They danced in synchrony around the lab with physical ease, almost elation, and a rare collaborative chemistry. But the most intoxicating aspect of Stefan was not the brilliance he brought into the room; it was the brilliance he brought out in her. Hannah had never experienced such exquisite insight. When he spoke of the possibilities of fission, she was aware of every molecule of chalk dust on her fingertips. Since she'd been a child, she'd known there was something inside her—something dormant and unsafe and exhilarating—

and now it had a context. When she closed her eyes and listened to the sound of his voice intercut with the frenetic *scritch-scratch* of chalk on blackboard, she felt herself on the verge of a universe reordered. The theoretical became physical. At last, all the long-imagined possibilities that lay in the harnessing of atomic power, the applications of her wildest dreams, everything her father had groomed her for—it was all within reach. This clarity, so close at hand, terrified her, but far more powerfully, it thrilled her to the core.

23

The party had deflated to a few last stragglers. The guy in the cowboy boots was now dancing with a bottle of Jim Beam. Jack lit his third Camel and offered one to Hannah, who declined, taking instead a tiny sip of her cold tea.

"Let me get this straight, Dr. Weiss. You're asking me to believe that you were on the brink of what might have been the pivotal scientific discovery of our time, but when Stefan Frei went to the opera, you just walked away? 'Meh, I think I'll head home tonight and see what's on the old Volksempfänger.' Come on."

"Major Delaney," Hannah said with genuine admiration, "you continually impress me with your knowledge of German culture. Unless you just like that funny word. Do you actually know what that is?"

"It's a little AM radio sold to the Germans as cheap entertainment. It turned out to be the most powerful propaganda tool ever deployed."

"Impressive."

"Down at the office, we call it the Goebbelsnout."

"Yes! Because of the big round nose," she said, remembering, rueful. "The idea of a radio in every home, this was a novelty, and it was a clever design—compact, quite reliable, and presented in a very attractive Bakelite case. You could get one in any color. Or tortoiseshell. My favorite. Sabine begged me to take her to the— oh, what would you call a store for incidentals?"

"Five-and-dime?"

"*Fivandime,*" she repeated, not really understanding the term but accepting it and committing it to memory. "I bought her one that was bright blue. She borrowed nail polish from me and painted little red flowers on it."

"Tell me about Sabine," said Jack.

"You already know." Hannah took a compact from her purse and touched up her dark red lipstick. "She's the one who sent the postcards."

"I believe that as much as I believe that you walked away from your work with Dr. Frei. We're more alike than you imagine, Hannah, you and I. We're both extremely ambitious—dangerously so. I wouldn't give up on something I'd been working toward for my whole life. And neither would you."

"I didn't give it up," Hannah said. "It was taken from me."

"Surely you could see where all these thrilling discoveries were headed, into whose hands this machinery would be placed. You knew about the camps."

"I thought I was safe," Hannah said. "I was assured by my employer that I was safe because I was needed for my work on critical project issues. I was an Austrian citizen and the daughter of a German war hero, which exempted me from—"

"But your uncle and cousin—"

"I thought I could protect them."

"How? By cooperating with the Nazis?"

"We didn't think of it as 'cooperating with the Nazis' to buy our bread after five thirty. We were obeying the law and doing what we had to do so we could continue to live our lives."

"What kind of life is that, crawling through the day with a jackboot on your neck?"

"You sound as naive as Sabine," Hannah said. The smallest hint of a smile tugged at the corner of her mouth.

"I could never live like that. I would have fought back."

"You Americans," Hannah scoffed. "You're so damn smug. 'Give me liberty or give me death!' You say that so easily because you've never been asked to choose between dignity and death. Between love and bread. You blame the Jews for their own extermination because you can't bear to say, 'There but for the grace of God go I.'"

"Point taken," Jack conceded. "But the people of the United States would never allow anything like that to happen. Fundamentally, we believe that all men are created equal—" He bit back the rest when he realized she was laughing at him.

"Oh, has the Alice Paul amendment been passed, giving women equal rights? Somehow I never heard about it," she said. "I'm confused. Are there not dedicated entrances and water fountains exclusively for those of Aryan descent? Japanese families in camps a few hundred miles from here? Country clubs and colleges where Jews are verboten?"

Jack's expression went stony. He rested his elbows on his knees, tenting his fingers as he contemplated the next question. "Then why are you here, Dr. Weiss? Why do you want the United States, this terrible, despotic country, to win a war if it will pretty reliably ensure the nation will be a superpower that controls the entire globe for generations?"

"Should I pretend some deep allegiance to my adopted country, Major Delaney? Pretend to have turned my back on the homeland I loved? We both know you would have immediately seen through that and assumed me to be a spy, so I've saved us both the trouble. But now you assume I'm a spy because I *haven't* pretended."

"I don't make assumptions, Dr. Weiss. I excavate facts and draw conclusions, same as you. My allegiance is to the truth."

"Truth! Liberty! Such lofty ideals. And yet I see a certain..."

"What?" Jack challenged when she allowed the statement to trail off.

"I'm not sure," she said. "Sadness, perhaps. Loneliness, definitely. And maybe disillusion."

"Let's get back to the facts."

"Yes, by all means."

"By whatever means become necessary," said Jack.

Hannah noticed that his tone didn't sound threatening, only assured, as if she'd come to a crossing and he was alerting her to an oncoming freight train.

"Finish telling me about the equations," he said.

"They were doing it wrong," said Hannah. "They were blind men with an elephant, and most of them were unwilling to ask a Jewish woman for guidance."

Jack leaned in closer. "Most of them?"

"There were a few exceptions."

"Such as…"

"Gregor Stern," said Hannah, "as you've already ascertained."

"And Stefan Frei."

"The Aryan golden boy?" She tucked a stray tendril back into her jeweled hair comb. "He was next in line to head the institute, about to broker a deal with Henry Ford and perhaps even win a Nobel Prize."

Jack, speaking quietly but with a hard edge of urgency and not a hint of give, said, "Dr. Weiss, do you understand what's at stake here? You were working with the architect of Hitler's atomic-bomb program."

"Stefan Frei didn't work with anyone. He just found people he could use."

"If you were so useful, why did he let you go?"

"You'd have to ask him."

"I'm asking you," he said. "I want to know why you, a Jew, were cooperating with the Nazis."

"We all did what we had to do to survive."

"Not everyone. So why did you?"

"Governments come and go," she said. "A little tyranny just felt like another swing of the pendulum."

"At first."

Hannah nodded. "The Nazis hate Jews. Hardly the first ones in history. They just happen to be exceptionally good at it."

"You have to pick a side, Hannah."

"Do I? Do I, really? A time of war is a time of amplified connection and disconnection. Our allegiance to everything we love takes on a dangerous primacy, while our fear of everything we hate dons the sheep's clothing of righteousness."

"And you don't believe that love will overcome hate?"

"Why would anyone find that sentiment comforting?" Hannah laughed. "Throughout history, love has been the source of more destruction than hate could ever aspire to. *In a time of war,* Major Delaney, love is dangerous. In a time of war, attraction becomes volatile. It is human nature to sexualize attraction, and it is the nature of nature to form attractions. In a way, it's simply nuclear physics."

"Hannah." Jack sighed. "If I had time to sit here and listen to this kind of thing, I'd be happy to do it all night. But I don't have time. And neither do you. You have one chance here to tell me the truth, and I mean the whole truth, or you will find yourself in an extremely difficult set of circumstances."

When Hannah didn't flinch, he charged on.

"Do you know what happens to spies in Leavenworth, Fräulein? Spies are not prisoners who enjoy the protection of the usual rules of battle or American citizens who enjoy the protection of the Constitution. In a time of war, spies are considered enemies of the state. They are *interrogated*"—he carefully enunciated the word, allowing her a moment to invest it with whatever connotations came to mind—"and then tried before a military tribunal.

No jury. No dainty appellate protocol. In my experience, sentencing tends to be both unforgiving and swift. The only hope you have now—"

"You've made your point," Hannah said, cutting him off. She studied the remnants of a party she could never be a part of, the dancing drunks and couples necking in darkened corners. "*In a time of war*. That idiom sets my teeth on edge. I have never known a time that was not of war, and far too often, I've heard that phrase invoked as the only reason necessary for whatever horrors need to be justified."

She leaned back, her delicate frame dwarfed by the armchair, and, for an instant, he thought he had frightened her, but she held his eyes without apology, determined to play the hand through. Then, still silent, Hannah scribbled something on a napkin, slid it across the table to Jack, got up, and walked away.

White's Diner
Santa Fe
Tomorrow at five.

24

FIELD NOTE

April 10, 1945

SUBJECT: COMPROMISE OF SITE Y PERSONNEL

To: Donovan

From: Delaney

SUMMARY: (1) Having deposed the 70-plus essential and nonessential Site Y personnel who signed REICHL petition, we can conclude, with a fair amount of certainty, that loyalty is thin, the food here is shit, and it is imprudent to trust European scientists with sensitive information beyond what is necessary to their function. (2) WEISS has proven less than forthcoming about her relationship with STERN, who is a bridge agent for whoever is actually on the tin can at the other end of this string. Suspicions strongly suggest FREI, S.

RECOMMENDATION: WEISS to be interrogated further at alternate location.

25

Jack paced in front of a window in the Quonset hut office, tossing a rubber ball back and forth between his hands and squeezing it hard. A blood-orange sun sank into the gap-toothed ridge beyond Los Alamos, turning the mountains amber, purple, and red. Jack appreciated the stunning vista, but the sacred serenity of the place remained out of his reach. Jack preferred the busy claustrophobia of the base with its crisscrossing webs of telephone wires, clotheslines filled with laundry that flapped in the wind, and jerry-rigged electrical cables. He was accustomed to grids: steel skyscrapers, blocks of tenement houses, the angled shadows of the elevated trains. One rarely saw the horizon in New York City; here there was nothing but horizon. The sky, a throbbing turquoise, stretched on for miles and made Jack feel uncomfortably exposed.

"Weren't you heading over to the diner in Santa Fe to meet up with you know who?" said Epstein.

"I thought I'd let her sit and simmer for a while. I need her to realize how much she wants to talk to me."

"Are you sure it's not the other way around?"

Jack dropped the ball and Epstein scrambled for it.

"Sorry, sir," said Epstein, handing him the ball. "It's not my place."

"Speak your mind, Lieutenant."

"Sir, with all due respect, from what I've observed, Dr. Weiss has a certain effect on certain people—and I'm not saying this is you, but take Peter Reichl, for example. He's been away from his wife for some time and maybe getting kinda…"

"Lonely," said Jack.

"That's one word for it."

"You're saying I'm not looking closely enough at Dr. Weiss?"

"The opposite," said Epstein. "You're so focused on her as a suspect, I'm not sure you're seeing the big picture."

Epstein checked the teletype machine. It was late afternoon, so the feed was occupied with the daily list of the dead, a seemingly endless march that reminded them with every drumbeat of the imperative of their task.

"Interesting," said Epstein. "Dr. Weiss listed her cousin Sabine as her next of kin in Chicago, but that's not who she listed here at Los Alamos."

"Hard to send postcards to a corpse," said Jack.

He didn't like being lied to and liked even less the way both Oppenheimer and Groves—and now Epstein—needled him with suggestions that some passing attraction for Hannah Weiss might influence his investigation. It was a red-blooded reaction, but Jack prided himself on being difficult to read, and Groves was a man who'd happily file away any little tidbit he could use for leverage in the future. Who wouldn't be attracted to a beautiful woman in a world of vests, lab coats, and olive-drab uniforms? Maybe Groves was thinking the same thing that had crossed Jack's mind: that she was lovely, that her presence in this arid place was a bit too much like the untouchable bloom of a senita cactus, protected by dangerous gray spines. Which made her all the more alluring.

The phone rang, and Epstein dived for it. "Major Delaney's office." He listened, jotting notes on the Big Chief tablet he always used. As if he were a grammar-school kid. It was one of the quirky things Jack liked about him. The lieutenant cupped his hand over the mouthpiece and said, "They got Gregor Stern."

"Excellent," said Jack, but a ripple of jealousy unsettled his gut. He should be there, in the European theater, not here in the desert poking under a rock for scorpions. Still, this was good news. Epstein was taking it like Hanukkah, a blow job, and cheesecake night at the mess hall all rolled into one. He clapped the phone down and crowed, "Stick that in your bratwurst and smoke it."

"All right, Gladys, just give me the information."

"Colonel Pash and the Alsos operatives have been staked out all night at the post office in Zurich. Couple hours ago, well, whaddya know—Gregor shows up. Goes right for the mailbox. Doesn't even look over his shoulder. They see him tucking something into his breast pocket and *zam!*—they swoop in. Beautiful. With hard evidence, there wasn't a damn thing the Swiss could do. And you know Pash."

"I do indeed."

Colonel Boris Pash, originally a White Russian, was built like a fireplug. A rabid Red-baiter, he was still waiting for the day the Romanoffs would be restored to the throne and he could return to the Motherland. There was not much anyone could do to get between him and his objective, and he didn't care who got hurt in the process. This Jack knew from experience. He squeezed the rubber ball in his right hand and followed the sizzling of the damaged nerve that ran up his arm from his wrist to the back of his neck.

"Stern took some convincing," said Epstein, "but he got religion a few hours into the conversation."

"And?"

"The postcards were intended for our Aryan friend Stefan Frei."

So there it was. Hannah Weiss had been working directly with the physicist who was now leading Germany's team of Nobel laureates in building the bomb. Despite her protestations, their communication, and perhaps their work, had continued after she left Germany. Jack felt the ticking clock ratchet forward.

"Stern's postcard—what did it say?"

Epstein handed Jack a hastily scribbled translation.

Let apes and children praise your art,
If their admiration's to your taste,
But you'll never speak from heart to heart,
Unless it rises up from your heart's space.

Jack folded the poem into his pocket, eager to engage in a bit of a heart-to-heart of his own. "Excuse me, Lieutenant. I have a date."

26

It reminds me of the forts Ulrike and I used to build in the woods," said Stefan, looking at the primitive prototype of a reactor they'd cobbled together on the floor in Hannah's basement lab. "We'd spend hours on it and plan to camp out there, but inevitably, Kurt would come and knock it down."

"Interesting," Hannah said absently. She was focused on her journal, noting the exact distance between the tank of water on the floor and the aluminum sphere suspended above it.

"Interesting?" Stefan laughed. "Clearly not."

"I was listening," Hannah insisted. "Ulrike, woods, camp out, Kurt, knock it down. Let's hope he doesn't do the same here."

Stefan adjusted the chain, and Hannah handed him the journal so he could make his notations alongside hers. "The less he sees of me, the more suspicious he becomes. These past few weeks—he knows I'm working on something."

"Ready?"

Stefan nodded. Hannah rotated a heavy crank, lowering the sphere into the water.

"If the shields work as we predict, the water should start to heat and bubble within days. If not—"

The ticking of the neutron counter rose to an agitated chatter and then a roar. Steam billowed up from the roiling water.

"The counter can't record the intensity," said Stefan.

"Switching to the chart recorder." Hannah made the change, and the recording pen zigzagged wildly on its wire swing arm. "Take it out! Now!"

Stefan heaved the crank, hoisting the sphere back into the air. For a moment, they stood there looking at it as if they were suspended from the same steel chain, each unprepared for the sudden burst of blue flame. Hannah cried out, covering her eyes as Stefan pulled her aside, shielding her body with his own. There was an eerie, static rumbling; a glass beaker shattered with a shrill cry. As if on fire, the air filled with the crackle and glow of blue coronas. The pile was engulfed in flames that sang with an escalating descant as gas escaped. Hannah pitched a bucket of water on it, but the flames burned higher and brighter. Stefan bolted over to the lab table for chemical retardant.

"Hannah, get out! It's going to explode!"

"No! The journal—"

Hannah groped for it in the haze as Stefan emptied powder over the hissing flames. The fire guttered down to a silky black core. They stood for a moment, and then they both dissolved into a mutual gale of nervous laughter.

"Shit." Stefan coughed. "Are you all right?"

Hannah nodded, struggling to breathe in the acrid fog. They opened windows, and fresh winter air swept into the lab.

"How about a walk?" Stefan croaked, and Hannah nodded again.

They pulled on warm coats and went out the side door leading to the alley. Hannah hurried to keep up with Stefan's long strides until she reached the corner of the building, where she stopped and waited for him to realize that she was no longer walking next to him. She watched with wry amusement as he continued halfway down the block, telling an animated story, breath-puffing clouds above his extravagant hand gestures. He stopped, spun around, and came back to where she was standing. "Is something wrong?"

"That's a matter of perspective, I suppose."

"I'm sorry. Curfew. I didn't think."

"It must be nice," said Hannah, "to go for a walk wherever and whenever you want without giving it a thought. When this is over, I'll never take that for granted again."

"You sound like my father." Stefan offered Hannah a cigarette, then held the light for her. "I don't know what makes otherwise intelligent and highly educated people think we'll wake up one morning and find the clock has been turned back ten years. *Good morning! Hitler's still a house painter in Bavaria. There's going to be a free election. And we're all eighteen again.*"

"But all the smartest people—Max and Gregor and my uncle

too—keep saying things will change. Even Sabine is convinced that if enough people push for it—"

"They don't know everything there is to know."

"But you do?"

He didn't answer, didn't meet her eyes.

"Stefan? What is it that you know?"

"If it's so damn easy to change the world," he said, "why doesn't it happen more often?"

"Because people rush by on their own urgent errands or they just don't care enough, but they—oh." Hannah pressed her finger-tips to her temples. "Of course! I don't know how we didn't see it, Stefan. It was right here!"

"Didn't see what?"

"This! This!" Hannah gripped his elbow and pulled him into a broad rectangle of light below the gas lamp. She dropped to her knees and scribbled furiously on the shallow snow. "One touches two, two touch four…and? And?" She looked up at him, drawing an impatient circle in the air. "Come on!"

"It's a chain reaction."

"So your question—that's the answer. Why doesn't it happen more? Or, more important: *When* does it happen? There are two ways." She scrambled to her feet and hooked her arm through his. "We're walking down the street in Berlin on a sunny day. People are in a hurry, rushing to get where they're going. They hardly notice the person next to them. But now, now we're walking down the street, and it's snowing—trudge, trudge—we're clomp-ing along."

"Hannah, I'm not following."

"Strangers greet one another, maybe even pause to chat. Think." She watched it dawn on him.

"The snow slows the reaction down; the snow's a moderator," said Stefan. "Like heavy water for neutrons."

"Exactly! Now take a different group of people, not strangers, but neighbors. Say it's a little town like Rothenberg instead of a bustling city like Berlin. If someone has a tragedy in that little town, how long is it before everyone knows about it?"

"Only the time it takes to make a few telephone calls."

"A few generations of phone calls," Hannah said. "Another chain reaction."

"But one needs a moderator, and the other doesn't."

"One is slow—perhaps it takes all day before everyone has passed through the snow." Hannah knelt again and traced an ascending curve in the snow, and Stefan squatted beside her. "The other is fast—the people know each other, so the message keeps spreading to new people and moving outward. One is a reactor—"

"And the other is a bomb." Stefan swept a straight line up from her arc.

"We've all been trying to turn a runaway reactor into a bomb—"

"—and it'll never succeed," said Stefan, "because they're two different...what? Why are you looking at me like that?"

"Because I finally get to see him," said Hannah. "The boy who loved Einstein."

"That was you. You did that." Stefan's gaze was fixed on her, yet she saw none of the calculated amusement or cool predation in it she had come to expect. There was a clarity and open admiration, a look that held hers frankly. She couldn't succumb to her learned instinct, cultivated by years of self-doubt, of ducking her head to avoid eye contact. She felt that he saw her, all of her, with no filter and no judgment.

Hannah shivered, teeth chattering, as Stefan placed a protective arm around her shoulder and pulled her close. She leaned into his body, feeling safely encircled, rough wool and soft cashmere against her cheek. Only the promise of their equations, scrawled across the frost on the cobblestones and already half obliterated by the falling snow, checked her desire to find oblivion in his embrace.

"Come on."

She jumped up and pulled him to his feet, and they ran down the alley to the basement door. In the lab, Hannah switched on the atom smasher. The crystal fluorescence blossomed green, turned greener, then went deep emerald. Hannah checked the data with a neutron counter as its cricket-like clicking rapidly increased, built to a roar, then died away.

"What's the highest yield you've ever gotten?" she asked.

"Three generations."

"We just got ninety."

"Ha!" Stefan whooped, threw his arms around Hannah, and swept her off her feet momentarily before he turned to readjust the spectrograph. "All right. Now. If we can figure out some way to reflect the nuclei back into the core..."

"Stefan," she said. "We did it."

They stood for a moment in the fluorescent glow. Hannah felt a shiver of electricity run through her body.

Stefan touched her arm. "Someone's coming."

He slipped the journal into his pocket as Hannah hastily erased the equations scrawled on the blackboard. When the door opened a moment later, she was perched on the lab assistant's stool, and Stefan was leaning against the table, lighting a cigarette.

"Good evening, Dr. Diebner," he said. With an expansive gesture toward the smoldering pile, he added, "We were about to have a grill party."

"What in hell!" Kurt Diebner waved one hand in front of his face and sniffed at the fumes like a bloodhound. Scholl stood in the hallway behind him.

"Commandant Scholl, what a pleasure to see you," said Stefan.

Scholl clicked his heels together. "Heil Hitler."

"Indeed." Stefan smiled, his jaw tight.

"What's going on here?" asked Scholl.

"All I have to do is put on a lab coat, and I become a fire hazard."

Diebner poked at the sphere. "You've been working with LEU?"

"Yes. Well. Whatever is lying around. Dash of pepper. Pinch of thyme."

"And you were able to produce this level of combustion?" Diebner said. "My God, man."

"Combustion," Scholl echoed, perking up immediately when he heard language he understood. "Excellent, gentlemen. This is exactly what the Reich Research Council has been hoping for."

"We can't—" Hannah started, but Stefan cut her off.

"Of course," he said. "That's been my goal all along, but clearly, it's still theoretical—not ready for a formal presentation."

Diebner shuffled through the papers on Hannah's desk. "May I see the lab journal?"

Stefan gestured to the smoldering mess. "If you find it, let me know."

"You and I should be working on this together." Diebner seemed wounded. "Upstairs. With proper equipment."

"And a proper lab assistant." Scholl sent a condescending glance toward Hannah.

"Of course, Kurt. I'd be honored," said Stefan. "As always."

After fingering Hannah's files, Kurt Diebner selected several papers and folded them into the pocket of his lab coat. "Good. I'll be in the lab first thing in the morning."

Scholl followed him out with a brusque "Good evening."

"And to you, sir." Stefan closed the door after them and whispered, "How much uranium was in there?"

"Eighty micrograms."

"And how many of those would fit into a Gotha bomber?"

"There isn't that much enriched uranium in the entire world."

"But there could be," said Stefan, "if someone was properly motivated to make it."

Hannah was silent for a moment, hollowed by sudden understanding, the weight of consequence settling on her shoulders. "'I shall never believe that God plays dice with the world.'"

"*Faust?*" said Stefan.

Hannah shook her head. "Einstein."

"Maybe God sometimes needs a little human help."

"What are you saying?"

"I'm not sure yet," said Stefan. "But we can't be seen together again. It's too dangerous. Whatever we do from this moment on, it's imperative we keep it from Kurt." He thumbed a bit of soot from Hannah's chin. "Can't have him knocking down our little fortress."

27

Jack studied Hannah Weiss as she sat across the table from him in a corner booth of White's Diner, a nondescript eatery with a handwritten menu and home-baked desserts. He found it interesting that she'd chosen this place because it was so quintessentially American, with oil-filmed Formica tables and sticky Naugahyde seats. Yet this piece of classic Americana was tucked into the arcaded colonnade of the ancient plaza across the square from La Fonda, the pink and coral of the adobes fading back into earth. Hannah did not strike him as being a chicken-fried-steak or make-your-own-omelet type. She'd scanned the menu quickly, not really reading the entries, then opted for a slice of apple pie. She'd eaten about a third of it—the center point—with a small splash of the cream the waitress had brought for their coffee. She'd been here before. He was certain of that, and he wondered with whom.

He'd heard rumors of a Russian safe house operating in Santa Fe—perhaps this was where she met with her handler.

"Why would Frei want to keep Diebner out of it?" he asked.

"Diebner already had a Nobel Prize," said Hannah. "I imagine Dr. Frei didn't relish the idea of sharing his with him."

"But he wasn't about to get a Nobel without you, was he?"

"I wouldn't flatter myself."

Jack shifted uncomfortably on his side of the booth. Sometimes when he sat too long, he had a sensation like a line of fire ants blazing a burning trail down his spine.

"Is something wrong, Major?"

"What could possibly be wrong?" Jack opened his hands on the table. "Here I am having dessert with a beautiful woman on a lovely spring evening. Coffee and apple pie. Birds singing. Sunset blazing. I mean, if the world actually is about to end—hey, what a way to go."

"There are worse ways, I imagine."

"And some worse than you can imagine."

Hannah sighed, tired of the game they'd been playing for almost two hours now. The waitress had brought their bill with a pointed "Y'all drive carefully, now" more than twenty minutes ago.

"Let me ask you a question, Major."

"Fire away."

"Have you ever been married?"

"I've never been in love."

"That's not the same thing, is it?"

"In my case it is."

"And why, do you suppose, have you never been in love?"

"People have a way of disappointing me," said Jack. "My turn?"

Hannah nodded.

"Why have you been working so hard to make me think that you and Gregor Stern are having an affair?" he asked.

"What makes you think we aren't?" There was a flirtatious lilt in her voice.

"You like to answer a question with a question, don't you?"

"Jews do that, don't they? Talmudic tradition."

Jack leaned forward and said quietly, "Don't be obvious, but check out the guy at the counter."

Without tipping her chin a fraction of a centimeter, Hannah took in a broad sweep of the diner. "He's been sitting there since you arrived. Looks like a salesman. Maybe an accountant."

"What's he doing here?"

Hannah shrugged. "Enjoying a cup of coffee. Reading the paper."

"He's been stood up," said Jack. "Since we've been sitting here, the waitress has offered him a refill several times. And he's already finished the crossword, which most people do after they're done reading the rest of the paper."

Hannah made another covert, searching gaze around the room.

"There are patterns to the way people hide things," said Jack. "Figure out the pattern, and pretty soon you know the truth."

"And your point is?"

"You're not as smooth a liar as you think you are." Jack waited for her to protest—or protest too much—but she held his gaze without missing a breath. "I'll show you. I'll ask you three questions, and I want you to lie about one of them. Ready?"

Hannah nodded and smiled playfully. "Fire away."

"What did you have for breakfast this morning?"

"Oatmeal."

"Where did you get the jeweled hair comb you always wear?"

"A present from my cousin."

"What's the last thing you think about before you go to sleep?"

"The piano playing next door." Hannah sipped her coffee and found it had gone cold. "Well? Which one is it?"

"Breakfast."

"Correct," she conceded. "How did you know? It's because I blinked, isn't it?"

"No, it's because all they serve in the canteen are powdered eggs."

They shared a laugh.

"Then you lied about the hair comb," said Jack, and Hannah's smile faded. "That's your pattern. You lied about breakfast, because you knew I'd catch you, and you wanted me to assume that was your only lie. And you're no doubt lying about the piano as well because it conjures the rather distracting image of you stretched out in bed on a very hot night listening to one of Chopin's languid preludes. And you're lying about the hair comb because…"

Rather than fill in the blank, Hannah said, "What about you? What's your pattern?"

"I don't have one. I don't lie."

"Oh, of course not," she said, "but even if I accepted the claim that you never lie—which is statistically improbable in the extreme—not lying is not the same thing as telling the truth, is it? So I have to wonder…" She traced one finger around the edge of her saucer. "What is it you're not saying, Major Delaney? What is it you're so very good at hiding?"

The burning that had crept down to the small of Jack's back felt like a branding iron. "You're enjoying this, aren't you?" he said.

"Aren't you?"

"Maybe not as much as you think."

"How could I know?" said Hannah. "The inscrutable Major Delaney offers neither clue nor telltale intimation."

"And now you're making fun of me."

"I don't mean to," said Hannah. "In fact, I feel great sympathy for you. I have a feeling that whatever secrets I've managed to keep, yours are bigger. Closer to the bone. More than anything else in the world, you fear being found out."

"Spare me the psychoanalysis."

"That's your pattern." The discovery lit a small fire in her eyes. "You don't lie, but you hide the truth. And that's why you've never been in love. When you love someone, there is nowhere to hide. When you love someone—"

"We're done here." Jack stood abruptly. "See you around, Dr. Weiss."

The waitress met him at the till. "Everything okay, hon?"

"Fine, thanks," said Jack. He dropped a ten on the counter, walked out, and strode across the square, ignoring Hannah, who had followed him out and was stumbling along behind him, her heels ill-suited to the dirt and loose gravel beneath her feet.

"Major Delaney? Major Delaney. Jack!"

He spun on her and said, "That'll be all for now, Dr. Weiss. If we have any further questions, Lieutenant Epstein will contact you."

"I'm sorry to ruin your dramatic exit, but the last bus back to Los Alamos departed more than an hour ago. You'll have to give me a ride."

"I don't have to do a damn thing."

"True," she said. "Major, may I please trouble you for a ride back to the Hill?"

Jack considered it. He was fine with a game of cat-and-mouse as long as he was certain he was the cat. Now he wasn't sure. Epstein's caveat echoed. She'd touched a nerve, and she clearly knew it.

"I'd be very grateful," she said, attempting a conciliatory smile. "I'm not sure I can walk thirty miles in these shoes."

He looked down at her pumps, trying not to think of the seam painted up the back of her leg, trying not to feel this grudging but growing admiration for the way her mind worked.

"If I've made you uncomfortable, I apologize," said Hannah. "We don't have to talk anymore."

"You won this round, Hannah, but believe me, we're not done yet." When they reached the car, Jack opened the passenger door for her and then got into the driver's seat. Before he turned the key in the ignition, he rested his hands on the steering wheel and said, "I'll say one thing for you, Dr. Weiss. You haven't disappointed me yet."

"Let's talk about something pleasant." She sighed. "Don't you get tired of your spy games?"

"Not until now," he said honestly. Another surprise. To both of them.

"I should think it would become exhausting after a while," said Hannah, "marching in circles like Joshua hoping that the walls of Jericho would tumble."

Jack ground the starter and pulled away from the plaza, leaving the lights of Santa Fe behind. Hannah rolled down her window and rested her elbow on the door, letting the cool, dry air move through her hair. When her tight French twist started to lose its shape, she resituated it, lifting her graceful hands behind her head. From the corner of his eye, Jack watched her tucking stray tendrils beneath the ever-present jeweled comb. He'd noticed her touching it while they were talking. She didn't need a mirror, so deeply ingrained was the habit. During a casual conversation, she merely seemed to be keeping her hair in order, but Jack realized now that she touched it to reassure herself that the ornament was still there.

The sough of the wind, with its slight high whistle, wove a web around them. How easy it would be, he thought, how tempting, to place a protective hand on her thigh. To feel the tension of her muscles ease under his touch and watch her head fall gracefully onto his shoulder. No one would know; they were utterly alone. The road was completely deserted, their headlights the only points of light. The stars rolled out in front of them, darkness dissolving the horizon. She leaned closer to the open window. "Mmm, smell the sage."

Her voice pierced the vanity of his fantasy. It was unnerving to realize how close he was to crossing a boundary; he could unravel years of painstaking work in one weak instant. Jack fiddled with the radio, but even the acoustic waves had been swallowed by the dark, gotten trapped on the other side of some unseen mesa.

"Do you mind if we stop for a minute?" she asked. "I love the desert at night; it comes alive."

Jack pulled to the side of the road, and when he cut the headlights, the sky above them stepped back into a limitless universe. The Milky Way was a chalk-white swath smeared across the black expanse. The stars were collectively and individually breathtaking, a reeling chorus of persistent, piercing lights.

"New Mexico gets impressive when there's no moon," said Jack.

Hannah got out and leaned her head back against the roof of the car, revealing the fine, long arc of her neck. Her warm breath created a soft cloud in the air in front of her lips. "When this war is over, you'll see. All this science happening now, all these hypotheses and logarithms and equations, will take us into space. We'll travel to the moon. To other planets. Other galaxies."

"Who's 'we'?"

"Mankind. The human race."

"But who'll get there first? Us or Russia?"

Hannah shrugged. "How far apart are the two when you're standing on the moon?"

"Standing on the moon," said Jack, "is a luxury I don't have. So the two look pretty far apart from my perspective, and I know which side I'm on."

"A luxury I don't have."

"Oh, yeah, I forgot." Jack shucked off his jacket and settled it around her shoulders. "Problem is, the whole woman-without-a-country, 'My allegiance is to science' bit—I'm not buying that.

I know what you're doing. I just have to figure out why you're doing it."

"And there's no room for the possibility that I'm doing it because it's the right thing to do?"

"I'm sure that in your mind, it is," he said, "but that's not going to cut a lot of ice in a military tribunal. They won't care why you did it, Hannah. And they won't care what happens to you in prison."

"Will you?"

"I haven't figured that out either."

Jack turned to find her studying him intently. In the starlight, her red lipstick took on a deep purple cast, like octopus ink. She raised her hand and drifted her fingers from her temple, behind her ear, to the base of her neck, then untucked the tight French roll. As her thick hair tumbled down over her shoulders, she leaned toward him, eyes soft, holding his frankly appreciative gaze. Jack was certain that if he kissed her now, she would respond with the urgent curiosity and tensile strength he'd observed in everything she did. That thought, like a barbed hook, drew him forward, but the poker-hot nerve endings that fired between his shoulders held him back.

"Let's play your game," she said. "Three questions, one lie."

"Ladies first."

"Where did you grow up?"

"West Egg," said Jack. "Like Jay Gatsby."

"Why are you in constant pain?" She touched his shoulder gently. "You're always shifting around to find a comfortable position."

"A sniper got me the day we liberated Paris." She gently massaged the rhomboid muscles under her fingers. "The bullet is still embedded in there."

"Is Delaney your real name?"

"It's my legal name," he said. "That's three. What did you have for breakfast?"

"Powdered eggs."

"Were you secretly having an affair with someone at Kaiser Wilhelm?"

"Yes."

"Where is the real Sabine?"

"I don't know. I'm desperate to find out." Hannah's eyes welled with tears, but she blinked them back and said, "Where did you grow up?"

"Above a butcher shop on Rivington Street."

"Were you thinking a moment ago that you'd like to kiss me?"

"Of course not," he said. "That was just a touch of indigestion."

Hannah laughed. "You're a terrible liar." The space between them, no more than inches, twisted and curved, drawing them together, closer and closer. Then she leaned forward and kissed him. She wore no perfume; his nostrils filled with the subtle scent of talcum powder along with the lavender sage that grew by the side of the road. He could feel how delicate she was with her narrow waist and tiny wrists. Jack braced his better hand on the edge of the car door so he could make the moment last. The pulse between them pulled their bodies toward each other until she broke away, leaned back, and scrutinized him. Still feeling the warm pressure of her lips on his, he whispered, "You get one more question."

"Major Delaney," she said, "are you a Jew?"

The silence between them vibrated with tension. Cicadas sang their call-and-response. Hannah drew back, studying him, and Jack watched the full understanding evolve in her eyes.

"You're a Jew," she said, "and they don't know. So all these years, you have been truly alone."

There was no frisson of gloating or triumph in her voice; there was only anguish. It was the first instance of true empathy Jack had known in his life. With panic and profound relief, he felt the crumbling of his carefully constructed walls. She was his Joshua. But at the same time, the spy catcher in him saw the opportunity, sensed her readiness. He knew from experience that a broken-down wall could be marched across from either direction.

"No more games, Hannah. No more lies." He held her jeweled hair ornament up to the starlight. "Where did you get this?"

He let her take however much time she needed. They stood together staring out into the darkness, companionable in their silence. He saw a rabbit flash its tail, but then it vanished into the brush, a dreamy white speck, and they were alone again. There were no signs, no telephone poles, no road markers. It was as if they had driven off the map and now stood teetering at the ragged edge of the known world.

"I'm going to need a drink," she said, "a whiskey."

He nodded and they got back in the car.

It was another half an hour before he saw the light. At first it was just a wink, but then, as they approached, it became a goose-neck streetlamp with a yellow bulb. Suddenly the radio picked up a signal from a station in Albuquerque, and the cascade of static brought the world along with it. Broken shafts of light were pouring out of the window of a roadside building. A few dusty pickups were parked by the door, their grilles catching the urine yellow reflection of a neon beer sign.

As he slanted the Buick into the dusty gravel lot, he saw that the place was as raw and makeshift as the buildings on the Hill. It seemed like a ghost town, a two-dimensional façade that had appeared momentarily real in the stark, empty landscape.

"It's just outside Indian land," she said, reading his thoughts. "There's always a place that sells liquor less than a mile over the border. Oppie takes the team out here when we've all got cabin fever."

Inside, at the far end of the bar, a few Indians in dirty Levi's hitched high and belted at the waist were drinking silently. Nearer the door, two ancient ranchers in Stetsons were parked in a booth; one of them hacked an asthmatic cough, noisy and bronchial. Everyone looked up when they came in, but the Indians retreated into their quiet huddle as Jack helped Hannah slip into the booth at the back, where they were shadowed, surrounded by a faint, smoky haze. He carefully placed the comb with the two jeweled moths on the wooden table in front of her, tilting it slightly so the diamonds caught and refracted the neon light from behind the bar. The silence was edged with a faint electrical hum.

"I'll tell you where I got it," she said, finally. "I'll tell you the truth this time."

28

The lace curtains along the street rustled with the arrival of the long black Mercedes, as if it brought a quiet breeze through the neighborhood. Stefan was not oblivious to this effect, as Hannah had originally assumed. No, he knew full well what people were thinking when he pulled up in front of her building. He simply didn't care. Observing him from the bay window in the parlor, Hannah tried not to smile. She didn't want to be glad to see him, but she was. Grinning like a schoolboy in the evening snow, he adjusted his cashmere greatcoat and retrieved his briefcase from the back seat.

She listened to the dance of his footsteps on the stairs and in the hallway. Her uncle Joshua opened the door and said, "Good evening."

"Dr. Weiss, I'm Stefan Frei. It's a pleasure to make your acquaintance. Hannah speaks highly of—"

"Is something wrong?" Hannah asked.

"And a pleasant good evening to you too, Fräulein," Stefan teased as he handed her a thick manila envelope. "We are about to be published, Dr. Weiss."

"Hannah! How marvelous!" Joshua looped his arm around her. "I could not be more proud of you, my girl!"

"I don't believe it." Flushed with excitement, Hannah tried to disengage the little tin brad that fastened the envelope, but she was so flustered, she ended up tearing the flap. "I never thought they would allow...oh."

The draft abstract was titled "Thermal Neutrons and Transuranium Elements"; its authors were Dr. Stefan Frei and Dr. Anthas Winik Sanheiser.

"Hannah, let me explain—"

"No explanation is needed. I understand." Hannah slid the abstract back into the envelope. "I'm thrilled that the work will be recognized."

"I'm scheduled to make the presentation tomorrow," said Stefan. "I should like very much for you to be there."

Hannah nodded and smiled, afraid to speak over the swelling heat in her throat.

"Won't you sit down, Dr. Frei?" said Joshua. "I'll get coffee. No—brandy! This calls for a celebration."

"I didn't mean to disturb your evening," said Stefan.

"Please," said Joshua. "It would be an honor. I've been hearing so much about you."

"Have you?" Stefan raised his eyebrows at Hannah, playful, teasing, flirtatious, and then he looked around the room, taking in the candles on the lace tablecloth and the family pictures on the piano. "You have a lovely home. It would be my pleasure to toast to your niece's success. In working with her over these months, I've come to see what an elegant mind she possesses."

"I'll get glasses," said Hannah.

Joshua followed her into the dining room and rummaged for a bottle behind the everyday port and cordials.

"Ah! Here's the good stuff." He winked at Hannah. "I suspect there's a little chemistry in that physics lab of yours."

"Don't be ridiculous," she said sharply. "He's a colleague and nothing—"

They were both startled to hear the piano in the parlor. It had gone untouched since Sabine's mother died. It was vaguely out of tune, but Stefan played superbly.

"Bach's Prelude in B-flat Minor," Joshua said. "I'd almost forgotten what it sounded like."

When he and Hannah returned to the parlor, Stefan turned away from the keyboard, self-conscious.

"No, no, please continue," Joshua said, pouring the brandy.

Stefan smiled and went back to the prelude, and Hannah stood, transfixed. When Joshua pressed a glass into her hand, she realized she was trembling. She wanted to close her eyes and listen to his music, to feel how it was nuanced by the sureness of his hands.

"How precious." Sabine stood in the doorway, surveying the amiable gathering.

"Dr. Frei, this is my daughter," said Joshua. "Sabine, come in and meet Hannah's guest, Dr. Frei."

"I know who he is."

"Good evening, Fräulein." Stefan got up from the piano and went to her, extending his hand. "Pleased to meet you."

Sabine kept her hands in her coat pockets and regarded Stefan with a cold, unflinching stare.

"Perhaps I should go," said Stefan.

Joshua placed his arm around Sabine's shoulders, but she shrugged him off. "Obviously my daughter has forgotten the manners my wife—*aleha hashalom*—taught her."

"And perhaps my father has forgotten whose piano—"

"Enough," Hannah said.

"What are you going to do? Send me to my room? Am I the only one who can see what's actually going on?"

"Nothing is going on." Hannah showed Sabine the abstract. "Look. Dr. Frei brought me our paper."

Sabine's disdain was undisguised. "Congratulations. It's good to know whose side you're on."

"We're not on a side," said Hannah. "We're scientists."

"Who's paying for your work? You're fueling their war machine."

"Sabine. Stop. Talking." Joshua tugged his daughter's arm, glancing uneasily at Stefan. "There is no war."

"Not yet. But soon. Isn't that right?" Sabine stood her ground in front of Stefan, her cheeks flushed from the cold evening air and her rising anger. "You know what's coming, don't you, Dr. Frei? Do you care? What are you doing to stop them? Anything?" When Stefan offered no answer, she turned to Hannah and said, "Then he's responsible. And so are you."

Sabine left them standing there in awkward silence. The slam of her bedroom door jarred Joshua into another flurry of apologies.

"No, please," said Stefan, "don't give it another thought." He downed his brandy and set the glass on the sideboard. "Thank you for your hospitality, Dr. Weiss. Good night, Hannah. Sleep well. Big day tomorrow."

The moment Hannah closed the door behind him, she spun around and strode into Sabine's room without knocking.

"What are you thinking? Have you lost—"

Hannah stopped short when she saw Sabine huddled on the floor in the corner between her dresser and the wall. Her face was streaked with tears. She was sobbing so hard, the little perfume bottles on her night table shivered and clinked. Hannah fell to her knees and gathered her cousin in her arms the way she had when Sabine was small. She stroked Sabine's hair away from her wet, creased face, asking over and over, "What is it? What's happened?"

"They took him," Sabine was finally able to say, gasping. "They took Daniel."

"He'll come back."

"No one comes back. No one. And it's my fault."

"It certainly is not." Hannah was hollowed out by the dawning realization of what might have happened. "Thank God you weren't with him."

"How can you even say that?" Sabine pushed her away.

"Because you are my responsibility, not him. As long as you're safe, I don't care what happens to anyone else."

"Get out of my room." Sabine's voice was laced with an icy deliberate fury. "I hate you…no, I hate your naïveté."

"Hate me if you need to, as long as you get to America." Hannah pressed her hands together, praying for patience, forcing calm. "This is not your fight."

"Then whose fight is it? It's my future at stake."

"Yes, exactly. You're a child; you deserve to grow up and have a full life."

"I'm seventeen. I'm a woman. And Daniel—he—" Sabine shook her head, her voice etched with resurging tears. "He knew that. And he loved me. And if I don't fight for him and you won't fight and Papa won't fight, then they'll keep breaking glass and taking people and—and who's left?"

Sabine cried for a while, and Hannah cried with her.

"The world is a mess, and I'm so sorry for Daniel, but none of this is your fault. He knew the risk he was taking."

Sabine looked up, blinking hard, struggling to breathe. "He was following orders."

"From whom?" Hannah said. "From *you?*"

Sabine nodded, unable to speak.

"This business with the leaflets—Sabine, tell me the truth. How deeply involved are you?"

"Daniel's father has a printing press in his basement. He took it with him when they shut down the newspapers. So I had an idea—because the soldiers—some of them are the same age as me, Hannah. They don't know—or they're afraid—and we just wanted to tell them they don't have to do these things, because if the soldiers refused, then there would be no more deportations. So

I write poems, and Daniel prints them, and the girls and I—we go in the bars where the soldiers are, and when no one is looking, we slip the poems in their pockets."

"How long has this been going on?"

"Since the beginning of the semester," Sabine said. "I thought I knew what to do, what was right. And they listened to me."

"All right. Let me think." Hannah pressed her fingertips against her temples. "Who else knows about this?"

"Daniel. The twins, Rudy and Rolf. Rolf's girlfriend, Gerte. And a few girls from the orchestra."

Hannah thought about the boy grinning at them from the sidewalk outside the café, Sabine's handiwork around his neck, and she shuddered at what they might do to make him talk.

"I never meant for anyone to get hurt."

"I know, sweet girl. I know. Everything will be all right, but you can't stay here."

"I couldn't bear it anymore—sitting in school day after day as if everything were normal. I'm such an idiot! I never thought about the consequences."

"You always thought about the consequences," said Hannah. "You just never let them stop you." Hannah kissed the crown of Sabine's head and pulled her to her feet. "Pack your things—only the brocade carpetbag, nothing else. I have an idea. All right? Be ready."

In the kitchen, Hannah picked up the phone and dialed with trembling fingers. A housekeeper answered with clipped efficiency. "Stern residence."

"Dr. Stern, please. This is Dr. Weiss from Kaiser Wilhelm."

"He and Frau Stern have gone to Bern for a wedding. May I take a message?"

"That won't be necessary," said Hannah, but in the moment between the housekeeper's question and Hannah's polite decline, there was an odd static on the line, like a cricket scurrying down the wire.

"Good evening, then," said the housekeeper. "Heil Hitler!"

Hannah's jaw clenched tight. "Heil Hitler."

She hung up the phone and stood in the darkened kitchen, her heart hammering. She searched her mind for someone—anyone—she could turn to, but even if there was someone else to call, she didn't know if she should; were they listening to Gregor's phone or hers?

29

Gaslight glow filtered through the basement window in Einstein's laboratory. The clock on the wall ticked toward four in the morning. In the half-light, Sabine looked like a little girl, sleeping as soundly as she always did. It was a trait Hannah envied, this ability to sleep, to stop the reeling of the mind and knit up "the raveled sleeve of care." Hannah's eyes burned with exhaustion. Her body ached from a long, cold night on the floor in the storage closet, but she didn't want to get up. There was no predicting when she would be this close to Sabine again, her arm over her cousin's shoulders, her body forming a protective arc at Sabine's back. She could feel Sabine's rib cage rise and fall with her soft, warm breaths—still breathing. Alive.

When Sabine was a little girl, she used to creep into Hannah's room at night, crawl into her bed, and curl up in a little ball against

Hannah's belly. Hannah imagined that this might be what it felt like to have a baby in one's womb—hearts beating in sync, lungs breathing in tandem—and she relished the tidal wave of love this child drew out of her. This love, fierce and unconditional, was the simplest and best part of Hannah, the one thing inside herself that felt unshakable.

The tumbler turned; someone was unlocking the laboratory door.

"Hannah?" Stefan said quietly. "Hannah, are you here?"

One hand tightly over Sabine's mouth, Hannah shook the girl's shoulder. Sabine's eyes opened wide. Hannah placed a finger to her lips. Sabine nodded. Hannah scrambled to her feet, pulled on a lab coat, and went out, closing the storage closet's door behind her.

"Good morning, Dr. Frei. You're here early. I was just—"

"You shouldn't have tried to call Gregor." Stefan's voice was hushed and steely.

"How did you—"

"Listen to me. There's very little time."

"For what?"

"Hannah, do you believe me when I say I am your friend?"

When Hannah didn't answer, he took her hand and led her to the blackboard. In quick, blocky capitals, he wrote ANTHIAS WINIK SANHEISER, and then, one by one, he erased the letters: H...A...N...N...A...

She seized the felted eraser from him and scrubbed away the evidence of his covert credit to her forbidden Jewish Physics.

"Hannah, I swear to you, someday the world will return to its proper order, and so will this." He tapped the board where the ghost of her name remained. "But the credit, the patents—none of it will matter if we don't survive this vipers' nest we've fallen into."

"Then why take such a risk?"

"Because I want to prove how much I care about you. We both know I need you to accomplish the work at hand. Ascribe whatever motive you like, but Hannah, you are important to me. Tell me you know this is true."

"I know," said Hannah, though she hadn't fully acknowledged it to herself until that very moment.

"We must remain calm," said Stefan. "We must be analytical. I asked you before. I'm asking again: Do you trust me?"

Given the narrow lane of choices, Hannah nodded.

"The girl," he said. "She's here?"

She couldn't bring herself to say yes, but he saw it in her face.

"Bring her out the back way. My car is waiting at the bottom of the fire escape behind the building. Hurry."

"Stefan, she never meant any harm."

"Hannah, I beg you—there's no time for this." He took her hands between his, kissed her clenched fists, and held them against his heart. "I swear to you on my life, I would never hurt you. I will do everything in my power to protect you, but you must do as I say. Go. Quickly. And bring the girl."

Moments later, she and Sabine were running down the long, dark hallway, each with a grip on the handle of the heavy carpetbag. When they came to the ironclad access door, Hannah went out first and crept up the concrete steps that led to the alley. She peeked over the curb and saw Stefan pacing in a haze of exhaust from the tailpipe of the Mercedes. She saw no one else in the alley, no light in any of the office or laboratory windows. She motioned to Sabine to follow her. Stefan hustled them into the back of the car, got in, and quietly closed the door.

The Mercedes prowled with hardly a sound and only its running lights on to the end of the alley. The capped chauffeur, silent as well, turned the steering wheel effortlessly, weaving the car through a maze of residential side streets. The back of the car was configured with two black leather bench seats that faced each other. Hannah sat across from Stefan, his lanky legs entwined with hers. Sitting close beside her, Sabine faced a woman who smelled like bourbon and musk. She lit a cigarette, and Sabine took in a startled sip of air.

The woman said, "Cat got your tongue, girl?"

"You're Lotte Scheer," said Sabine. "I've seen you in the movie magazines."

The car bumped over a curb in a roundabout, lurched out into a main arterial, then picked up speed, passing other vehicles at a rapid clip. Hannah gripped Sabine's hand.

"Darling," Lotte said to the chauffeur, "you drive like a fucking Italian. If I didn't love you, I'd jump out and show a little leg like Claudette Colbert. I'm sure someone would be tempted to give me a ride."

In the driver's seat, Ulrike gave a low, guttural laugh. "But you do love me, darling. Like it or not, you've thrown your lot in with me and my penchant for race cars."

"When we were ten," said Stefan, "Ulrike stole the groundskeeper's van and convinced me we should run away from home. We got two miles, hit a tree, and trudged back to receive the flogging of our lives."

"I've always reserved my worst impulses for my closest friends," Ulrike said.

Hannah caught Ulrike staring at Lotte in the rearview mirror; this was not the benign gaze of a friend but, undeniably, the intimate smile of a lover. No longer the louche society girl Hannah had seen draped along Stefan's arm, Ulrike had pulled back her hair under a leather cap. She wore a tweed jacket and tie. She looked like—no, she *was*—Lotte's girlfriend. Ulrike was no doubt protected by her status as Kurt's sister and Stefan's friend, but Lotte was a childless woman who performed openly on the stages in Berlin—perhaps even at Damenklub Violetta. If she had not already been labeled an amoral, she surely would be soon.

As the world had changed around her, incrementally, Hannah had accommodated it. Her worldview, she was certain, had always pointed toward true north. Now, suddenly, there was no north. The magnetic fields that surrounded her were all in motion; her compass, too, was spinning like the stars around Polaris in the night sky. Her legs were trembling; her knees shook uncontrollably. Hannah, who prided herself on understanding the rigorous structures that governed the universe, realized that her hypotheses, the very beginning of true understanding, had been wrong or, worse, built on false assumptions.

She had put the life of the person she loved most in the world in the hands of people she didn't trust, people she barely even knew.

"Where are we going?" she asked, hearing the break in her voice and her shallow, quick breathing.

Stefan leaned forward, his legs pressing against hers to stop the trembling. He spoke in a deliberate, careful tone, low and comforting. "You and I will get out in Stendal," he said. "Take the train back to the institute, attend the presentation, and then go about our day as if nothing unusual has happened. Can you do that, Hannah?"

"What about Sabine?"

"She and Lotte will sail from Hamburg this evening." Stefan took a blue folio from his breast pocket and handed it to her. "Identification, ship's passage, and papers to debark in Cuba. It's the best I could do on short notice."

Hannah nodded, not sure yet if she should thank him or grab Sabine and leap out of the car. She opened the folio and stared at the identification papers. The grainy photo featured a plain girl with bobbed black hair and glasses—Gisella Proust, age twenty, born in Strasbourg.

"Do you speak French?" Lotte asked Sabine.

She nodded.

"'I am Mademoiselle Scheer's secretary.' Say it."

"'I am Ma—'"

"In French!" Ulrike barked. "Little idiot."

"'Mademoiselle Scheer—je suis sa secrétaire.'"

"'Mademoiselle Scheer does not wish to be disturbed,'" said Lotte.

"'Mademoiselle Scheer ne veut pas être dérangée.'"

"What is your name?"

"It's…Gisella?"

Lotte slapped her smartly on the cheek. "What is your name?"

"Gisella. Proust."

Lotte seized a handful of Sabine's hair and pulled her face close. "What. Is. Your. Name."

Hannah saw something die in Sabine's eyes. Her answer was calm and freighted with years of maturity and disappointment. *"Je m'appelle Gisella Proust. Je suis né à Strasbourg."*

"You will keep your eyes down and your mouth shut, Mademoiselle Proust," said Lotte. "You will not leave the cabin without me, and whether we're in the cabin or elsewhere, we will speak French. We will speak quietly, and you will not speak at all unless you are spoken to." She leaned forward and took hold of Sabine's ear, hard. "This is not a game, little girl. My life hangs from the same piano wire as yours, and if you fuck this up for me, I will not hesitate to put you over the railing. Understand?"

"Oui, Mademoiselle Scheer."

"The look on her face! I can be quite terrifying when I choose to be." Lotte rummaged in Sabine's bag. "Take off the coat. You can have Ulrike's, yes? Can she, darling?"

Ulrike sighed dramatically, but she shrugged off her gray tweed jacket and passed it over the seat. "The hair is a problem," Lotte said.

"Does she have a decent hat?" Ulrike asked.

Sabine pulled her beret from her pocket, and Lotte took it between her thumb and index finger, her aversion undisguised.

"I believe I specified a *decent* hat, did I not?" said Ulrike.

"She can have mine," Hannah said quickly, handing over her brimmed cloche.

Lotte opened the elaborate multitiered etui that functioned as her makeup kit. She took out scissors, motioned for Sabine to kneel on the floor in front of her, and began lopping off Sabine's curls in thick handfuls. "Stop whimpering. The androgynous look becomes you."

Ulrike glanced at them in the rearview mirror when Lotte was done. "It does! Look how pretty her face is without that witch's broom on her head."

Lotte donned a pair of Sabine's gloves, dipped her fingers in a small pot of shoe blacking, and expertly worked the color through what remained of Sabine's hair. "We'll even it up and dye it properly on the ship. For now, nice and slicked back. Like Josephine Baker. Very stylish. But these shoes—they're for a schoolgirl."

"She is a schoolgirl," Hannah said.

"Not anymore." There was no acid in the assertion. She was simply stating a fact. Lotte tapped Hannah's knee. "These will do."

Hannah took off her Spanish T-straps and exchanged them for Sabine's oxfords. Lotte took mascara from the makeup etui and darkened Sabine's eyebrows, filling in the carefully crafted arch. She took a pair of brass-rimmed spectacles and parked them on Sabine's nose.

"I wore these in *The Merry Widow*," she said. "Don't lose them."

Lotte shoved Sabine's coat, her shorn curls, and the soiled gloves into the carpetbag and latched it shut. Sabine gripped Hannah's hand, her eyes wide and pleading.

"I'll find you," Hannah said. "I'll find you."

The car swerved abruptly to the side of the road.

"Stendal Station," Ulrike sang out.

Lotte handed the carpetbag to Stefan and said, "Be a dear and dispose of this."

"No!" Sabine cried, but he was already out of the car. "Hannah!"

Hannah took Sabine's face between her hands and pressed her lips to Sabine's forehead. "I'll find you. I'll find you."

"Hannah, come along. Please." Stefan got a firm grip on her arm and dragged her from the car.

"I'll find you!"

Hannah caught a last glimpse of Sabine's frantic face in the rear window, and then they were gone.

Stefan steered Hannah across the deserted platform to a dark corner away from the curious gaze of the ticket agent. He closed his arms around her and held her tight against his body, supporting her weight when her knees failed. Hannah buried her face in his chest, grateful for a passing train that covered her muffled sobbing. Then the train was gone, and there was no sound but Hannah's small, strangled sobs and the songs of early-rising birds that nested in the eaves and pecked at crumbs on the platform. Stefan murmured her name and hushed her, his lips brushing her temple.

"I'm so sorry, Hannah. I'm so sorry."

"Oh God, what have I done?"

"The only thing you could do," he said.

Hannah searched his eyes, pushing against his solid embrace. "Promise me she'll be all right. Swear to me she won't be—"

"You know I can't. If I could change anything—"

"Let me go with her. I could take the train and be in Hamburg before—"

"Don't be naive. Every one of us is walking on a razor's edge. Do you know what Ulrike risked in order to help you?"

"Why?" Hannah needed to know.

"She did it for me—think of it as a favor for those many dull nights at the opera."

"But why you? Why would you risk this?"

"It was somewhat humbling to find myself less courageous than a schoolgirl," Stefan said with a tired version of his boyish grin. "Beyond that, I told you, Hannah—you are important to me. Just as Lotte is important to Ulrike. The two of them know the risk they're taking, what would happen if people knew, but how we feel—how the heart—it's not always convenient to…to love someone."

Somehow the stumbled declaration was more potent than the well-polished charm he usually kept at the ready. Hannah allowed him to pull her close again, comforted by his broad hands on her back and his warm breath on the top of her head. She was accustomed to the high Spanish heels that placed her almost eye-to-eye with Stefan; now, in Sabine's flats, Hannah fit comfortably under his arm, her nose at the level of the top button of his starched white shirt. She felt, for the first time she could remember since she and her father had played scales together, that she was protected, that someone cared about what might happen to her, that she alone wasn't responsible. She stood as still as she could, dreading the approach of the next train. When they could no longer deny the rumble of it in the distance, she pushed away from his embrace and straightened her jacket.

"I'll go to the last car," she said. "You should go to the first."

"You'll be all right." Stefan stroked a hot tear from her cheek.

She nodded. "If I hurry, I can be in my lab before Karin arrives."

"Be careful."

The train ride back into Berlin was brief but grueling. Hannah felt the real and imagined stare of every passenger who passed down the aisle, the soldiers in their crisp brown shirts, the children singing Nazi Youth jingles.

"*Vorwärts! Vorwärts!* Blare the bright fanfares..."

30

Hannah sipped her whiskey without breaking eye contact with Jack. The booth where they'd been sitting—a tight half-circle banquette built into a back corner—was dimly lit with small, dusty wall sconces, but somehow, in the half-light, her face had become more readable than it was in the broad light of day. She was less guarded. Or maybe she was just exhausted. It was after midnight now, and Jack had seen her out walking at sunrise that morning. In any case, he finally felt as if he was making some headway.

"I want to know what's in this for you," said Jack. "I get what's in it for him. You're brilliant. You're beautiful. You know your way around an atom. Obviously, it serves his purposes to keep you hidden in the basement like—"

Jack stopped himself, but Hannah said, "No, please, say it. Like a Jewish slave."

Jack nodded.

"And that's not your situation at all, is it, Jack? You've sworn to defend a society in which you feel the need to hide lest anyone discover your second-class citizenship—but I'm the Jewish slave. That's rich."

"Go ahead and judge me. The Allies aren't packing us into freight cars and shipping us God knows where."

"Everyone knows where! The Americans were aware of it long before they entered the war. They know. No one returns." Hannah closed her eyes and breathed the word *"Oswiecim."*

"Auschwitz," said Jack. "You've heard of it?"

"Of course I've heard of it. You've heard of it. Don't be coy."

"I processed the maps, aerial reconnaissance—"

"What did you learn?" Hannah's posture betrayed her eagerness. "What did you see?"

"It's the size of Lower Manhattan. Mostly crematoria."

"Have the Allies bombed it?"

"Not to my knowledge."

"Have they bombed the tracks leading to it?"

"I doubt it," said Jack. "It's not a strategic target."

"No," she said bitterly. "Of course it isn't. Because Jewish slaves are expendable—even to the Allies."

"That's not true."

"Why do you say that? Because it would be too painful for you to accept? Because you might have to remember that you are a Jew?" She threw back the last of her whiskey, glanced toward the bar, signaled the bartender for another. "Do you even remember your name, Jack? Do your parents know…"

The half-formed question trailed off. As she turned back to him, Jack watched the flare of defiance in her expression disappear; her eyes glazed over and went dark, as if blackout shades had been drawn across a window.

"Hannah? What is it?"

Abruptly, Hannah slid around the banquette and snuggled her hip close to Jack's. She tugged his chin over and kissed him, an open-mouthed kiss filled with insistent desperation.

"Hannah—" Jack felt her hot breath on his neck.

"That man…" she whispered. "The man from the diner."

Jack lowered his eyes, made a brief sweep of his surroundings.

The man from the diner was perched on a stool at the bar next to the Indians, not so close to them as to be conspicuous, but close enough that his view of their booth was unobstructed. He'd taken off his hat, which sat on the bar beside him, but it was definitely the same guy; the beer bottles on the bar in front of him told Jack he'd been there for a while. It was a gut punch for Jack to realize that Hannah had spotted him first.

"I see him." Jack brought Hannah's hand up to his mouth and murmured along her wrist, "Who would be following you, Hannah, and why?"

She touched her pinkie finger to a smudge of lipstick at the corner of Jack's mouth, took her compact from her purse, lifted the lid, and looked in the mirror. "We need to get out of here."

"I'm open to suggestions."

"This isn't a joke. Don't they train you for situations like this?"

"Like what? Public crossword-puzzling? His being here could be sheer coincidence."

"Do you think it is?"

"No."

Jack rose abruptly from the booth, crossed to the bar in quick strides, drew back his elbow, and coldcocked the crossword-puzzler with a hard right to the center of his face. The man's barstool went over, and he hit the floor like a bag of wet cement. A thunderclap of agony ripped through Jack's shoulder and spidered down his arm.

"Hey! Hey! Hey!" the bartender bellowed. "What the hell, mister?"

"I don't like the way he's been looking at my wife. Come on, Mindy," he called to Hannah from across the room. "Let's go."

"That's right!" The bartender barreled around the long transom. "Get the hell outta here, ya friggin' hothead. And don't come back!"

On their way out the door, Jack glanced over his shoulder at the man on the floor. He wasn't unconscious, but his nose was gushing blood, and he seemed to be having trouble sitting upright, even with an assist from the bartender. As Hannah and Jack crossed the parking lot, Jack groaned and gripped his shoulder, muttering through clenched teeth, "Damn it! Damn it to hell."

"I'll drive," said Hannah.

He nodded and handed her the keys, hating it when she opened the passenger door for him and helped him in as if he were an old lady, as if he were infirm.

"I'm fine," he barked. "Just get in and drive."

Hannah hurried to the driver's side, tossed her shoes in the back seat, and roared out of the parking lot, spraying dirt and pebbles in her wake.

"You're going the wrong way," Jack said.

"If we go toward the Hill, he'll follow us. We'd be the only car on the road. If we go toward Albuquerque, we'll be in traffic."

"At two in the morning?"

"Fine, Jack. Where would you like me to go?"

"I don't know. Let me think for a minute." Jack drilled his thumb into the socket under his arm, trying to gently rotate the joint. Waves of electrical shocks traced the fragile architecture of his right shoulder and traveled down his spine. "Son of a bitch. That hurt."

"You need ice."

"We need to continue our conversation," said Jack, "and whoever your secret admirer is, I need to understand how he knows you're here."

As Hannah drove through the darkened streets on the outskirts of Albuquerque, Jack kept his eyes trained on the rearview mirror. When he was satisfied they weren't being followed, he tipped his thumb toward the patchy blue neon of the Blue Swallow Motel.

"Ice machine," he said. "And a quiet place to continue our conversation without an audience."

Hannah slowed to a stop on the deserted Route 66, nudged the blinker, but didn't turn into the driveway.

"You have my word—" Jack started.

She waved the assurance aside. "It's not that."

"Then…"

176

"If I agree to go on," said Hannah, "will you tell me your name?"

"What does that have to do with anything?"

"You expect me to trust you. I need to know you trust me."

"I don't."

"Ah. Well, then. I appreciate your honesty."

Hannah parked at the dark end of the motel lot, as far as she could from the chill of the neon-blue lights. She waited in the car while Jack arranged for the room, then he waited in the room while she took a pillowcase to the ice machine.

"When Stefan said it was too dangerous for Kurt to see the two of you together again," said Jack when she returned, "you took that to mean what?"

"At the time, I assumed he meant that if it was known that he was working at a fraction of his potential, more would be expected of him. He would lose the lifestyle of…" Hannah searched her English vocabulary for the right words. "I don't know the expression. Bon vivant?"

"Playboy."

"Playboy," she repeated, dropping the word into her well-ordered memory. "Later on, however, I understood that if the work we were doing should fall into the wrong hands…" She shook her head. "It's unthinkable."

It was becoming clear to Jack that a lot of people had already left their greasy fingerprints all over the gadget, and everyone associated with it had a different opinion of which hands were the wrong ones.

If someone has to have it, he thought, *I guess I'm glad it's us.*

31

Sabine's feet were half a size smaller than Hannah's, so the oxfords, brand-new at the start of the semester, cut into the back of Hannah's ankles, creating nagging heat and then raw, open blisters as she walked briskly from the train station to Kaiser Wilhelm. Hurrying down the steps to her lab, she felt a warm trickle of pus down her right heel. She paused to remove the shoe and was surprised to see the light come on in the lab.

"Karin?"

When there was no answer, Hannah removed the other shoe and padded in her laddered stockings to the doorway. Karin was there—Hannah could breathe—but rather than her usual morning routine of drinking coffee and reading transcripts, Karin was busy packing a file box with personal items from her desk. Hannah cleared her throat and said, "Good morning, Karin."

"Dr. Weiss! You startled me. You're early."

"As are you." Hannah tipped a nod toward the file box. "What's all this?"

Karin shook her head and continued to clear out the wide, flat desk drawer.

"Are you leaving?"

"I'm sorry, Dr. Weiss. But what am I supposed to do?" Karin set her hands on her hips. "Hide gypsies and deviants in my kitchen cupboards? Let my sisters starve while people who don't belong here take all the jobs? You could be grateful, you know. Grateful that Dr. Frei allows you to have this lab. Grateful that I've stayed as long as I have. A lot of the girls have been telling me I can do better—telling me I could get caught up in things I'd rather not be caught up in."

"Like what?" said Hannah. "Have you ever seen me say or do anything that compromised the integrity of the institute?"

"No, Dr. Weiss, and that's what I told them. I said, 'Dr. Weiss has no time for political or personal affairs, she has no life but science.'"

"That's what you told whom?"

Karin took care in placing a little potted cactus on top of the other items in her box and then she hoisted the carton by slits cut into the sides. She paused as she was about to go out the door. Without looking back, she said, "I wish you well, Dr. Weiss. I hope you won't bear me any ill will."

As the dull *chuck* of Karin's footsteps receded down the hall, Hannah went to the closet where she kept a first-aid kit and cleaned her wound, wincing as the hydrogen peroxide bubbled against her blistered skin. She located a pair of fur-lined ankle boots she kept under her desk for snowy days, then made a perfunctory attempt to press the wrinkles from her skirt with an iron cylinder heated on the hot plate.

The lab was a silent catacomb. Hannah busied herself organizing and reorganizing papers and equipment to best utilize the empty spaces Karin had left. At the stroke of noon, she called her uncle, as they had arranged, and said, "Ophelia sends her love. She's learning to swim."

Joshua's response was unintelligible, more of a hiccup than a word, but Hannah could feel his profound relief.

"I may be late again tonight," she said. "Please don't wait up."

The job at hand was a muted exercise in remedial theory compared to the energized mandate of her collaboration with Stefan. There was no point to it. Hannah could see this now. It was Max's way of keeping her occupied while the truly important work was accomplished by the Aryan males clearly destined for greatness, or at least for the wealth and prizes that accompany it. The afternoon crawled by, the hours marked by a specific brand of envy that gnawed like hunger. The bald meanness of it surprised Hannah and made her ashamed. The long day in the wake of a sleepless night dragged on her shoulders and weighted her eyelids. She would not stay late after all, she decided at half past three. She was assembling notes and packing up her valise for the trek home when Gregor appeared in the doorway. "Am I interrupting?" he asked.

"Please do," said Hannah. "You're the only visitor I ever get anymore."

"I'm sorry I haven't come more often."

Hannah shrugged and smiled. "You're here now."

"With a mission," said Gregor. "Stefan asked me to escort you to the presentation and park you in the front row with your peers."

"It's not a good idea for you to be seen with me."

"What will they do? Send me home to sit by the fire with Annalise and little Carl?" He clutched the front of his vest. "I'd be forced to eat lamb sandwiches, help Carl build block castles, and scratch our dogs behind the ears. And all that violin playing—how would I endure it?"

"May I ask you a question, Gregor?" When he gestured her to go ahead, she said, "Why do you stay?"

"Why wouldn't I?" said Gregor. "They pay me good money. I enjoy my work. I hate what's happening in Germany right now—hate it like hell—but it's not for me to judge, so I stay out of it. I concern myself with what concerns me, and I advise you to do the same." He folded his arms. "What? Why that face?"

"I suppose I'm not as certain as I used to be about the boundaries between what concerns one person and another."

"You're not going to get political on me, are you?"

Hannah shook her head. "It's been a strange day, Gregor. I don't quite know how to go forward from it."

"Start with this," he said, handing Hannah her valise. "See where it leads you. Not all science takes place in the lab, you know. Not all life either."

They started up the stairs to the lecture hall, gradually becoming aware that most of the other scientists, assistants, and students were walking in the opposite direction.

"What the devil…" Gregor stopped one of the young lab assistants and asked, "Aren't you all going to the presentation?"

"It was canceled," he said.

"How unfortunate," Gregor said as the assistant walked away. "Are you all right, Hannah?"

"Relieved, actually. It doesn't matter. The work is out there now. That's the important thing."

"I doubt Frei the Younger is feeling so magnanimous."

"Please thank him for trying," said Hannah. "I really just want to go home."

Gregor squeezed her hand, and they parted ways at the stairwell. Hannah turned down the hall toward Einstein's lab, wanting to reassure herself that there was no trace of Sabine's sojourn there, but when she reached the foot of the stairs, she heard Stefan's voice and then Max's, both edged with frustration. The light banks shut down in quick succession, like a series of shadows tumbling across the floor. Hannah crouched on the steps, listening to the heated confrontation between father and son.

"You thought Kurt wouldn't notice this little game you played?" Max seethed. "The moment he realized it was her name on the paper, he called the Reich Research Council. It's no longer physics. It's Jewish Physics."

"Father, I know you don't believe that."

"What I believe doesn't matter. Now it can never be published! All that work, wasted. If we don't placate them, the consequences will be worse, much worse. I will not give my institute to the Nazis."

"You're already giving it to them one piece at a time." Stefan's voice was freighted with his lifetime of expectation and regret. "You've even given them your own son."

"I'm trying to do what's best for everyone and act in the greatest interests of science. Dr. Weiss is extraordinary. I understand the value of her work, and I know you care for her, Stefan. I see it in your face every time she enters a room, and it's idiotic. Idiotic! You could have any woman you want. I'm desperate to keep her out of sight, away from the madness, and you're not helping." Max sighed a deep, beleaguered sigh. "This insanity will blow over. Everything will go back to normal. We must keep our wits about us until—"

"The insanity, Father, is that you keep telling yourself that."

32

The days of Max Frei's staunch self-deception were numbered. A week later, as Hannah entered the building, she was directed to the lecture hall. Nazi banners backdropped the stage, floor to ceiling, and at the podium Max Frei stood trembling, dwarfed by the enormous black swastikas, flanked by Commandant Scholl and several other high-ranking officials. When he addressed the gathered scientists and staff, his voice was measured and clear, but even from her place high in the balcony, Hannah could hear the broken heart beneath it.

"Kaiser Wilhelm has been declared a model institute of the Reich," he said. "Effective immediately, I will step down and take a position in the physics department so that our important work may continue uninterrupted under the wing of our glorious führer and his Reichstag."

Scholl's arm rose like a javelin to the requisite angle. "Heil Hitler!"

Stunned silence was followed by an uncertain spatter of applause and murmurs of "Heil Hitler."

"I thank you all," said Max, "for allowing me the privilege of working with you."

As he moved away from the podium, Scholl stepped up to the microphone, but before he could speak, Stefan Frei stood up and began to applaud. Diebner and the rest of the physicists immediately stood and joined him, and then the remaining audience members got to their feet, applause building to a thundering crescendo. Max bowed his head, courtly but clearly moved. Hannah pulled her knees up in front of her and hugged her arms around her shins, drawing herself in like a pill bug. She was startled by a hand on her shoulder. "Gregor—"

"Hannah, two Gestapo agents are waiting in your lab to arrest you." He lifted the flap on his bulging messenger bag and Hannah glimpsed her purse, the pewter edges of a few framed photographs, and her Shabbat candlesticks. "I took what I could. Come. Quickly."

"I have to warn my uncle."

"There's no time, Hannah."

"Please! Please, Gregor, I'm begging you. If I can't do it, go to my apartment and break the mezuzah. My uncle will know what it means."

"Fine. I will, I promise, but I'm not leaving you here. Please. We're wasting time."

Keeping low behind the banks of the balcony seats, Gregor scrambled to a large window that opened for the film projectors.

"Ladies first," said Gregor, and Hannah crawled through without hesitation or modesty. Gregor crawled after her and pulled down a rickety ladder that led to the catwalks where the spotlights hung, trained on the stage far below.

"I join you in honoring Dr. Frei for his many years of dedicated service," said Scholl, patting the air with his hands to quell the long ovation. "You'll be pleased to know that his successor is one of your own: Dr. Kurt Diebner."

There was another ovation, though somewhat less enthusiastic, as Diebner ascended to the stage and saluted his new superiors.

"This morning," he said, chest puffed, "I spoke with our führer personally. He has commanded that our focus be directed entirely toward the production of atomic energy—for the glory of the Reich!"

Looking down from this dizzying height, Hannah saw a sea of raised hands, a surreal scene from a melodrama that depended entirely on hackneyed tropes of war and twisted patriotism. Gregor tugged at her sleeve, and she followed him to a spiral staircase that led to the rooftop. The zigzagged fire escape on the side of the building was open to the view of several long black cars.

"This way," Hannah said. She took off her boots and held them in her hand as they followed the shallow eaves around the copper turrets to the back. She used Gregor's messenger bag to break an attic window, and they climbed inside a storage area.

"I'll take the freight elevator down to the incinerator room," she said.

"Perfect." Gregor raised an eyebrow. "Almost as if you'd thought all this through in advance."

"It's always prudent to have a plan," said Hannah.

"Wait there for me. It'll be dark soon. If I'm not back in thirty minutes, then…" He shook his head. "I'm blank. I have nothing."

He brought down the elevator gate, and Hannah toggled the switch that lowered her down into the bowels of the building. She stood in the shadows in the incinerator room, skin prickling at the occasional sound of scuttling rats. After an eternity, she heard Gregor whisper her name.

"This way." He took her hand, and they hurried to the ramped coal hod. "When we get to the street, walk naturally to the end of the block."

A taxi waited beyond the glowing reach of the streetlight on the corner. Gregor opened the door for her, and Hannah was overtaken by a tide of emotions when she saw Stefan extending his hand to help her in. She threw her arms around Gregor and kissed his cheek. "You're a good friend. You've risked your life for me. I don't know what to say."

"Do you know what they have me working on?" he asked, and she shook her head. "A valve gear for steam locomotives. I may never be a brilliant scientist or a great humanitarian, but every one of us gets a moment to show whether or not we're worth a damn. And you've given me that."

Hannah dug into the bag and brought out one of her grandmother's silver candlesticks. "I want you to have this."

"I couldn't."

"Please. Every time I light mine, I'll think of you and thank God."

Gregor took the candle holder and gave Hannah a quick hug. "Now go before we all start weeping."

"Thank you, Gregor," Stefan said.

"Another farthing in the favor bank," said Gregor. "I'll let you know when I'm prepared to make a withdrawal."

As the cab sped away from the curb, Stefan set her bag on the floor between his feet and said, "Are you comfortable?"

"I won't know until you tell me where we're going."

"I don't want to ruin the surprise." Stefan's eyes flicked toward the driver in the front seat for a fleeting second. He took the cashmere scarf from his neck and wrapped it around her shoulders, covering the gold star on her coat. "Here. We don't want you to catch cold."

Neither of them spoke again as the taxi wound through the afternoon traffic to the train station, where they got out and Hannah rushed to keep pace with Stefan's long-legged stride. They boarded a train and sat quietly in a private compartment, attempting to read as travelers hurried by on the platform outside the window. After a small eternity, the train lurched forward.

They were rolling through the lush countryside when the porter came for their papers. He rapped twice, then opened the door. "Heil Hitler!"

"Heil Hitler," said Stefan, handing over two tickets and his own identification. "For me and my assistant."

"May I see her papers?"

"I assure you, my papers will be sufficient," said Stefan.

The porter studied him, then stepped out to the corridor to consult with one of the soldiers who stood smoking near the transom.

The soldier looked at Stefan's papers and then came to the door of the compartment. Stefan greeted him with an unflappable smile.

"It's an honor to meet you, Dr. Frei."

"And a pleasure to meet you, Lieutenant…"

"Fuchs."

"Lieutenant Fuchs. Excellent," said Stefan. "Who's your commanding officer?"

"Captain Ramsauer."

"Ah! Fritz, yes. He'll keep you on your toes. Is he still insisting on those Belgravian pugilist sideburns?"

The lieutenant laughed. "Yes, sir."

"I look forward to seeing him and Commandant Scholl next week at the institute. I'll make it a point to commend your excellent performance."

"Thank you, Dr. Frei." The soldier kept his eyes purposefully away from Hannah. "Enjoy your evening."

"You as well, Lieutenant Fuchs."

The soldier returned to his post; the porter handed Stefan his papers, punched the two tickets, stepped out, and closed the door behind him. Hannah exhaled her held breath, thinking how convenient it must be to skip so lightly over the barbed wire of bureaucracy. A moment later, there was a muffled disturbance in the corridor, and Fuchs bustled past the compartment door wrangling an elderly man by the back of his neck. An old woman shuffled along behind them, weeping and imploring in Hungarian, struggling with bulky bags. She fell, and her husband tried to help her up, but Fuchs cuffed him on the side of his head. Hannah tensed and sat forward, but Stefan set a firm hand on her thigh. She could see the passengers in the neighboring compartment averting their eyes as the familiar scene played out. When the corridor was quiet again, Stefan said, "It was a good impulse, but you're in no position to help anyone."

Stefan drew down the shades on the compartment door and windows and resettled next to Hannah.

"So, tell me, where are we going?" she asked.

"A little town in the Black Forest," said Stefan. "Haigerloch. Do you know it?"

Hannah shook her head. "How far is it?"

"About eight hours. My family has a country house there. It's where I spent the happiest part of my childhood." Stefan stretched his legs and tipped his hat down over his eyes as if he intended to nap. "I was thinking the change of venue might inspire us."

"To do what?"

"You have my word, Dr. Weiss." Stefan placed one hand over his heart. "I'm far too lazy to live up to my reputation for mischief-making."

Hannah turned toward the window. The deep green of pine trees laced with silver snow flashed by, and between each blaze, she saw the reflection of her own soft smile. As they left Berlin behind, the sun rolled low, dodging and disappearing between the trees and tin rooftops at the edge of the city. A cart came down the corridor; Stefan bought sandwiches and coffee, and they traveled along for another hour or so, each with a sandwich in one hand and a book in the other. It didn't occur to Hannah until later how unusual it was to share such comfortable silence. The train made its occasional stops, and they kept their eyes on their books as fellow passengers and patrolling brownshirts came and went in the corridor. Every now and then, she heard sharply raised voices out on the platform and noticed a slight tip of Stefan's chin, but nothing in his face or the cadence of his breathing betrayed a hint of uncertainty.

Eventually, Hannah slept, curled on her side on the leather seat, suspended between an exhausted dreamscape and the metallic rattle of the train on the tracks. When she opened her eyes, she found that Stefan had covered her with his greatcoat and was snoring softly on the seat across from hers, his book—a worn copy of Goethe's *Faust*—still in his hand. She peered through the crack between the wall and the window shade, but it was too dark to see anything more than a scribble of dawn on the horizon.

"Good morning," said Stefan.

"Good morning." Hannah handed him his coat. "Thank you."

"You looked like that painting by Frederic Leighton. *Flaming June,* isn't it?"

"I don't know it," she said. "Is it modern?"

"Victorian. But not prudish Victorian. In fact, it's very sensual."

"Ah."

Stefan cleared his throat and stood abruptly. He raised the window shade and peered into the half-light. "Haigerloch is the next stop. It's a bit of a hike over the hill to the house. Do you mind?"

It occurred to Hannah that this was the first time since she had gotten into the taxi in front of Kaiser Wilhelm that Stefan was actually asking her to express an opinion about an aspect of their journey. In the next moment, she realized that she wanted to be here, with him; she would gladly endure any inconvenience or discomfort for the pleasure. She gathered her things and followed him down the corridor. As the train pulled into the station, the porter fetched a bag of outgoing mail and deposited a bundle of newspapers outside the Dutch door where the stationmaster stood marking his morning log. Hannah waited off to the side while Stefan spoke briefly to the stationmaster. The elderly gentleman used a switchblade to cut the string on the bundle and handed Stefan a paper, and Stefan gave him a few coins. He met Hannah at the edge of the platform and, noting her curious expression, said, "Gregor's not the only one with a farthing in the favor bank."

"What does that mean?" Hannah asked.

"I'll show you." Stefan thumbed through the morning paper, going past the propaganda and political news to the human-interest pages. "Yes. Here we are."

He showed Hannah the headline: "Diva Lotte Scheer Bids Fond Farewell to Germany." Hannah seized the paper and searched the grainy figures in the background of the photo. The young woman who had once been Sabine stood on the high side of the gangplank, one elbow on the rail. She was wearing those brass-rimmed spectacles, which caught the light and glinted, making her expression unreadable. But she was there, on the boat, the SS *St. Louis*. At this very moment, Hannah thought, Gisella Proust was safely on her way to Havana under the stern and exacting orders of Lotte Scheer.

Hannah breathed a deep sigh of relief, leaving a frosted cloud on the air.

"They're well out of German waters by now," said Stefan.

"You'll be able to contact Lotte in Cuba and make arrangements for Sabine's transport to America."

"Thank you. Stefan, I don't know what to say."

"Tell me that you trust me."

"I'm here, aren't I?"

"You are." He touched her cheek.

Hannah followed Stefan down the steps, glad for her snow boots, unfashionable as they were, and they set off on a steep trail that led away from the main road and into the woods. They reached the top of the hill as the sun rose over a distant ridge. Morning bells echoed down the valley from an old church situated on a palisade above the river. The imposing basilica had been built to accommodate the noble Schloss family and other denizens of the quaint village.

"There's the house." Stefan pointed to a rambling stone-and-timber cabin with high gabled windows and a wraparound porch. "It's only a few kilometers on the road. Or we can shortcut across the pasture if you're game."

"I'm game." Hannah nodded.

"I thought you might be." Stefan took her valise from her, and they started down the hill. The sky was streaked with rose and amber. The air was stinging cold, edged with the sharp smell of pine, and full of raucous birdsong. Hannah kicked through the scattered pockets of snow.

"I see why you were happy here," she said. "What a wonderful place to be a child."

"The only place where my father was closer to me than to his lab assistant."

"Then I imagine he must have been happy here as well."

"Your imagination is better than mine," Stefan said.

"What about your mother?"

"What about her?" Stefan hastened to smooth the sharp edge with a sheepish smile. "She's a lovely person who's had a lovely life. It's hard for her now. She has moments of terrible conscience. The news on the radio is very upsetting to her. She hates what's happening, but she doesn't want to do or say anything that might cause trouble for Father or me, so she retreats into her garden. She's taken up oil painting. She raises funds and brings food baskets to the war widows. She's trying to be a good person."

"I'm sure she is," said Hannah. "So many good people are taking up oil painting these days."

Stefan pointed to a glen by the river. "See that dead tree?"

"The one that looks like a shipwreck?"

"It does, doesn't it! Thank you. Ulrike always insisted it was a fairy castle. I wanted it to be my pirate ship. The Diebners rented a place on the river every summer; our parents were friends. When Kurt and Ulrike were around, there was plenty of trouble to get into. When they weren't around, I'd dog my father in the lab, always under his feet. There are worse ways to grow up, I suppose."

"I loved being at the clinic with my father," said Hannah. "He used to hold me up and let me look through his microscope. I worshipped that world—secret, invisible. He always told me, 'If you haven't found the answer, it's only because you haven't looked hard enough.' He said there's a pattern—an explanation for everything that happens."

"But there isn't, you know."

Hannah pondered that, hands in her pockets.

"He was killed in the Great War, your father?"

"Yes," she said. "Mustard gas."

"I'm sorry. That's a hard way to go."

"My mother kept asking, 'Why did this happen?' I never found the answer. Eventually, she stopped wondering. She made a new life for herself."

"But you decided you'd rather live in the invisible world."

"To the extent that I can."

"Sounds very lonely," said Stefan. "It's fine to look for answers under the microscope, Hannah, but you can't live your life there."

They emerged from the shaded grove by the river. Linden trees and larch pines lined the banks. A flash of gold and indigo caught Hannah's eye—a large butterfly perched on Stefan's coat sleeve.

"You have a passenger," she said.

"So I do."

He set down the bags and tried to coax the butterfly onto his finger, but it fluttered in a tight circle around his hand and rode the breeze up into the sunlight. "That's a mountain blue, member of the swallowtail family. The top of her wing is a bright brilliant blue, while underneath, it's dull brown. They keep their wings closed when they aren't flying so they stay camouflaged. Ah—here she comes back."

Hannah stood still. Stefan stepped close to her and tried again to coax the butterfly into his hand, and this time it fluttered up and alit in Hannah's hair.

"I admire that about the mountain blue, keeping her beauty

hidden, not showing off or wasting herself on the rabble. Don't move," he whispered.

Hannah felt the beat of the butterfly's wing next to her temple. She felt its weight the same way she felt the weight of Stefan's gaze—breathless unfamiliarity heightened by intense will. She would not breathe if the price of breathing meant the end of this moment. She felt the gentle tickling of his fingers on the nape of her neck, underneath the wing of her hair, dusting over the top of her spine.

Stefan brought his lips close to hers, holding back the last centimeter that separated the gesture from a kiss. He brushed the butterfly from her hair, and she watched it arc up into the branches, flickering blue, until it disappeared into the blue of the sky.

"Did you catch butterflies when you were a boy?" she asked.

"I did. But I hated the idea of a killing jar, so I'd let them go," said Stefan. "Actually, I prefer moths. Everyone thinks of them as drab, fluttery things, but many of them are even more beautiful than butterflies. My mother showed me how to attract moths at night. She'd heat brown ale in a pot, stir in a cup of dark brown sugar and a tin of black treacle. Then she'd add a couple of drops of rum. Sometimes she'd even let me have a sip. A few hours before the sun set behind that hill, I'd brush the sugar mixture onto the tree trunks and fence posts surrounding the garden. After dark, I'd lie in the middle of the garden with my torch pointed toward the sky—above me this great firmament of moths, like shooting stars in the canopy of heaven."

Hannah closed her eyes and could see that boy protected from the harshness of the world by his imagination, the beating of tiny wings like a delicate shield in the air above him.

Stefan was leaning so close to her that Hannah could hear his heart beating, the blood rushing through his veins and arteries. Her own heart seemed to be synchronized to his and she felt a dizzying rush of blood to her head, so much so that she had to steady herself by moving a step back. "Maybe we should be going?" she said.

"Should we?"

"I think so."

"That's up to you. It's the duty of a shallow cad to attempt to lure beautiful women into his lair."

"But you're not shallow," she said, "and I'm not—"

"You are a beautiful woman."

"No. I'm the smart one. The hardworking one."

Hannah retrieved her bag, and they continued along the sloping bank to a footbridge that took them over the river. They followed a narrow road through a copse of trees and emerged at the edge of the pasture.

"Almost home," Stefan said. "Wait till you see my father's lab. Every modern gadget you can think of." He broke into an easy lope, arms outstretched like airplane wings, coattails flapping behind him. "Come on, slowpoke!" he called over his shoulder, all grinning, infectious gladness.

Running to keep up with him, Hannah felt a spark of forgotten joy. She physically felt the shift of her posture—the worry-wired neck, the averted eyes—as the tension of the city slid off her soul, and she tipped her face up toward the clear morning sky. She'd been aware for a long while now of the finely tuned fight-or-flight instinct that hummed constantly under her skin, but this was the first moment she realized how much stronger it had made her. As she climbed the steps to the expansive porch, Stefan opened the door with a flourish.

"Welcome. The staff is gone after summer," he said, "but I shall do my utmost to make you comfortable."

A low winter sun filtered through the closed shutters inside the main floor of the large country house. The piano and furnishings were covered with white sheets, a silent vanguard of ghosts waiting for the return of the living. Even so, there was an elegance about the stone, a quiet poetry in the slant of the dust motes in the air. The wall in the stairwell was a towering gallery of family portraits framed in pewter, ebony, and gilded tin, some inset with little etched nameplates identifying Stefan's stalwart forebears at various stages, from towheaded childhood to wrinkled dotage.

"I think you'll find whatever you need upstairs, last room on the left," said Stefan. "That's where Ulrike and Lotte store their summer clothes."

"Thank you." Hannah paused on the first step, one hand on the newel-post. Stefan was still standing on the hardwood floor, so they were eye to eye when she asked him, "Why did you bring me here?"

"Because you are the smart one." His lips brushed her temple. "And the hardworking one." He kissed her neck. "And the beautiful one." He leaned down to kiss her mouth, and Hannah didn't shy away. She opened her mouth to his, kissing him back, her arms now behind him, pulling him closer, falling deeper and faster.

Then she stopped and caught her breath, as if shaking herself out of a trance.

"How I've longed to do that," he said, "since the very first time I saw you."

He touched her hair, and, as he caressed it away from her face, she moved her cheek into his hand, bending her neck, calm.

He leaned forward, placed his hands on her cheeks, and kissed her again, very gently this time. "Would you like to see the lab?"

"Yes," Hannah said. "But it can wait."

She took his hand and led him up the stairs, and it was nightfall when they came down again. Making use of the last light of day, Stefan hiked through the woods to a neighbor's house and borrowed eggs, butter, and milk from the kitchen staff while Hannah scavenged in the pantry and root cellar for canned peaches, wine, and potatoes. They stayed up late readying the lab for the work, made love until morning, slept until midday, and woke so eager to get to the lab, they had to flip a coin to decide who would stop by the kitchen and prepare the coffee.

For three days, the cycle of science and sex, sex and science, fed into each other to cyclonic effect. There was no part of Hannah that Stefan was reluctant to touch or taste and no part of Stefan exempt from Hannah's diligent experimentation. In the lab and in bed, he made her laugh, made her more certain of herself. Sitting like a lotus on the edge of a steel table in Max Frei's solarium lab, feeling like Katharine Hepburn thanks to Lotte Scheer's white blouse and gabardine pants, Hannah was a freer, funnier, wiser version of the self she had been in the basement at Kaiser Wilhelm. For the first time in years—or perhaps ever—Hannah experienced a nuanced happiness that took her away from the world around her and turned her inward, toward her own abundance.

On the fourth day, they opened the bedroom shutters to find a heavy snow falling, creating a finely spun cocoon around the house. Restless, Stefan paced the great room, toying with a metal paperweight etched with the continents and vast oceans of the globe. The silver sphere was roughly five centimeters in diameter, about the size and weight of a cricket ball. He tossed it over his shoulder and caught it behind his back for so long that the repetitive *thwok-thwok* of it started to drive her mad.

"No matter how we bombard it," said Stefan, "the chain reaction won't sustain."

"When Niels Bohr is stuck," Hannah said, grabbing the paperweight midair and placing it atop the piano, "he asks himself, 'What would Mozart think?'"

Stefan sat down at the piano and thumped out a few bars of Mozart's Piano Concerto no. 12. Hannah sat down beside him, her fingers skimming across the keys an octave or two above, transforming the staid classical piece into a fusion of jazz and outright silliness. Stefan leaned his shoulder against hers, and they let their hands wander up and down and, finally, away from the keyboard.

"I keep getting distracted," he said.

An hour later, they lay in bed, spent and tangled. Stefan drifted his finger along Hannah's spine, spelling out letters and symbols.

"E equals mc squared," she said. "Way too easy. My turn."

Stefan rolled over. "No tickling."

"Guess." Hannah traced a complex equation in the sweat at the small of his back, and he laughed, arching his spine.

"I said no tickling!"

"Guess and I'll stop."

"I give up."

"Rutherford's transmutation of the nitrogen atom."

"I was going to say that." Stefan shifted to lie on top of her, propping his elbow by her shoulder. "I don't want to leave."

"Don't make me think about it."

"There will be a war. I'm certain of it, and I know it's selfish, but I want this place to survive."

"Haigerloch, you mean? Or this house?"

"Both. And the peace and lightness of these past few days. I have no right to expect it, but I want to bring our children here someday. Our grandchildren. I want to grow old with you here." He kissed her mouth and eyelids. "This is what it would be like," he said, "if we never had to go back."

"If we could live in the invisible world."

"We could keep on working together. And keep on…" He nudged with a sly smile, and she took him in, refusing to yield a moment of happiness in anticipation of the hour when they would have to leave this place. She knew that hour would come; even if they chose not to return to the real world, the real world would eventually return to them with a crushing vengeance.

On March 12 they heard on the radio that Austria had been annexed. Hannah was no longer protected by her foreign status. It was sealed now; she could never return to Berlin as long as the Nazis were in power, and they would be waiting there when Stefan went back, expecting him to take his place in the ascending Reich. If they tried to hide at the summerhouse, it would simply be a matter of time before they were found. Hannah would be sent to a concentration camp. Stefan would stand accused of racial defilement. His scientific collaborators would lose their credibility within the Reich, and his family would lose everything, including this home where he had been happy as a child and where Hannah was so happy now.

There was no fantasy between them that they could grow old together. Their time together was finite, so in these hours, in this place, they felt an obligation to drink deeply and completely. To reframe love in terms of depth and richness, as opposed to longevity, was to know love without limit. Untethered from time, love existed for them as a pure and measureless energy. But it did not exist in a vacuum.

The next day, they walked to Haigerloch Station and boarded the train back to Berlin, careful to sit across from each other and avoid eye contact. Hannah held Stefan's worn copy of *Faust* between her hands. Neither of them looked up when the young family in the compartment across from theirs was challenged for papers and then dragged weeping down the corridor. Everything they could do to change their fate—and the direction of history— they knew they had already done.

They got off the train at Lichtenberg Station and took separate paths to the newsstand, where Gregor Stern browsed the tabloids and periodicals. Standing close to each other, as strangers must in the confines of a crowded station, they spoke softly behind their papers.

"As far as the Gestapo is concerned," said Gregor, "Hannah Weiss is about to be arrested on her way to Copenhagen." He slipped a train ticket and freshly minted passport into Hannah's pocket. "Meet Susannah Rosbaud, who'll be working with me in Zurich. I've always wanted a lab assistant who's smarter than I am."

"Were you able to reach my uncle?"

"I'm sorry, Hannah. He's gone."

She tried not to make any noise, but her ragged exhale sounded like the death throes of a mortally wounded animal.

"I'll call General Volker," said Stefan. "If he's been taken to one of the camps—"

"Stefan, you can't," Hannah whispered, hating the words as they emerged from her mouth, even though she knew her uncle would have said the same thing. "You can't jeopardize our work. We agreed. You will be a model citizen of the Reich."

"How will I know you're safe?" he whispered.

"We'll find a way."

The train whistle shrilled, and Gregor said, "I'll get our seats."

Stefan shifted to stand with his back to Hannah's, and she leaned against his solid warmth. She felt him slip something in her pocket.

"Send this back to me," he said, "if you stop believing in what we're doing. Or if you find someone who—if you find a way to be happy."

"I won't."

Stefan tried to say something else, but his voice rasped and broke. He cleared his throat and walked briskly away.

Sitting next to Gregor as the train pulled out of the station, Hannah put her hand in her pocket and felt the sleek shape of the silver box. She opened it and smiled when she saw the two night moths, understanding now what she hadn't the first time he tried to give it to her. Then she'd seen it as nothing more than a shiny object, an idle and frivolous distraction, and she'd assumed Stefan saw her the same way. Now she knew it was his story, that private part of himself with which he had entrusted her, a symbol of his belief in her strength. She would need all that now.

Hannah gathered her windblown curls, pulled them away from her face, and tucked the comb high on one side where he would be able to see it. She searched the platform until she saw him walking, walking faster, then running to keep pace with the window where she pressed her open hand until the train reached a bend, and the station dropped out of sight.

33

The motel room smelled of old carpet and furniture oil; the olive bedspread and faux-wood paneling had a drab anonymity in sharp contrast to the lush romance of Haigerloch—or what Jack, shot through with equal pangs of skepticism and envy, envisioned Haigerloch to be. The silence between them was filled with the whine and grind of the wall heater. Hannah seemed smaller somehow, Jack thought, as if giving up this part of the story had taken something of her substance.

"If the postcards were really nothing more than love poems," said Jack, "why didn't you tell me that from the beginning?"

"I didn't know if I could trust you."

"But you trusted him."

"With my work and with my life."

"Why the obsession with *Faust*?"

"My uncle always said a good book is like a doorway."

"To what?"

Hannah shrugged. "To the whole world."

"In the newspaper clipping—'Diva Lotte Scheer Bids Fond Farewell to Germany'—she was aboard the ship in Hamburg." Jack recalled the item from the rummage of Hannah's quarters and searched his memory of the photograph, trying to summon up the image of a young woman with short dark hair and brass-rimmed glasses.

"It's the last photograph I have of her," said Hannah. "I would be very grateful if it could be returned."

"You thought it meant she was safe."

"It's the evidence that Gisella Proust made it out of Europe before the worst of the transports, before the bombing began. I have no way to contact her. She has no way to find me. I've tried to locate Lotte, but she seems to be in hiding. Which is understandable. She made no secret of her Communist leanings or her homosexuality. I don't see either as being an asset if one is trying to make a new life in the United States."

Without agreeing or disagreeing, Jack said, "If you trusted him, why did you send the telegram?"

"The postcards stopped coming. I begged Peter Reichl to send the telegram, hoping Gregor would reply. I still don't know why I haven't heard from him."

"They picked Gregor up in Switzerland a few days ago," Jack said. "He's been a little preoccupied."

Hannah winced. "What did they do to him? He's done nothing wrong."

"They got what they needed and sent him home to his wife and son. What did Frei do with your research?"

Hannah waved the question aside. "Just because you can sustain a chain reaction doesn't mean you can build a bomb. Any physicist worth his or her salt understands the principles. It's the mechanics of it that matter now."

"How does that make what you're doing anything less than treason?"

"Treason." Hannah studied her palm as if she were holding the word, examining it like a butterfly on a pin. "Is it possible to be treasonous when one's country no longer exists?"

"Maybe you didn't gift Hitler with the bomb before you left Germany, but you and Stefan certainly set the ball rolling. Let's not pretend he's still there years later, pining for you and writing love letters. You and I both know, Hannah, that he and Kurt Diebner are posted up somewhere drinking *Hefeweizen* and figuring out how to bomb the Eastern Seaboard into glass."

"Such certitude," said Hannah. "What a luxury."

"Well, it's not rocket science, is it?"

"If only it were. The V-two is a child's toy in comparison."

"Seven years," Jack said. "What makes you think he's still in love with you?"

"I know him."

"Oh, please."

"You don't believe it's possible to know someone so completely?"

"No."

"Because you refuse to know yourself," Hannah said.

"This isn't about me."

"Then why won't you tell me your name?"

"Because it's not relevant to our discussion."

"Is that it, Jack? Because I think it's the story that seeps into our bones: *You're a filthy Jew. You will hide or be persecuted because that's the way of the world and there's nothing you can do to change it. Juden.* That was the Nazis' triumph—making that word itself dehumanizing. You know it's a lie, but eventually it becomes a part of you, like that bullet in your back or numbers tattooed on a wrist. You choose to live with self-loathing because the pain is easier to bear than the idea that your life has been a betrayal of those you love, and of yourself."

Jack rose from the bed abruptly; the springs wheezed. "Excuse me. I need some air."

He stepped out into the motel breezeway and closed the door behind him. Pebbles crunched beneath his feet as he crossed the parking lot to a phone booth outside the office. There was a telephone in the room, but he needed isolation and the cold night air in his lungs. Hannah's physical proximity and the persistent scour of her questions were peeling away layers of self-protection. He was flailing and needed to grab onto something solid to regain control of the investigation. The icy blue neon and the hard slap of the night air were reminders that he had to keep his head in the game, eyes front. He had no contingency plan if Hannah decided to bolt, and he wasn't sure he wanted to be responsible for the consequences of her staying.

If Hannah was telling the truth, Stefan Frei had risked his own life to save Sabine, in which case either he was a genuine prince whose one small character flaw was heading up the atomic-bomb squad for Adolf Hitler or he did it to win Hannah over and then got her in the sack to seal the deal. If Hannah had concocted the whole thing, then she was Scheherazade and Jack was the dupe who couldn't get enough of her stories, who was so obsessed by her fairy tales that he hadn't noticed that dawn was breaking and he'd wasted an irredeemable amount of valuable time. For every hour Jack had sat there listening to her romantic fancies, Stefan Frei was one step closer to determining who would get to end the world.

Jack plugged a nickel into the pay phone and waited through several rings before Aaron answered, fumbling the receiver, mumbling, "Yeah. Epstein. I'm here."

"It's me."

"What in hell, Jack—what time is it?"

"Oh-three-hundred."

"Where are you? Is she with you?"

"That's none of your business, Lieutenant."

"Jack, don't do this," said Epstein. "You need to get back here now. Groves has been breathing down my neck since Collier told him you and Dr. Weiss were both off base. You're about to blow this investigation and throw away your career for a woman who—"

"Lieutenant," Jack said, cutting him off, "shut the hell up. That's an order."

"Yes, sir."

"Did you ever get the location on Lotte Scheer?"

"Not yet. Why?"

"Find her," Jack said, "and get the manifest for every passenger vessel leaving Cuba during the first two weeks of November 1938."

"Jack, why are we wasting time on this? We know it was Dr. Weiss. We know what she's doing."

"But we don't know why she's doing it."

"Who cares!" Epstein flared. "Money. Ideology. Blackmail. I could give you a dozen reasons. What difference does it make?"

"Your concerns are duly noted, Lieutenant."

"Something else you should know—Kaiser Wilhelm Institute's been bombed." There was a dry rattle of telex paper as Epstein read off a succinct litany of details.

"Thanks, Aaron. Tell Collier I'll be back in time for breakfast."

"Jack, Groves has been threatening—"

Jack hung up and stood in the sickly blue glow of the phone booth long enough to light a cigarette. He heard the ticking of moths as they endlessly circled the bulb overhead. He didn't like the way his hand trembled when he was weary. Every muscle he'd ever taken for granted in the past now demanded its due on a daily basis. The simple act of throwing a poorly timed punch was enough to straitjacket him for days. In the crack of a single gunshot, he'd ceased living in a young man's body, and in the seventeen months since it had happened, an unwelcome desire for Hannah was the closest thing he'd felt to being fully alive again.

If she was playing him, her method was unorthodox, to say the least. Jack had been tested by some beautiful women in both personal and professional venues; the standard approach was to make a man feel bigger, smarter, and more powerful than he actually was. Hannah made him feel exactly the opposite, to far more devastating effect. While Jack didn't necessarily agree with her assessment of him, he wasn't about to underestimate her. If she was in as much of a bind as he suspected she was, the smartest thing she could do was drag Jack down with her. *She's a sly one,* his furtive companion hissed from its dark corner beneath his right shoulder blade. *She's a schemer.*

A shvartse hun ken oykh leygn a vays ey, his grandfather used to say. "A black hen can still lay a white egg." Jack hadn't thought of the Yiddish expression in a long time. Whatever uncanny skill he had in the realm of interrogation, he owed to his ever-suspicious *zaydeh.* He took a last deep draw on his cigarette, stubbed the butt against the bottom of his shoe, then dropped it down a sewer vent. It was time to go back to Los Alamos.

When he opened the door to the dingy room, a rectangle of light fell on Hannah, who was curled on her side, sleeping, at the foot of the bed.

Jack bent down, his lips close to her ear. "Jakob."

She smiled without opening her eyes and shifted her body so he could sit beside her.

"Jakob," he said. "Son of Rachael and Benjamin."

"How did Jakob become Jack Delaney?"

"Gradually," said Jack. "But it wasn't hard. There was this girl…"

"I knew there'd be a girl," Hannah said as she rolled over, rested her chin on her hands, and looked up at Jack. "Every good story begins with a girl."

34

At fifteen, Jakob Abramson vowed he would rid himself of everything he associated with his childhood—the kosher butcher shop with sawdust on the floor, the blood in the gutters, the constant buzz of filth flies, the stench of rotting meat. On a summer day, in a city infused with the odor of garbage and sweat blasting on waves of hot air out of subway grates and building vents, a pretty girl brushed by him on the street. She smelled of lemons, clean sheets, and money. Her name was Janie Winthrop. Two years older than he and enough of a rebel that she'd allowed him to take her to the movies for a double feature of air-conditioning and heavy petting. The fact that he was Jewish made him even more forbidden and, therefore, even more alluring.

With her shiksa good looks and a voice lifted with the breathlessness of infinite possibility, Janie invited him to spend Memorial

Day at her parents' country club in Tuxedo Park. It was a re-
stricted club and his friends bet that he wouldn't be allowed in. But
when he got there, Janie put the pen in his hand to sign the guest
register and smiled. "The magic is, people don't know you, so you
can be anyone you want. Besides," she whispered, thrilled with her
little intrigue, "you're with me, so no one will even guess."

He could be anyone he wanted to be. Anyone. So he wrote
down a name he'd seen in a novel. *Jack Delaney*.

He wasn't being deceitful; he was outsmarting them. He
wasn't shaming his parents; he was making them proud. Jakob
couldn't go to prep school, but Jack Delaney could. And by
making the name change legal, Jack Delaney got into Harvard,
where he played tennis and rowed crew. Jack Delaney went to
the winter gala and danced with any great-granddaughter of the
American Revolution he chose. And Jack Delaney was assured a
stellar future at any of the white-shoe Manhattan law firms that
recruited him.

In those days, Hitler was far from the front page. When Jack
bought his Park Avenue co-op, Pearl Harbor was still a lovely
place to vacation. Then came the Olympics in '36—the banners,
the chilling rhythm of the goose-steppers. The spectacle stirred
something across the sea and, like the subtle introduction of ter-
mites, began breeding in all the dark crawl spaces where the Great
Depression had fostered an existential rot of hopelessness and
thrashing blame. The movement hardly registered on Jack's radar
until February 1939, when the German American Bund gathered
more than twenty thousand people in Madison Square Garden.

The gathering was listed on the marquee as a pro-American

rally, right above Tuesday night's hockey game (Rangers versus Detroit) and Wednesday night's basketball game (Fordham versus Pittsburgh), as if these three events were on par with one another, spirited but friendly face-offs—may the best man win—but prior to the rally, the expected turnout was enough to raise potential liability issues that brought Bund officials to the wood-paneled enclave of Cravath, Swaine, and Moore.

"Jack," said Lowell Moore at the morning briefing, "you speak German, don't you?"

"It's rusty, at best," Jack hedged. The German dialect he'd picked up as a kid was not the *echt* German that Bund enthusiasts had brought with them from Berlin.

"They need someone to read these over and flag anything that might be actionable." Moore handed Jack a program mock-up and several pages of copy organized for a tabloid-type printer. "They don't want to be misrepresented in the press. You know how the *Times* slants everything to the left—Commies, labor unions, Hollywood—thanks to Franklin D. Rosenfeld and his Jew Deal."

Jack studied the documents, letting Moore's hateful spiel—not the first of its kind he'd heard—become background noise. A drum corps and color guard would usher in a chorus of beautiful girls beneath a forty-foot image of George Washington. American flags would stand beside swastikas. The crowd would be galvanized by a rousing keynote address from Fritz Kuhn, leader of the American wing of the Nazi movement. Commemorative spoons, soap dishes, ascots, and chocolate bars would be available for purchase. The Bund tabloid was an impeccably organized, cheerily illustrated screed about the dangerously immoral Jews, the murderers of Christ, who were plotting to rob, convert, and persecute Christians throughout the world. It spoke of America's best and only hope—racial purity—and explained how the science of eugenics was key to this glorious future.

Jack called the American Jewish Committee and the ACLU and was lectured about the sanctity of free speech even for those with whom one disagrees. He called the mayor's office and was told, "Mayor La Guardia says the best cure for these international cooties is to expose them to sunlight." Jack looked into permits, liability insurance, fire codes; the Bund had done everything by the book. Ultimately, he handed the documents back to Moore with the reluctant verdict that nothing about the rally was illegal or actionable in civil court. If anything, those gathering to protest the event would be the ones getting arrested. Moore was pleased to hear it, and he assured Jack that Fritz Kuhn would be as well.

"I told him we'd be in the VIP gallery," said Moore. "He's eager to meet you. This thing is really gathering steam, Jack. Lindbergh and William Randolph Hearst are on board. I want us in on it from the beginning."

It took Jack only six minutes to type his letter of resignation, but he sat at his desk for several hours considering it carefully before he signed his name at the bottom.

Qui tacet consentire videtur, the letter said. *"One who chooses to remain silent is taken to agree."* I do not agree.

35

Hannah shifted to lie on her back, unguarded for the moment, her eyes closed, allowing his story to unfurl in her imagination. Jack inhaled the scent of talcum powder that lingered along her neck, allowing himself to imagine what her skin would feel like under his hands, what it would be like if he had it in him to compromise. There was a tiny scar under her mouth that he ached to touch; it was shaped like a slender white crescent moon.

"You took a brave stand," Hannah murmured.

Jack longed to agree, to accept the unexpected gift of Hannah's approval, so rare, precious, and almost impossible to achieve. But he knew that his brave stand was burdened by his past silences, the misconceptions he'd done nothing to correct, the jokes he'd rewarded with a collegial chuckle.

"What happened to the letter?" she asked.

"I gave it to Moore's secretary after I'd cleared out my desk."

Hannah turned toward him and opened her eyes, that pale, pale blue; it was as if drawn curtains had been pulled back to reveal a startling view of the sea. He saw something delicate in the arc of her lids, in the way she was curled up on the motel bed like a woman in a painting. She looked at him, slightly perplexed, as if his story—like an incorrect equation—didn't quite add up. Then a moment of understanding passed between them, electricity through a completed circuit.

"Who signed the letter?" she asked. "Was it Jack or was it Jakob?"

"Jack," he admitted. "But you already knew that, didn't you?"

Hannah nodded, but her gaze was soft, compassionate; he could find no judgment there. "It takes more than one letter to deconstruct a life built on lies."

"I couldn't atone enough for what I'd allowed," Jack said. "I know myself well enough to know that. I'm still atoning."

"Sometimes…" Hannah mused. "Sometimes one can do more good in the world by staying in disguise."

It seemed to Jack that she was confessing something, conveying a message of some kind, although he didn't understand what. Then Hannah leaned over, smiling, and kissed him delicately on the cheek—it was a blessing, acceptance, absolution.

"So, Jakob, why tell me this now?"

"Because you asked."

She laughed. "You never answer a question just because it's asked. Neither of us do."

She sat up, straightened her spine, and adopted a mock

serious tone. "Your interrogator will ask again: Why did you tell me?"

"Because I don't want every man who says he loves you to be a liar."

Hannah slid her cool hand along his wrist and into his coat pocket.

"If we could drive away from here..." Jack laced his fingers through hers. "If I could take you away from all this..."

"I know. You can't, but thank you for wanting to."

She leaned her head into the soft spot between his shoulder and chest, and he put his arm around her, let her nestle into his body like a child. He lowered himself back onto the bed, her head still safely supported by the protective curve of his forearm. They could stay like that forever, suspended in time. Maybe they'd be awakened by the sharp shock of the motel-room door being staved in, or maybe they'd be forgotten, fall off the edge of the known world.

Then he understood that he'd made a bargain, not only with her, but also with himself—there could be no more lies. No more half-truths. Not even comfortable lies of omission.

"Hannah, I need to tell you something."

She sat up abruptly, her eyes wide. "How bad is it?"

"They bombed the Kaiser Wilhelm Institute. It was a primary target."

"Stefan..."

"It'll be a while before the bodies are identified."

"He's not dead. He's not dead. I would feel it." She put her feet on the floor, clearly processing her thoughts, prioritizing her questions. "What about Max? Is there anything left? The library, the archives—"

"Please, don't ask me to say any more, Hannah. I've already said too much."

"Thank you for telling me." Hannah rested her head in her hands. "I'm so exhausted. I don't know what's left for them to fight over anymore. Potsdamer Platz, Monbijou, now Kaiser Wilhelm—parks, architecture, science, art—everything beautiful about Berlin is ash and rubble. There's nothing to go home to but dogs fighting over dry bones. Everyone I care about is dead or vanished...the rest have all gone mad."

She dozed on the long drive back, her head on Jack's shoulder. He had to blink hard and crack his window to stay awake. As he approached the guard shack on base, the lights haloed in his tired eyes.

"Hannah." He set his hand on her thigh. "We're here."

She sat up and settled her purse in her lap, prepared to hand over the appropriate documents when the guard rapped on the window and said, "Papers."

Jack left her at her quarters and went to his office, where Epstein was sifting through dispatches from the telex.

"Military intelligence slipped me something on Lotte Scheer," he said, handing Jack the yellow carbon copy of an old field report. "Whatever you wanted to ask her—somebody else wasn't asking so nicely."

36

The sky over Berlin. A city of classical beauty, monumental buildings, sprawling parks, and high ideals. A full moon emerges from passing rain clouds, and its rippled reflection floats on the slow-moving currents of the river Spree. The streets are wet and quiet. The beer gardens are empty, draped with strings of life-less light bulbs that shudder and clink in the breeze until—after a moment of silence, as if the city itself takes a deep breath—the air-raid sirens shriek. The immense double doors of the building fly open, and a swarm of fireflies descend the wide stairway in front of Kaiser Wilhelm—scientists and assistants with little red miner's lights pinned to the lapels of their white lab coats. Some clutch books and personal effects in their arms; others do their best to balance sensitive lab equipment and fragile experiments.

A dark Mosquito swoops low over the city, its thin wings inked black, its small engine whining a telltale song, softly at first, then louder, louder, louder still, until it drops a tiny phosphorous flare, a brightly lit Christmas tree dangling from the pale puff of a parachute. Just above the grand old turrets, it bursts, blinding white, like fireworks, illuminating the primary target for the on-slaught. Searchlights slice upward, scanning for the first sortie of RAF bombers. Antiaircraft batteries open their iron bellies, and great gusts of silver flak burst into the air. The bombs rain down in bellowing waves. A fireball transforms the night sky. The institute crumbles. Books burn. Blackboards and tables turn to splinter and ash.

Einstein's lab is a crematorium, confined by barred windows beneath the level of the molten street. I want to believe Stefan isn't there, but I know he is. At first, I pray to wake before I see the flesh melt from his body, but then I pray to stay, to stand with him in the choking haze of heat and smoke as he labors to save what he cherishes most—his books, his experiments, his father—refusing to accept that all these things were lost years before, in the clear light of a promising day.

37

FIELD REPORT

EYES ONLY

SUBJECT: LOTTE SCHEER

To: Delaney

From: Donovan

SUMMARY: As requested, autopsy details on body retrieved from the Seine by Vichy Milice on August 20, 1943.

(1) Body of female subsequently identified as SCHEER, LOTTE, thirty-three. Occupation: entertainer; nation of origin: Luxembourg. (2) Examination of remains reveals (a) captivity of some significant length indicated by low body mass and evidence of shackles on wrists, ankles, and neck, and (b) enhanced interrogation via techniques known to be employed by both Gestapo and KGB. Hard to say whose side this one was on.

RECOMMENDATION: Deceased was known homosexual who socialized with Hollywood types in highbrow circles in Germany, Russia, Poland, the USA, Italy, and France. Identification should be kept classified and remains disposed of per protocol.

38

Jack jolted awake, feeling as if he'd been yanked from the metal bed where he'd been dozing, stretched out, with the passenger manifests in his hand, still wearing his shoes and overcoat. Someone was pounding on the door, yelling something about...something. He rubbed his hand over his face and mumbled, "Just a second," but less than a second later, the door was kicked open. Collier stood there, grinning, flanked by two burly MPs.

"Good morning, Doris."

"What's this?" Jack asked.

"Time for a ride."

With a weary shrug and little patience for Collier's theatrics, Jack followed the MPs out to their transport. Epstein was in the back seat, arms tightly folded, jaw squared with annoyance. He met Jack's eye for a moment and then stared out the window as the MP drove away from camp and across the endless desert. Gray dawn and a thin skiff of snow settled a ghostly veil over the vast lava basin between the Oscura Mountains and the Sangre de Cristo Range.

"Into the volcano," Jack muttered. Epstein glared straight ahead, refusing to meet his eyes. For the next three hours, there was nothing but the white noise of wheels on flat road interrupted by an occasional artillery-fire bang and vibrational death rattle when the transport hit deep ruts.

Jack saw a flurry of white flakes against the windshield and, surrounding him, a bleached moonscape willed into existence overnight. Light from a frigid moon whitewashed the volcanic rocks. An old metal windmill rattled and wheezed, and lonely cows foraged for whatever bits of grass they could find. In jarring contrast with the desertscape, a steel skeleton jutted a hundred feet high on the horizon. Weaving through construction equipment and the necessary trappings of a small encampment, the jeep bumped over rocks to the base of the tower. Groves was there, his bulk even bulkier in cold-weather gear. He was chewing on an unlit cigar, surveying the upward progress. He waved Jack over to join him.

"Welcome to Jornada del Muerto, Major Delaney. History books will say it was on this spot that we won the war."

"This is your test site?" said Epstein.

"Oppenheimer convinced me this would be the perfect spot," said Groves. "Now the winds are gale force and it's covered with snow. Fucking snow in the fucking desert, for Christ's sake." He turned his baleful gaze toward Jack. "Tell me what you know, Major."

"The postcards were just love poems."

"Love poems," Groves echoed. "Ah, sweet. That's nice. And I guess she wouldn't have any trouble convincing you of that, would she?" He sang a bar from a Rodgers and Hammerstein song, the cigar still clenched between his teeth, and did a soft-shoe shuffle, kick-stepping sideways to set his arm on Jack's shoulder.

"Here's a little love note from Colonel Pash over in Zurich." Groves produced a dispatch from his breast pocket. It was attached to a glossy photograph of a postcard that was signed *Ich liebe dich—H.*

"How long have you had this?"

"Long enough to have it decoded," said Groves.

Jack stared at the yellow carbon copy of Pash's terse report. They were still trying to decipher Hannah's elegant encryption, a code intricately woven into the penmanship itself rather than a reconfiguration of letters or words, but there was damning evidence that she'd been bleeding secrets from Oppenheimer's laboratory to Frei's.

"You were supposed to get into her head," said Groves, "not the other way around."

"General, I assure you—"

"Maybe you missed day one of spy school where they told you not to think with your dick. Did you imagine that if you confessed your big secret, she wouldn't lie anymore? Or were you so busy trying to get between her legs—"

"That is not what happened, sir."

"A scorpion is a scorpion, Major Delaney, and you got stung. I hate to think what it'll mean for an Ivy League up-and-comer like yourself when your intelligence cronies find out what you really are."

"What I am, sir, is an officer of—"

"You're a kike." Grove's tobacco breath was hot in Jack's face. He pointed a finger at Epstein and said, "You and your snip-cock lackey over there—I never trusted either one of you. Now I understand why."

Before the question *How did you know?* could form in Jack's mouth, he knew the answer, and the realization kneecapped him. Hannah had told them. She'd broken him down, element by raw element, deciphering a secret he'd spent a lifetime shielding. While he was outside the motel room, trying to grope his way back to reality, she'd had the time she needed to pick up the bedside phone, cast doubt on every scrap of intel he'd come up with, and make sure that when she went into the volcano, she wouldn't be going alone. Jack focused on the single point of solid lead near his spine, forcing himself to distill a single purpose from the stew of fury and sickening foolishness roiling in his gut.

"I'd give my left tit to drop-kick your ass out of here right now," said Groves.

"Unfortunately," Epstein piped up, "Delaney is the only one she trusts."

Jack could see in Groves's face that this thought had already occurred to him.

"General, if you have your people bring Dr. Weiss to interrogation," said Jack, "I'll find out exactly how much Frei knows."

"If you can't get it out of her," said Groves, "Pash has some off-shore associates who can."

"That won't be necessary, sir."

Groves put his index finger in the center of Jack's forehead and pushed hard enough to move Jack back a step. "Get your head out of your ass, Major Schmuckstein."

39

Hannah stood beside Oppenheimer in the Critical Assemblies lab, both of them shadowed by a ten-foot iron frame that looked for all the world like a guillotine. At the base of the structure, a table had been carefully set with blocks of uranium hydride; at the top, a core the size of a blackboard eraser dangled from a wire above a reinforced containment chamber. While Hannah checked meters and indicators, Oppenheimer tested the wire. His knobby Adam's apple bobbed in his throat.

"A reading of three hundred thousand watts means we've got enough reaction to detonate," he said. "Anything less, and we've failed."

"Anything more," said Reichl, "and we kill half a million people—including ourselves." He managed an apprehensive smile. "Either way, my friends, it's been a pleasure working with you."

Hannah squeezed Oppie's hand and nodded, and without further ado, Oppie let the wire slip through his fingers. The core dropped, gained velocity, and passed through the hydride blocks in a burst of neutrons punctuated by the stifled static and ominous rumble of the contained explosion. Glass covering the indicator needles spidered with a loud pop, prompting a hiccup-y gasp from Reichl, and the next moment, terrible blue bolts of lightning flashed through the room. Hannah felt a frisson of energy and magnitude up and down her arms and neck. Oppenheimer stepped to the indicators and cautiously assessed the readings through the shattered glass.

"Twenty million watts," he said, and for a long moment after that, none of them were able to speak.

They stood, faces frozen in half-smiling expressions of nervous wonder and abject despair. Oppie recovered first, exploring the next step, his voice still hushed with awe. "We must surround the core with a tamper material, a material that will reflect any escaping neutrons back into the uranium."

"A jacket of reflective, nonreactive material," said Hannah. "Tungsten, maybe."

"Exactly. Pen the neutrons in like a pack of wolves and let them tear themselves apart."

A sharp knock startled them out of stillness.

Oppenheimer threw the door open and said, "I asked not to be disturbed."

Collier walked past him and took hold of Hannah's arm. "Dr. Weiss, come with us, please."

"Wait!" Reichl stepped between Hannah and the MPs at the door. "What is this?"

"The major does not control my lab," said Oppenheimer.

"But General Groves does," said Collier.

"Oppie, it's all right." Hannah removed her white lab coat and took her purse from a shelf near the door. On her way out, she touched Reichl's elbow and said, "It's been a pleasure working with you too, Peter."

Hannah relished the cool air outside the laboratory tower and kept her gaze fastened on the far mesas as Collier drove to a cinderblock building on the farthest perimeter of the compound. She followed him down a windowless hallway to a starkly lit interrogation room with a plain steel table and two wooden chairs, one of them occupied. The air was charged and formal, the walls barren except for a framed photograph of Franklin Delano Roosevelt posed by an American flag. When Hannah sat down at the table across from Jack, she saw not a trace of the man she knew as Jakob. Lieutenant Epstein arranged a selection of file folders and lab books in front of her and then stood impassively in the corner.

Hannah glanced up at the bare light bulb suspended overhead and said, "I guess we've progressed beyond the simple background check."

"Identify this, please." Jack slid a paper across the table, body taut, voice unyielding.

Hannah glanced at the page copied from Oppenheimer's lab notes and said nothing.

"It's your work, isn't it?" said Jack.

"I've been here three years. We've done thousands of—"

"Maybe this will refresh your memory." Jack laid the photograph of Hannah's postcard next to the hastily scrawled Rosetta stone from Pash's code breaker. "We have Gregor Stern in custody. This is the last postcard you sent him. It's an encrypted version of this page from Oppenheimer's lab notes. Tell me again, Hannah, about how we mustn't let the truth fall into the wrong hands."

"A matter of perspective, isn't it?"

Jack sat silent, refusing to take the bait.

"What will you do when your troops discover the Germans don't have the bomb?" said Hannah. "Pack us up and send us home?"

"Once the Japanese know we have it, we can stop the war in the Pacific. We'll never even have to use it."

"What a comforting thought."

"Do I detect a note of sarcasm?"

"Let's ask your friend General Groves." Hannah leaned in close to the microphone. "Why have the Allies firebombed almost every major city in Japan but deliberately left two untouched? Is Peter Reichl imagining monsters under the bed, or have the Allies very purposefully left two pristine targets that might work well for a grand demonstration of absolute power?"

"That's not what this is about."

"There are so many ways to build a crematorium."

"Enough!"

Jack slammed the heavy lab book on the table, and Hannah felt the percussion in her breastbone. She shrank unwillingly from the cold, pure rage in his face; it was impossible to sit stoically the way she'd always thought she would.

"Clear the room," Jack said.

Epstein cleared his throat. "Major—"

"Out!"

As the MPs made a hasty exit, Epstein shot Jack an imploring look, but Jack's granite expression was fixed on Hannah. Epstein left the room and closed the door.

"Jakob—"

Jack ratcheted his chair back, strode to the far end of the room, and wrenched the portrait of FDR off the wall, exposing a microphone wire that dangled like a rat's tail. He returned to the table and stood looming over Hannah's shoulder.

"No more lies," he said with icy quiet. "No more machinations. No more tender moments or doe-eyed bullshit." He placed the book down with chilling precision and flipped it open. "Your initials—here, here, here, and here. Yes or no?"

"I can explain."

"You don't explain, Hannah. You lie. And then you lie about the lies. I want the truth. What did you tell them?"

"Nothing! Jakob—Jack—you must believe me. I didn't tell them anything."

"You. Told. Them. *Everything.*" Jack straightened to his full height and his shoulder hit the naked bulb, sending it swinging on its chain like a hanged man.

"I sent them false experiments." Hannah searched for a shallow sip of air. "I made it seem as if—"

"I'm looking at Oppenheimer's handwriting right here. They weren't false, Hannah. You didn't change a thing."

"Of course I didn't change anything, you ass!" Hannah flared. "You think Kurt Diebner is as stupid as that? I sent them experiments that ended in blind alleys—"

"So they wouldn't waste time going down them."

"So they *would*. I deliberately sent them in the wrong direction."

Jack laid the postcards on the table in an unforgiving grid. "Our cryptologists already know what you said to him."

She stared at the table.

"Where is he now? What is he doing?" Jack asked.

"If I tell you, they'll kill him."

"Right, right. I keep forgetting. He's one of the good guys." Jack paced, circling back to the empty wooden chair. "Who did you call from the motel? Collier?"

"What? Why would I?"

"How do they know about me, Hannah? Because I haven't told anyone since I was fifteen. I managed to get through Harvard Law and God knows how many background checks, and you want me to believe this is a coincidence?"

"I'm sorry, Jack, but I didn't tell them anything. I didn't tell them your secret."

"Then how do they know?"

Hannah glanced toward the dangling rat's tail. "They know everything."

There was a soft knock, and the door swung open.

"Jack," said Epstein, his face ashen, "something's happened."

Jack barked an order to the MPs in the hall, and they came to the doorway.

"She stays here," he said, ticking his thumb toward Hannah. "Epstein, you're with me."

As they made their way down the slushy street, Epstein

muttered, "This is fubar, Jack. This whole mess. This is fubar like fucking...*fubar*."

"Lieutenant," Jack said with the smallest of smiles, "I believe that's the first time I've ever heard you use an expletive."

"I save it for appropriate occasions," said Epstein. "Pretty sure this qualifies."

Generally, when the bullhorns called the citizens of Los Alamos to gather for an announcement, there was a palpable surge of hope in the air, everyone praying to hear that the Axis powers had been defeated or at least that some major piece of the Reich had fallen. As Groves stepped to a lectern set out on the front porch of the ranch house, Jack could see in the general's face that good news would not be the substance of what he had to say. The gathered scientists and service members fell silent under the dazzling sun. There was no sound except the flapping of a flag in the wind that whistled down from the mesas. Groves tapped the microphone, and the assembled winced at the shrill feedback.

"Ladies and gentlemen," he said, "it is my duty to inform you that our great president and commander in chief, Franklin Delano Roosevelt, passed away at fifteen thirty-five hours eastern standard time."

There was a collective inhale, then muffled sobs rippled through the uneasy crowd. Jack and Epstein stood there, stunned. Two servicemen cranked the billowing flag to half-mast. A petty officer at the end of the porch played a mournful taps. Peter Reichl wept, one hand clamped tightly over his mouth, as Oppenheimer stepped up to the microphone beside Groves.

"In Hindu scripture," he said, "in the Bhagavad Gita, it says,

'Man is a creation whose substance is faith. What his faith is, he is.' The faith of Roosevelt is shared by men and women in every country in the world. For this reason, we must dedicate ourselves to the hope that his good works will not have ended with his death. Friends, fellow scientists—"

"This tragedy will not affect our great task," Groves cut in. "I've already briefed President Truman about our work here, which will continue unabated."

Oppenheimer looked like he wanted to say something else, but Groves turned the microphone toward the floor. "Company dismissed," he said, but it was as if an ice storm had passed through, leaving everyone's limbs and feet frozen. In the suspended moment before the crowd dispersed, Jack saw Hannah's secret admirer, the crossword-puzzler from the diner and the bar, standing on the knoll beneath a grove of piñon trees. Fedora firmly in place, he was scanning the yard with binoculars, first settling on the porch where Oppenheimer lingered, bent and skeletal, then sweeping over to settle on Jack.

Jack tapped Epstein's elbow. "Escort Dr. Weiss back to her barracks and keep an eye on her until I get there."

Epstein blinked as if he were trying to wake up from a bad dream. "What?"

Jack was already gone, loping across the yard, pushing between the scientists and lab assistants milling near the porch. The fedora disappeared into a dense stand of trees. Jack plowed in after it, crashing through the low-slung pine boughs. He scrambled up the bouldered hillside until he reached a steep trail a few hundred feet below the timberline. He leaned forward, hands on his rib cage, breathing hard, listening for any man-made noise in the under-brush. The ambient wind was punctuated by the faint chirping of birds, but as Jack's heart slowed to a normal rhythm, it seemed that the birdsong was a little too consistent, a little too monotone. He followed the sound, keeping to a sparsely worn but distinct path.

The little radio shack sat perched on a rocky outcropping from which one could enjoy a relatively unimpeded balcony view of Site Y and the surrounding compound. From the shack's open window came the jumpy chirrup of Morse code and the steady drone of a teletype machine. The man in the fedora and trench coat stood in the doorway. He tapped a pack of Lucky Strikes against the side of his hand. His eyes had puffed up with deep pur-ple bruises, and there was a blunt white line of tape across his nose.

"Well, this is a hell of a thing, isn't it?" he said.

"It is," said Jack. He glanced at the radio shack. "You're FBI."

"Agent Hicks."

The man grinned and extended his hand, offering Jack a ciga-rette, but when Jack reached out to take it, he was blindsided by a swift left hook. It wasn't enough to lay him flat, but it sent him reel-ing back a few steps and provided Hicks considerable amusement.

"Okay, then," Jack said, cradling his jaw. "Got that out of your system, Agent Hicks?"

"For now." Hicks proffered the pack of Lucky Strikes again. Jack warily took the one that was sticking out the farthest. "Actu-ally, I should thank you. Now Uncle Sam'll have to fix my deviated septum."

"Glad it worked out for you," said Jack. "Why are you tailing Dr. Weiss?"

"I was tailing you, Hymie."

Jack nodded robotically, not really hearing the words. Then the echo came, clear as day: "I was tailing you."

"So she didn't tell Groves. You told him." Jack sighed and pinched the bridge of his nose. "Goddamn it."

"I got no pleasure from it. I don't like that fat Commie-lover any more than you do, but there's a war on, right? Following orders, chain of command, all that rigamarole."

"But—at the diner—you didn't have time to plant a microphone."

"I read lips."

"Of course you do."

They leaned against the wall of the shack, smoking in silence for a while, a strange truce. Inside, the teletype rasped and clattered. Jack took a flask of whiskey from his overcoat.

"Got a couple coffee cups?"

Hicks gestured toward the door, and they went inside his humble quarters. He took two metal mugs from a shelf.

"Technically, I'm still on duty," he said. "Better make mine a double."

Jack poured a generous shot into each cup and perused the hand of solitaire Hicks had laid out on his cramped writing desk. "Try putting the three of clubs on that four of diamonds. Then you can move that row to the five of spades."

Hicks nodded his approval and clinked his mug against Jack's. "Thanks, neighbor."

"Why were you following me?"

"Donovan wanted to know how you were doing. If you were

gonna bounce back from the whole Paris thing. He's had you pegged for a position in this new central intelligence agency that's supposed to get funded."

"Interesting."

"Of course, the whole, um..." Hicks made an odd hand gesture. Jack didn't know or want to know what it meant. "The woman. That probably doesn't bode well for you."

"Probably not."

"But who knows? You've always been on Donovan's golden-boy list, and now you've got the dame on ice—"

"The dame?" Jack mimicked. "On ice? What is this, a Humphrey Bogart movie?"

"That's exactly what it is," said Hicks without a hint of humor. "This is the part where it finally dawns on the gumshoe that he can complete his mission or throw away his career for a mouthful of Yid titty." He finished off his whiskey and returned to his game. "Let me know which way you decide to go. I'll inform Donovan."

Jack didn't dignify his slur with a response; he just nodded toward the teletype. "Mind if I check out the chatter? If you're done busting my balls, that is."

"Help yourself." Hicks shrugged. "Use that security clearance while it lasts."

The long scroll of mustard-colored paper was set up to fold into itself in a milk crate positioned in front of the machine. Starting with the most recent dispatches, Jack read back through the feed. The first several yards of type pertained to the untimely death of the president. Then came a long series of weather reports, followed by the daily list of the dead. And then Jack spotted the name Frei.

40

Once there was a boy who loved Einstein. He sat in Einstein's lap, interested in the oddness of the man—that ponderous nose, the inexplicable sprouting of hair from the old man's ears—but blissfully indifferent to Einstein's great words.

Imagination is more important than knowledge. Knowledge is limited; imagination encircles the world.

Those words spun down like whirlybird seeds from a tall maple tree, one after another, glancing off the crown of the boy's blond head, grazing the sleeve of his blue school jumper. The boy was too busy skipping stones and examining moths to pay them any mind, but the seeds were planted nonetheless.

I have no special talents; I am only passionately curious.

As the boy grew, he applied himself to the understanding of science and life, but always the first more readily than the second, for science was the logical aim of his own passionate curiosity, and life was a mystic parabola that eluded his grasp every time he became certain he had solved the equation of its inevitable arc.

Try not to become a man of success, but rather try to become a man of value.

If only his mother could have found the boy by the side of a stream in the quiet countryside and whispered in his ear, *Don't listen. Don't think. Keep to your innocent pleasures. You must never set chalk to blackboard. The result will be calamity.*

41

Making her way up the slushy gravel path to her quarters, Hannah was grateful when Epstein offered his arm. The long day and sleepless night had left her dizzy with hunger and deeply rattled. Passing by the lab, she looked up and saw Reichl at the window, face grim, watching as she was marched to her quarters by two MPs. More than anything, she wished to be high in the tower with him, lost in the cascading numbers. At Hannah's quarters, the MPs took up their posts on the doorstep. They were both in their early twenties, their faces resolute but streaked with tears. The sight of them provoked a fresh lump in her own throat. She was familiar with loss, but Roosevelt's death was something different. Every potential path that forked outward from this moment was fraught with uncertainty at best, and at worst, one could say without hyperbole, could lead to the end of everything. She and the rest of the scientists who'd signed Reichl's petition had comforted themselves with the notion that Roosevelt's better angels would stand firm in the face of unspeakable power. The scientists were less confident when it came to Truman, a man without an ounce of poetry in him, a politician with not just a war but also an election to win.

"After you." Epstein opened the door and gestured for her to go in.

"Aren't you coming?"

"I'll wait out here."

Hannah went inside and curled into the chair in the corner, too hungry to eat, too exhausted to sleep. She stared at the pages of a book for an hour or so, then set it aside when she finally realized she was reading the same paragraph over and over. Outside, Epstein, lacking the heavy overcoats worn by the MPs, paced and stomped in the cold, sneezing and barking like a sea lion. Hannah eventually opened the door and said, "Please, come in, Lieutenant."

"No, thank you," he said. "I'll wait for Major Delaney."

"Don't be silly. You're freezing. Come in. I'll make coffee." She turned to the young MPs and asked, "Would you care for coffee, gentlemen?"

Neither of the soldiers shifted so much as an eyelash.

She sighed, impatient. "It's not treason unless you put sugar in it."

Epstein didn't laugh, but she detected a twitch at the corner of his mouth as he stepped in and put down Jack's heavy satchel. The leather valise bulged with the thick file folders that had been set out on the table in the interrogation room. The nape of

Hannah's neck itched with the desire to see what was in them. Epstein perched uncomfortably on a wooden chair at the table while she set the kettle on the hot plate and measured coffee into a French press.

"Will Jack be very long?" she asked.

"You mean Major Delaney."

"Probably wise to avoid becoming too familiar. But considering your history—"

"He told you about that?"

"Of course," she said.

"I would prefer we not talk anymore," said Epstein.

"How disappointing to discover he isn't the man he seemed to be."

"I'm sure you'll get over it."

"I meant for you," said Hannah.

"If anyone understands why he's made the choices he's made, I certainly do," said Epstein. "You don't know what it's like."

"To be denied a country-club membership? You're right, Lieutenant, I can only imagine."

"You don't know him."

"Apparently, neither do you."

"He has a bullet in his back because of me." Epstein pushed his chair away from the table and stood to face her. "The day Paris was liberated, as we were on our way to secure the Joliot-Curie laboratory, he saw a German sniper on the roof across the street and stepped in front of me. Later, when they were interrogating the sniper, they asked him why. 'War's almost over, Paris is liberated, you could have walked out of here, so why?' He said, 'I wanted to kill one more fucking Jew.' Just scanning the street with a spotting scope, he decided I looked like a person who didn't deserve to live. Jack saw him up there, and instead of—"

"Lieutenant."

Epstein came to crisp attention, startled to find Jack standing in the doorway. "Major Delaney. I didn't—"

"You're dismissed." Jack set his hand on Epstein's shoulder. "Thank you, Aaron. I need you to head back to the office and address a few issues. You'll find a list on your desk."

"Yes, sir."

Hannah took two mugs of coffee out to the MPs while Jack retrieved his files and sat down at the table. She sat down across from him, trying not to feel anything when she saw the purple swelling along his jawline.

"Looks as if you've had a complicated day," she said.

"Haven't we all." Jack laid the folders out in the same careful order he'd arranged them on the interrogation table. "Before we start, Hannah, I'm sorry."

"Sorry you jumped to an unfair conclusion or sorry you were caught in a lie?"

"Sorry I allowed my personal feelings to impede this investigation," said Jack. "That will no longer be a problem."

Hannah turned her gaze toward the window. Out on the snow-covered streets, trucks and transport vehicles bumped over potholes.

"We've lost one of the greatest leaders the world has ever known," she said. "He gets two minutes of silence and then everyone goes back to work."

"Isn't that what you did after they took Sabine?"

"Hardly the same. I believed she was safe. I still do."

Jack unfolded a short run of teletype paper from his breast pocket and smoothed it flat on the table. "Max Frei is dead."

Hannah hugged her arms around her rib cage as if to protect herself from a hard body blow. She couldn't bring herself to say Stefan's name, so she asked, "Who else?"

Jack handed her the list and watched her skim down the columns with her finger, flinching with each recognition, color draining from her face.

"Max, Karin, Heiden, Ramses, Gottler...so many...so many. Everyone except..."

"Except Stefan Frei."

She hadn't realized until that moment that she'd been gripping the teletype so tightly it had crumpled under her fingers.

"Anyone else conspicuous by absence?"

Hannah shook her head, but then she said, "Kurt. Kurt Diebner."

"These scientists were Hitler's equivalent of the Critical Assemblies Team."

"That's a gross oversimplification."

"Kurt Diebner is Hitler's Oppenheimer. Stefan Frei is Hitler's Reichl. The only one they don't have is you." Jack dragged his chair next to hers and took her hand. "Hannah. They don't have you. Do they?"

She sat still as a mantis, eyes on the wall. Jack moved his thumb back and forth across her wrist. Her pulse fluttered like a hummingbird beneath her cool skin.

"Was he that good?" he said. "Good enough that you would help him even though you knew he was one of them?"

"Will it keep you up nights if I say yes?" Her tone was teasing, but beneath it, there was blunt defiance. "You look tired," Hannah said. "Maybe we should call it a night."

"It's exhausting, isn't it? Being a liar."

"It is. But you can't stop."

Jack shrugged. "Turns out you can."

"Why should I trust you?"

"Because you're not in Leavenworth yet."

Her breath hitched in her chest before she said, "You're wrong."

"About what?"

"He isn't one of them," said Hannah. "He's trying to stop them. That's why he didn't leave with me."

"You still believe he loves you."

"He does."

"Then why seduce you into his scheme? Why endanger your life? You think he doesn't know you could be tried for espionage? Hanged for treason?"

"He's in greater danger than I am," said Hannah. "That's why I didn't tell you, Jack. You want to see the Nazis as imbeciles, but Kurt Diebner is a brilliant scientist. Stefan needed me to help steer them in the wrong direction."

"I see." Jack got up and paced for a bit, hands in his pockets. "So you were sending him the results of the Critical Assemblies—"

"Only the dead ends!"

"Right. Right. So Stefan could mislead them."

"Exactly," said Hannah.

"But there's one thing that doesn't add up. If you hadn't sent the telegram, Hannah, we would never have known. So I have to wonder…" He sat down next to her again, the hard bone of his kneecap touching hers. "How can someone so smart be so stupid?"

"What?"

"You know what I think? I think you wanted us to catch you. You wanted it to end because deep down, you knew he had deceived you."

"I didn't hear from him for many weeks. I was desperate to know—"

"Know what? If he still needed you? If he still wanted you?"

"No," said Hannah. "That's the one thing I never questioned."

"Never?" Jack shook his head. "Huh-uh. I know you, Hannah. You question everything."

"Not that."

"You wanted us to catch you because you were terrified that he'd been using you, and you were desperate to know if it was too late—if you'd already put the bomb in Hitler's hands."

"He swore to me that would never happen."

"Oh, that I believe." Jack got up to pace again, working out the equation in the air. "I'm Stefan Frei. Brilliant but lazy. Tired of being in Diebner's shadow. Eager to be seen as more than a playboy. I discover down in my very own basement someone who makes me look like a first-rate scientist. I steal her ideas, let her work with me—but always in secret—and, to ensure her devotion, I tell her I've fallen in love with her. I convince her my public allegiance to the Nazis is all a ruse. I pretend to help her family escape, and I actually help her escape. I even make her believe that I'm the one at risk when I send her out into the world like a virus. I know someone will want to use her the way I did. Fermi, Bohr, Peierls, someone else. Eventually she'll end up exactly where I need her to be. I persuade her to send me secrets. Nothing big. Diebner's got the main ideas covered. No, I just need enough failed experiments to fill in the blanks so I'll avoid the blind alleys and move twice as fast, because time—time is everything."

"You're wrong." Hannah struggled to be still, overtaken by a gut-deep trembling. "You're wrong. You're wrong."

"Then comes the truly brilliant part: There's no second place here. Whoever gets there first gets to rule the world. So I don't give the bomb to Hitler. That would be insane. I'm too smart for that. I give the bomb to Russia."

"Do you hear yourself?" Hannah scoffed. "You and Collier— you see a Communist behind every tree."

"How did he know the Allies were going to bomb Kaiser Wilhelm?" Jack said. "If he wasn't tipped off, how did he know that he and Diebner needed to get out?"

"Leaving his father and all of our colleagues? He wouldn't do that."

"You said it yourself—Stefan Frei never worked with anyone. He only found people he could use. That's what you told me. I can play you the tape if you want the exact words."

"I lied! To protect him. He loves me. That's the truth."

"Give me one piece of evidence that proves he loved you, that he ever gave you a moment's thought except when your postcards arrived with new secrets he could use."

"You've seen the evidence."

"What—this?" Jack wrenched the jeweled comb from Hannah's hair and tossed it on the table. "That meant nothing to him. You're clinging to it because believing he loves you is the only way you can believe Sabine is still alive."

"You saw the newspaper photo. You know he saved her life!"

"Did he, Hannah?"

Jack pushed through the scrambled files, came up with a murky autopsy photograph, and thrust it in front of her. Hannah recoiled from the gruesome image—a woman's body, broken and decomposed—but she forced herself to study it with a scientific eye before she wheeled on Jack, triumphant.

"Nice try." Hannah flung the photograph in his face. "That's not Sabine."

"No," said Jack. "It's Lotte Scheer."

"You're lying."

"I'm Stefan. I have to put on a good show for Hannah, so I make sure there's very public proof that it all happened just as I said, but I also make sure I don't leave any loose ends that might ultimately prove inconvenient." Jack laid a series of passenger manifests on the table. "The SS *St. Louis* never got permission to dock in Cuba. It wallowed around the Straits of Florida hoping to get an authorization to dock in Miami. No go. FDR sent the boat back to Europe, where it dropped a few passengers in Holland and France. The rest of the people on board got shipped right back to the countries they were trying to escape. They fished Lotte Scheer's corpse out of the Seine. She'd been tortured. Mutilated. And they haven't found Gisella Proust's remains, but that doesn't change the fact that her body is in that river, Hannah, or in a shallow grave, or reduced to ashes that are mixed with thousands of others' on the floor of a crematorium."

"Liar!" Hannah slapped him hard across the face. He caught her wrist and shoved the photograph in front of her again.

"You see what they did to her, Hannah? That's what Stefan did to her by handing her over to the Gestapo. That's what *you* did to her by handing her over to him before you went with him and let him fuck you and betrayed everything and everyone you ever loved."

"Please stop. Please. I'm so tired, I can't think." She covered her mouth with her hands to stifle the guttural wail that came from deep inside her body. Hannah slumped into her chair, keening Sabine's name, heaving hoarse sobs. Jack sat next to her, stroking her hair, whispering below the reach of the microphones secreted around the room.

"I wish there were a way out, Hannah. I wish it hadn't played out like this."

"I just want it to end." Davening, weeping, Hannah ground her fists against her lap. "I hope they take me out of here and kill me. Tell them to kill me, Jack. Don't let them take me to that place. Tell them to shoot me in the head."

"Listen to me." He held her face between his hands, forcing her eyes to meet his. "Hannah? *Listen*. You have to be strong now. You have to hold on. I don't know yet how to help you, but I swear to you, I will try. Will you trust me to do that?"

She shook her head, hopeless. "What difference does it make?"

"I know you never meant for any of this to happen," he said. "I can make a case against the death penalty. I'll protect you if I can."

Hannah closed her eyes for the duration of two or three ragged breaths as Jack kissed her wet cheeks and mouth, and in the brief silence that followed, Jack heard the sound of an out-of-tune piano next door.

"See?" she said like a child craving approval. "I told you, the piano is the last thing I hear every night before I go to sleep. I didn't lie about everything, Jakob. Not everything."

He pressed his forehead to Hannah's, his wide hand on her slender back, and they stayed this way while the mournful melody played to its inevitable conclusion.

"*Yitgadal v'yitkadash sh'mei raba b'alma di-vra...*" Jack had not heard the mourner's Kaddish since the day his mother was buried, but he tried to say the words. Hannah whispered with him, grasping his hand with the desperate grip of someone dangling over the side of a cliff, and they fumbled toward the end of the traditional prayer for the dead—for Sabine, for Lotte, for the many lost souls at Kaiser Wilhelm, for all the men and boys Jack had killed and seen killed.

"*Y'hei shlama raba min-sh-maya v'chayim aleinu...v'al-kol-yisrael, v'im'ru: amen.*" May there be abundant peace from heaven and life for us and for all Israel, and say: amen.

Hannah lowered her head onto the crook of her arm, and Jack sat with her for a while, hushing her and stroking her wild curls away from her wet cheeks. As her jagged breathing settled to an exhausted but even cadence, Jack felt the adrenaline seep out of his veins, replaced by numbness, sorrow, and self-loathing. He rose carefully, stepped outside the door, and closed it with a soft click. Epstein was loping toward him through the predawn ground fog. Jack met him at the edge of the gravel road.

"You were listening?"

"Yes, sir. If you want to review the tapes before—"

"That won't be necessary," Jack said, hoping it would prove true. "Arrange the transport. Make sure it's people we can count on to be…" He couldn't find the right word, but Epstein nodded, knowing what he meant.

"On it." Epstein handed Jack a thick envelope. "The logistics intel you asked for."

"Digest it for me."

"Exactly what you thought it would be."

"Thanks, Aaron." Jack tucked the envelope in the breast pocket of his coat and took up a position near the two MPs on Hannah's doorstep. He turned away from them as he lit a cigarette. He didn't want them to see that his hands were shaking.

After a brief eternity, Epstein was back with the transport. Groves and Collier rolled up just as the MPs were opening the steel gate on the paddy wagon. Jack hoped they'd maintain a distance for compassion's sake or at least that they'd be too lazy to get out of their jeep.

"I'll get her," Jack said to the MPs. "Give me a minute."

He went inside and found Hannah sitting dry-eyed and erect in the eerie silence, studying the jeweled night moths on the table in front of her.

"I am by nature a gatherer of empirical evidence," she said. "Before Stefan, I had been with two men—almost three, but physiology mercifully intervened. All of them scholars. None of them insensitive or detached. Each of these men made a commendable effort. I would have been glad if my own desire had risen to those occasions, but…" She made a dismissive gesture with her hand. "In the end I was left feeling that my time would have been better spent in the bathtub with a good book."

Jack, uncomfortable, cleared his throat. "Hannah, we need to go now."

"Stefan was different. More accurately, I was different when I was with him. It was the difference between being naked and being without clothes."

"Hannah, please."

"Jack." She held up one finger. "This is important. You asked a question. Now I know the answer."

"What question?"

"You asked me, 'How can someone so smart be so stupid?' And the answer is: *I can't*." Hannah stood, calm and certain. An unsettling smile played across her lips. "I am not a fool. I am not some naive and needy girl who opened her legs to a clever lothario. Stefan is a good man, and he loves me. I know this in every molecule of my being. He's always told me the truth."

Jack forced his eyes away from her face. "Hannah, I wish that were true. But it isn't. And we have to go now."

"Germany doesn't have the bomb, Jack. Stefan swore to me that he and I—together—we wouldn't let that happen. That's the truth. The Germans have nothing. Not even an atomic pile."

Jack steeled himself and opened the door for the MPs. Hannah's pulse was quick and shallow. She was terrified, but still there was that unsettling smile, lucid and resolved. He grabbed the jeweled comb from the table, took her arm, and led her out to the transport vehicle, speaking softly in her ear.

"It's going to be hard. Be strong. Don't let go." He helped her up the iron steps into the back of the transport vehicle and connected the manacle to an eyebolt on the bench. "I'll protect you if I can."

"No!" Hannah said, urgent and intent, with a quick glance over her shoulder at Groves. "Protect Stefan. Everything depends on him now."

"Protect *him?* How do you expect—"

"Swear to me, Jakob, if I tell you where to find the evidence, you'll use it to protect him."

"What evidence?"

"You'll find it in *Faust*. Promise me. Don't stop looking until you find it."

The MPs swung the steel gate closed and slipped a thick pin through the hasp to keep it in place.

"Well, you're out of the shitter." Groves clapped Jack on the back. "Seventeen minutes to spare. I trust you enjoyed the petunias. Donovan's waiting for you in Washington. So I assume you'll be getting out of my hair forthwith."

"Yes, sir," said Jack. "I just want to make sure I don't leave any loose ends."

As the transport clattered away, Jack realized he had Hannah's comb clenched in his fist. When he opened his hand, there were jagged imprints of wings and a trickle of blood, as if the poisonous little bastards had stung him.

42

FIELD NOTE
CONFIDENTIAL

April 28, 1945

SUBJECT: URGENT REQUEST TO JOIN ALSOS IN GERMANY

To: Donovan

From: Delaney

SUMMARY: As stated in previous communiqués, agents of this detachment urgently request permission to join Alsos team in Germany. Site Y scientist HANNAH WEISS has provided valuable intel re whereabouts of German ATOMIC RESEARCH team including FREI, S., and DIEBNER, K. FREI is dangerously manipulative and possesses balance-shifting information that may tip future advantage to Soviets.

RECOMMENDATIONS: (1) Execution of DR. WEISS be stayed until value of her continued cooperation can be assessed. (2) Bill— give me a chance to make this right. Let me join Alsos Black Forest insertion. OBJECTIVE: Locate, interrogate, and eliminate STEFAN FREI.

43

The road roars beneath my feet. The paddy wagon is an iron echo chamber through which every muddy rut and flung stone reverberates. Wind whistles through the infinitesimal holes that provide ventilation but little light. Occasionally I hear the scrape of sagebrush and manzanita. We have left behind the familiar grounds of the laboratories where my colleagues, their families, and the indigenous people who cook and clean for them sleep or work late into the night. Where bright stars dance in the endlessly open sky, small, winking, silver, and others glow like tiny suns, as though heaven had opened its inky cloak to reveal a tantalizing glimpse of gold.

I'm startled awake, mouth bitter with the taste of fear. The metal door rasps open, revealing fields turned cobalt in the moonlight. I see an MP relieving himself at the side of the road. His colleague slides a bucket toward me.

"Ma'am," he grunts, then partially closes the door to shield my modesty. This passes for compassion in a time of war, and I'm grateful for it. Did the German officers show my uncle compassion as they herded him into a cattle car? I doubt it.

After an eternity of long, cold darkness, followed by hours of oppressive heat, we arrive at the prison. They unchain me, and I stand, unfolding like a rusted gate. I walk proudly, back straight, under the glare of the searchlights that sweep through the darkness of unfurling night, pinning me in their harsh light. The cold stones of Leavenworth loom, pitiless, above me. I look directly into the eyes of the guards as they strip me naked. I try not to flinch as the razor slices across my head, taking brown locks along with a piece of my scalp. Blood drips down my forehead and into my eye. An ice-cold shower washes red down a black drain.

Dressed in a stiff gray prison shift, I pass through the concrete gauntlet to my cell. I meet the stare of every prisoner, all of them banging on the bars of their cells and jeering: "Traitor." "German traitor." "Treacherous kike." Thirty cells on each side, two prisoners in each cell, one hundred twenty eyes filled with virulent hatred. We stop as the guard unlocks an enormous wooden door at the end of the cellblock. "Traitor!" The cries are thunderous now, the cries of brothers who lost brothers, fathers who lost sons, soldiers who lost comrades. They want revenge for their losses. I want to tell them that my work and the work of my colleagues saved thousands—perhaps even hundreds of thousands—of lives. They wouldn't hear. They'll judge me the way history will—as a treacherous German spy.

I feel something hit my arm, then the side of my head. Not mud, I realize; the clumps are warm to the touch. Human feces.

I count the steps...seventy-one...seventy-two. My solitary cell is ten meters belowground, carved into the hard dirt, cold and damp. The guards throw me a thin blanket, then slam the heavy door. There's a finality in its terrible, reverberant clang. I will never see light again. I will vanish with the ashes of my era. If my story—all the equations and divisions that led me here—remains untold, will anyone even wonder whether it could have ended differently?

The laws of physics are finite and inflexible. There was a time when I took great comfort in this. I thought it meant that I could control the outcome by correctly predicting the path of the chain reaction. The naive belief that anything was in my control was a futile fantasy; once a chain reaction has been set in motion, there is no alteration, there is no escape.

44

Having finally secured the permission he needed, Jack rolled into Jornada del Muerto to say his farewells. Under a searing sun, the only shade lay in the slivers of shadow east of small huts that baked in the glare. The wasteland that was fast becoming the Trinity test site bustled with anxious activity. The desert tundra was strewn with miles of cable and wire. Shirtless men, backs nut brown and gleaming with sweat, strung wires overhead; they wore bulky canvas gloves to protect from electrical shocks and goggles against the wind-blown grit and sand. Reinforced concrete bunkers were under construction. The site lay in a hollow bowl whose far sides, the Oscura Mountains, were too distant to be more than a painted cyclorama for the main event—the one-hundred-foot tower, which exuded a skin-crawling aura of dread and wonder.

Groves, Oppenheimer, and Reichl stood off to one side, supervising the operation. Groves looked as smug as a dealer holding a stacked deck; clearly he'd seen the same intelligence dispatch Jack had in his pocket now. Oppenheimer was inscrutable, as always, but Jack was certain no one at Reichl's clearance level or below had been informed of what he knew. After two weeks of futile banging on Bill Donovan's door, Jack finally had the key. Now all he had to do was get Groves on board with the idea that they would all be better off with Jack on the ground in Germany when the news went global.

"So you're still going ahead with the gadget?" Jack called out to Groves, knowing he had Oppenheimer and Reichl within earshot as well. "Even with no credible intelligence indicating the Nazis are close to having the bomb?"

"There's no credible intelligence indicating they don't have it," said Groves.

"What difference does it make now?" Jack offered the dispatch from his pocket. "Hitler is dead."

The information dropped like a stone in a pond, making no echo. The gravitational waves rippled out toward the mountains, where the shock was dampened and absorbed into absolute silence. Jack could hear the sound of his own body: his heart beating, the pulsing of blood in his vessels. Finally Reichl's quavering voice broke the silence.

"Hitler is dead? *Hitler is dead?*"

"Ding-dong," said Jack. "Der führer burrowed away in his underground bunker and popped a cyanide capsule, tested first for its efficacy on his beloved dog, Blondi. Then, for good measure, he shot himself in the head as his thousand-year Reich collapsed above him."

"Oh God! Thank you!" Reichl clasped his hands together above his head and then bent forward as if in prayer, palms against his knees. *"Endlich sind wir für seinen bösen Griff freigelassen worden! Oh God. It's over. It's over."*

"Not quite over," said Jack. "Is it, General?"

Jack turned his gaze on General Groves, who glared at Jack to try to shut him up. Jack smiled placidly as they all listened to Reichl's elated babbling.

"Well, the Japanese, of course," said Reichl, "but they're on their last legs. Without the Nazis, the Axis is irreparably crippled. There's no need to detonate the weapon now. If we stage a demonstration, invite the Japanese generals to the desert—include the Russians, if that makes you feel better—we can show them that all war is pointless now."

Reichl looked to Oppenheimer for support, but Oppie's jaw tightened and all trace of empathy drained from his face. Jack almost felt bad for Oppenheimer; his magical juggling act in the desert was coming to its inevitable end in a hailstorm of indisputable facts. The good doctor, who'd kept his cards so close to the vest, was finally going to have to show his hand. He could no longer afford sympathy, engagement, or even neutrality—he had a mission to complete.

"What if the trigger mechanism jams?" Oppenheimer said harshly, turning on Reichl. "What if the plutonium degrades? What if it simply doesn't work? Our enemies would be emboldened by our failure."

"But—but—the petition, Oppie. You agreed!" Reichl sputtered. "We're talking about *people*. Human beings—thousands, potentially millions—*obliterated*. How can that be justified?"

Oppenheimer's eyes turned cold as lead. "We all knew what we were building."

The indignant righteousness that had kept Reichl puffed up was slowly seeping out, like air from a deflating balloon.

"We should not have this weapon," Reichl whimpered to the air. "Nobody should have this weapon."

"It's too late, Peter." Oppenheimer, face grim, nodded toward Groves. "They already have it. It's theirs, and we gave it to them." The blunt finality of this statement, a fact, left Reichl shell-shocked and speechless.

Groves saw his opening and pounced, seizing control of the moment. "In the two minutes we've been standing here arguing about morality, hundreds of our boys have died in the Pacific. Meanwhile, Truman's at Potsdam with Churchill and Stalin preparing to carve up Germany. We didn't sacrifice four years and forty thousand men so we could take Europe away from one dictator and hand it to another. The Reds need to know we've got the bomb."

"But it's not enough for them to know you've got it," said Jack. "You want them to know you're ruthless enough to use it."

"It's a deterrent, Major."

This, Jack realized, was the justification Groves had used, a phrase he'd repeated over and over to assuage the consciences of "his" scientists and to keep them working: *It's a deterrent.* Jack looked at Groves with newfound respect. His dogged focus on the mission, on building his bomb, wasn't primal animal instinct, like a dog peeing to mark its territory; it was what was necessary to bring a bomb from a scientific fantasy to a reality that would soon be tested on this very site. Groves had created and sustained in his army of Nobel Prize winners and eccentric geniuses exactly what he'd needed: a clear, unmistakable, specific objective.

"I'm curious to know what you make of this logistics intel, General." Jack produced the bitter fruit of Epstein's diligent digging, a communiqué containing an assessment by General Curtis LeMay.

He opened it and started reading it aloud. "'Strategic bombing of Japan nearly complete. Availability of future targets could be a problem.' Seems to me, General, if you don't have your gadget ready soon, there won't be anything left in Japan to destroy. That's why Hiroshima has been left untouched."

As Jack was handing the communiqué to the general, Reichl grabbed it. He stood staring at the words without seeing them, without comprehending. For a moment, even Groves was quiet; the silence was broken only by the low moan of the bomb casing swaying in the wind.

"You need a pristine target," said Jack, "a perfect place to show the world the total devastation this weapon is capable of. But if your scientists find out the truth—that they haven't been fighting Hitler for months—what happens to your precious gadget?"

"Get control of this, General." Oppenheimer, wraith-like, turned on Groves and hissed, as if speaking to an underling, "Every second is critical. I cannot afford to have my scientists questioning what we're doing. Reichl's petition for ethical oversight has already gained hundreds of signatures."

Oppenheimer glanced at Reichl, still standing motionless, the dispatch in his hands.

"How will the other scientists react, Dr. Oppenheimer," Jack said, "when they discover that you and the general deliberately lied to keep them working?"

"General," said Oppenheimer, "give him what he wants."

"Not if he wants that woman." Groves folded his arms over his belly.

"I want Stefan Frei," said Jack. "He's still at large—with our secrets and theirs. Let me find him before he moves into the arms of the Russians. Dr. Weiss is on her way to Leavenworth, and we all know what will happen to her there. I won't let her hang while that Kraut bastard goes free. Frei should face a firing squad."

"No one knows where Frei is," said Groves, "or if he's even alive."

"If he's alive, I'll find him."

"What am I supposed to tell Donovan?"

"Tell him we kikes stick together." Jack walked over to Oppenheimer, who was now staring at the ground, his face sunken and tortured.

"Doctor," Jack said, glancing up at the tower, a black guillotine silhouetted against an angry white sky, "I know it's a little late in the day for this question, but please indulge me. How is this damned thing going to work?"

As if reading by rote from a textbook to a delinquent student who probably wouldn't understand, Oppenheimer said, "Inside that casing, we will place a small fissile plutonium core surrounded by explosives. They'll produce shock waves of different speeds.

Von Neumann calculated a configuration that will focus the waves inward, rapidly compressing the plutonium core."

"And the core—how big is it?"

Oppenheimer framed a small orb with his hands. "The size of a baseball. Approximately nine centimeters in diameter."

"And the destruction will be…"

"We have no idea, really. My colleagues are making wagers on the explosion's yield. Enrico Fermi is betting that it will incinerate the entire state of New Mexico."

"If that baseball of plutonium doesn't explode…"

"God help us all."

"And if it does?"

"God help us all."

"Then why?" Peter Reichl, spitting with rage, strode up to Oppenheimer, waving the LeMay dispatch in his face. "Why are you doing this?"

"Why did you, Peter? Why didn't you turn on your heel and walk away?" Oppenheimer's remorseless gaze settled on the horizon. "I'll tell you why—no true scientist would walk away from the possibility of releasing the energy of matter itself, literally transforming the composition of things. You're the same as all of us. Our curiosity is boundless. Our morality is convenient."

45

After nine hours sitting in the back of a Flying Fortress on a metal bench wedged between a backhoe and a stack of propane pallets, Jack despised *Faust* with the white-hot hate of an eleventh-grade English student. He read, cover to cover, the book Epstein had taken from Hannah's quarters. He read it backward. He held each page up to a naked light bulb. He tried isolating and juxtaposing letters and numbers related to the passages on the postcards that he laid out on a makeshift plywood table, running his hands over them as if they were the scarred ivory keys of an old piano.

"You'll find it in *Faust*," she'd said, but Jack had no idea what he was looking for. The encryption key, maybe. Or some clue to the whereabouts of the meticulous lab notes from the summerhouse. Some kind of journal must certainly exist, but he and Epstein had dissected Hannah's quarters after she was taken away and hadn't found it, supporting Jack's assumption that Stefan Frei had kept that valuable artifact close to his vest.

"Are we hearing anything from the ground?" Jack asked. "Have they located the scientists?"

"Not a trace," said Epstein. "Pash is ready to pop a vein, chasing rumors from Basel to Saarbrücken. He's not about to let Uncle Joe get the scientists into a bear hug." Epstein rolled out a map on the table. "The search is focused here, in the Black Forest."

Jack experienced a frisson of pure instinct like a cool breeze on the back of his neck. "I know where they are."

A few hours later, the Allies rolled into Haigerloch in a continuous column of tanks, trucks, and armored cars. As they entered the picturesque village, shuttered windows and Dutch doors were thrown open. Broomsticks waving white dish towels and pillowcases emerged. Colonel Pash stared, steely-eyed, from the turret of the lead tank, flanked by Sergeant Rhodes, who gazed at the scene through army-issue binoculars. In the armored car behind the tank, Pash's voice crackled over the radio.

"You're on thin ice, Delaney. This is a goddamn farm town. There's no place to hide a lab."

As if on cue, a slow, solemn cadence of bells drifted down from the old church tower on the palisade, each long note followed by its half-muffled echo.

Jack thumbed the radio handset and told Pash, "Hang a left."

At the outskirts of the sleepy village, an ancient church was perched at the edge of an eighty-foot cliff. Pash's tank and Jack's armored vehicle peeled off from the rest of the column to climb the narrow, winding cobblestone street. When the tank lumbered to a stop in front of the ornately carved church doors, Jack thumbed the radio again. "Before you do anything—"

The tank lurched with a single percussive judder, part belch, part thunderbolt, and the front of the building blew apart in a hailstorm of stained glass and stone.

"Or there's that approach," Jack said dryly.

Weapons drawn, he and Epstein followed Pash's small contingent into the shattered nave, stepping over shards of stained-glass saints and chunks of broken angels. Jack moved toward a narrow door behind the altar. He pointed to it and put a finger to his lips. "Remember, we need Frei alive."

"We need him on our side or we need him dead." Pash grunted. "Open it."

Two noncoms splintered the door with machine-gun fire. Smoke and dust settled to reveal a dank tunnel reaching deep into the rock. Rhodes led the way, weapon in one hand, flashlight in the other, followed by Pash and his men. Jack and Epstein brought up the rear, pausing to examine cots, chairs, and tables still set with recently used utensils. The tunnel eventually opened into a storage area and then a primitive workroom with makeshift desks and blackboards.

Rhodes stopped abruptly, shining a thin beam of light beneath a lab table where several men cowered. They flinched away from the sound of heavy weapons rising to shoulder level.

"Out of there! Now!" Pash barked.

"Herauskommen!" Jack said. *"Jetzt!"* The men came out.

"Tell them to keep their hands where we can see them."

"Halte deine Hände hoch. Wo ist Stefan Frei?" When the scien-

tists stared, eyes forward, in silence, Jack raised his revolver to the cheekbone of the man standing nearest to him and bellowed, *"Wo ist Stefan Frei?"*

The scientist bent forward and vomited on the floor, prompting a rolling belly laugh from Pash. A dapper, silver-haired avuncular gentleman stepped forward and set one hand on the shoulder of his terrified colleague.

"You're Diebner," said Jack.

The gentleman nodded. *"Frei ist weg,"* he said. *"Frei ist tot. Er wurde vor Wochen getötet."*

"Delaney?" said Pash.

"He says Frei is dead. Killed weeks ago."

Pash yanked Diebner forward by the front of his coat. "What's the Kraut word for 'bullshit'?" he asked Jack.

"Bullenscheiße."

"That'll come in handy." Pash gestured his front man to roust Diebner out, and Jack followed them back up the tunnel into the light of day. Pash's men shoved Kurt Diebner into the armored car. Jack and Epstein got in too, one on either side.

"Take us to the train station," said Jack. "I think I know the way from there."

The armored car scrabbled up the hillside like an industrious dung beetle and stopped at the crest. Jack got out, studied the summerhouse briefly, then handed his binoculars to Epstein.

"I'll take the shortcut," he said. "Wait for a few minutes after I get in, then come down the road. If he's in there, either I'll be dead or I'll have him by the balls."

He descended through the scrub brush, finally understanding

fully the story Hannah had told him, why she'd taken the time to describe the tree that reminded her of a shipwreck, the copse where butterflies congregated, the ancient stone wall with seven stones missing. From its beginning, the story was a carefully detailed map drawn on his memory with Hannah's invisible ink. All along, she'd known that he would see it only if he loved her enough to listen.

Jack stayed low as he crossed the pasture and approached the porch. Through the murmur of the distant river and the shrill song of the birds, he heard a piano. Pausing with his back flat against the wall, he drew his weapon, then stepped inside the open front door. He allowed the music to lead him through the portico and into the spacious front room where Stefan Frei sat at the piano playing Bach's Prelude in B-flat Minor with nuanced prowess.

The interior of the house was almost exactly as Hannah had described it, though it was seven years older now and that much further from its former glory. Jack could feel that moment of her story here. He couldn't escape the memory of her telling it, how her skin had come alive with an energy that was so uniquely hers—sensual, intellectual, and secret. He couldn't erase the thought of her body when Frei opened his arms to Bach's wide glissando, shoulders broad and sculpted, hands dexterous and finely trained. Something like acid poured down Jack's spine, and he raised his revolver, left hand supporting the right, steady despite the agony that underlay his scapula, as he sighted the dead center of Frei's brain.

The music turned mournful, and Jack felt the part of Hannah's story that would never be told, everything he knew he was powerless to prevent, the details he hadn't allowed himself to dwell on. It all came to him now as clearly as if she were whispering it in his ear.

46

There is a reason we light two candles for Shabbat. My uncle explained it to me like this: "The Torah talks about the Sabbath in different ways. We're told in Exodus to remember, *zachor,* and keep it holy. In Devarim, it says to observe, *shamor,* and keep it holy. *Zachor* speaks to the positive, the bread, wine, prayer, and song—everything we celebrate, eat and drink, and rejoice in. *Shamor* speaks to the negative—that which is prohibited, the work and play we set aside, the pleasures from which we abstain. This isn't to say these things are good or bad, Hannah. It does not refer to right or wrong. More like inhale and exhale. That which we choose to keep and that which we choose to let go—both are holy."

47

Leaving the last notes of Bach's prelude hanging in the air, weaving among the floating dust motes, Stefan Frei rested his hands in his lap. Without turning from the keyboard, he said, "Thank you for allowing me to finish. You may shoot me now."

Jack heard Epstein's voice from the doorway behind him, measured and calm: "Major Delaney, would you like to question Dr. Frei here or in the kitchen?"

"Turn around. Slowly," Jack said. *"Drehen Sie sich langsam um!"*

Frei turned. His demeanor was easy and affable, but his face was haggard. Instead of rakish charm, his eyes contained the same haunted sorrow Jack had observed in Hannah.

"We should speak English," Frei said. "Easier for the transcriptionist. And quite honestly, your accent sets my teeth on edge."

"Because I speak German like a Jew?"

Frei shrugged, and they stared at each other in silence as Epstein unpacked the recording setup, connected the battery, and positioned a bulky microphone on a side table next to a file box of evidence.

"I'm going to ask you a few questions," Jack began.

"And if I refuse?"

"That's your right. The Allies are preparing a war-crimes tribunal. Any help you give me now would surely place you in a more favorable light."

Stefan looked unimpressed but said, "I see no harm."

They moved to the table and sat facing each other.

"Dr. Stefan Frei," said Jack, "you are the chief theoretician for the German nuclear research project?"

"A very fancy title for what little I did."

Jack opened a file from the evidence box and laid down a densely scribbled sheet of pale blue paper. "Is this one of your experiments?"

"Possibly."

"And these?" Jack slid a second and then a third page across the table.

"How did you gain access to our experiments?" Stefan asked.

"We didn't."

"Then how do you explain—"

"These aren't really your experiments, are they?" Jack said. "Tell me about Dr. Hannah Weiss."

"I believe she was a scientist at Kaiser Wilhelm Institute," Stefan said.

"And..."

"And she left. I have not seen her in many years."

Jack placed the battered copy of *Faust* on the table, and Stefan raised a stiff rendition of a grin. "Ah. You caught me, Major. I did keep this little secret from my colleagues—for obvious reasons. It was a minor indiscretion, but some in the Reich have very little sense of humor."

Jack set out the postcards like a game of solitaire, watching Frei's face for any trace of recognition or remorse, seeing nothing but cool self-possession as smooth as the surface of the black pond across the pasture.

"If she meant so little to you," said Jack, "why did you go to so much trouble to stay in touch with her?"

"Wouldn't you do that to keep a beautiful woman on the hook?"

"So it wasn't related to the fact that she's a spy and you got her to glean sensitive information covertly from a top secret military operation?" Jack saw the first shiver of indecision at the corner of Stefan's eye. "Cutting to the chase."

"Hannah would never have said that."

"She's been taken to Leavenworth," said Jack. "Do you understand what's happening to her right now?"

"Ah, I see." Stefan tented his long fingers, elbows resting on the table. "You're here because you care for her. I understand completely the lengths a man would go in order to have her, Major, but she's of no use to you."

"They are interrogating her."

"She knows nothing."

"Torturing her."

"I tell you, she is of no use!"

"She's going to hang," said Jack. "For you. For what you made her do."

Stefan twisted away from the table and paced a few steps before he struck the wall with the side of his clenched fist, leaving a powdery crack in the plaster. He returned to the table, forcing composure.

"If the only thing that will satisfy you is to kill someone," he said, "take me. I willingly submit to whatever judgment is rendered by your tribunal, but Dr. Weiss—Major, I beg you, Dr. Weiss has done nothing wrong."

"Let's hear your version."

"Whatever I say, you won't believe me."

"Then you might as well tell the truth." Jack nudged the microphone toward him. "Why did you bring her here? To work with her or to sleep with her?"

"Both."

"To manipulate her."

"To do that, one would have to be as smart as she is." Stefan grew serious then, looking out the drawing-room window at the frostbitten field where Pash's men had set up a camp stove and were brewing coffee. "You won't believe me when I say it, but I loved her. Long before she allowed me into her laboratory. For years, I tried to ignore her, tried to keep my distance. The way things were turning in this country—like fruit rotting on a shelf—I knew it would be dangerous for her if she knew how much I loved her."

"If you loved her," said Jack, "why didn't you let her go?"

"I tried."

"If you truly loved her, and you truly had no intention of providing Hitler with this weapon of mass destruction, why didn't you give Hannah the lab journal and send her out of the country?"

"I did."

"Then where is it? Where is the lab journal? Because I'm certain it's not in Los Alamos."

"No." Stefan laid his hand on the leather-bound *Faust*. "It's here."

Jack opened his hands, impatient. "Show it to me."

Stefan took a Swiss Army knife from his pocket and selected a slender blade. He opened the book and, with surgical precision, slit the endpaper inside the front cover, separated it from the embossed leather, and peeled it away to reveal several dozen tightly rolled scrolls, each the length of a standard notebook and half the circumference of a pencil. He drew out the delicate cylinders one by one and laid them side by side on the table. With great care, he unrolled the first page, smoothed it flat, and traced a finger along the lines of Hannah's small, perfect script intertwined with his own angular chicken scratches.

"She called it our mezuzah," he said.

Epstein groaned and dropped his chin to his chest.

"Because her uncle always said a good book—"

"Yeah, yeah, we get it," said Epstein.

"Okay. She had the journal," Jack said, trying to find another way in. "That's why you couldn't leave her alone. That's why you pursued her and coerced her to spy for you."

"I told her to take the journal and never look back."

Jack cut his eyes to the recorder, knowing Pash was outside listening to every word. Time to play his trump card. He set the jeweled comb on the table between them. The night moths winked in the slanted light. Stefan took in a sharp breath.

"Dr. Frei, she needs you to let her go now. She needs you to tell the truth."

"I am telling you the truth."

"No. The truth is, you coerced her," said Jack. "You deceived her. You made her believe you loved her and that you intended to sabotage—"

"I wanted to run away with her, wanted us to live out our lives in some quiet place. She was adamant that we couldn't allow such unspeakable power to fall into the wrong hands."

"Then how did we get here, Dr. Frei?"

"Diebner promised Speer that we would have a major contribution to the Wehrmacht at the Harnack-Haus conference in Switzerland. Gregor Stern was there. He gave me a postcard." Stefan went to the writing desk by the window and retrieved a bound packet of cards similar to the one Jack had removed from Hannah's quarters. He shuffled through them to find one in particular and laid it on the table in front of Jack. "The first of many."

Vielleicht braucht Gott ein bisschen menschliche Hilfe. Ich liebe dich—H.

"'Maybe God needs a little human help,'" Jack translated, raking his fingers through his hair, sorting through the implications. "Sending the secrets—you're claiming it was her idea?"

Stefan nodded. "That's correct."

"You're almost as good a liar as she is."

"It's the truth."

"At least she lied to protect you, not to save her own skin." Jack, his voice soft and low, leaned right over Stefan, almost whispering in his ear. "You condemned her to death. You murdered her!"

Stefan labored for air. "If you say so—"

Jack fixed the revolver's sights between Stefan's eyes. "One more word and I'll kill you." Pressing the gun barrel against Frei's skin, he said to Epstein, "Tell Rhodes to get Diebner in here."

Ushered in by Rhodes and a young MP, Kurt Diebner was looking considerably worse for whatever he'd experienced out in the armored vehicle.

"Stefan," he said, "please believe me. I didn't tell them you were here."

"Stay calm," said Stefan. "It's almost over."

"Dr. Diebner," said Jack, sitting him in the chair closest to the recorder, "did you attend the Harnack-Haus conference?"

"Of course. Yes. Why?"

"What was the purpose of that conference?"

Diebner directed an anxious glance toward Stefan, who nodded and said, "Tell the truth, Kurt. Save yourself."

"Albert Speer wanted us—Dr. Frei and myself—we were to report on the possibility of new weapons."

"In particular..." Jack prompted.

"The atomic bomb," said Diebner. "It's no crime to defend your country. The Allies are doing the same. We have reliable intelligence, so don't bother pretending."

"Is it fair to say," asked Jack, "that Dr. Frei was pressuring Speer to fund your research?"

"Certainly. We both were. A device of that size—obviously, the expense of engineering, manufacturing, and transporting it is beyond anything ever undertaken."

"That size?"

"The sheer bulk of the thing has always been the prohibitive factor," said Diebner. "Surely Oppenheimer's people have reached the same conclusion."

Jack glanced at Stefan, waiting to see the nod of assent both he and Kurt were expecting. Stefan's eyes were averted, focused intently on something outside the parlor window. Perhaps it was a slow-moving cloud, parting to reveal just the briefest ray of sun, or the quick flare of the camp stove as one of Pash's men opened the fuel-control valve. In that swift, subtle angle of light, Jack observed what Hannah had so often mentioned—Stefan Frei's look of inscrutable charm.

48

High marble columns reached into a cloudless summer sky and reflected on the placid lake in front of Harnack-Haus. Banners billowed like sails on a tall ship, blood red and emblazoned with black swastikas. Kurt Diebner was in his element, eager to share a discovery he was certain would shift the course of history and ensure him a second Nobel. He stood at the head of a table populated by military officials, industrialists, and the nation's finest scientific minds.

"We can create a weapon," Diebner announced, "that will reduce London to ashes in a single blast."

Excitement rippled through the room. Looking around the table, Stefan saw not one uncomfortable pair of eyes dropping downward, not one hesitant hand going up. Albert Speer voiced the questions on everyone's mind: "What would be required? How soon can you have it ready?"

"Our experimentation attests to the need for at least two tons of enriched uranium," said Stefan.

"Two tons?" Speer turned to Scholl. "Is that feasible?"

"With adequate funding," said the commandant, "we could dedicate our factories exclusively to production."

"And the Luftwaffe will have to design an aircraft big enough to transport it," said Stefan. "The device will be too big to fit into our Heinkels or Gothas."

"How big would the bomb core have to be?"

"Approximately twelve meters in diameter." Stefan opened his arms. "Envision a sphere the diameter of a giant oak."

Speer huffed, skeptical. "So what you're saying, Dr. Frei, is that if your experiments finally succeed, and if we pour billions into the production of enriched uranium, and if we devote additional resources to designing and building an aircraft large enough to transport this massive device"—he paused as an uneasy titter swelled to a wave of derisive laughter—"then we can have an atomic bomb."

"Correct," said Stefan. "Surely it's worth the Reich's commitment to create a weapon that will guarantee our führer a victory of unparalleled—"

"Questioning the Reich's commitment," Speer said, cutting him off, "is not the way to get what you want, Dr. Frei. Our resources are entirely focused on supporting our men in the field."

Kurt Diebner attempted to rehabilitate the presentation. "Dr. Speer, at least we can all agree that it warrants further consideration. And we can console ourselves with the knowledge that our American counterparts face the same obstacles—and their commitment to this war has never been as great as ours."

49

A sphere the diameter of a giant oak,'" said Jack. "You're certain that's what he said?"

Diebner nodded, miserable and spent.

"A giant oak tree," Jack enunciated. *"Eine riesige Eiche."*

Diebner turned to Stefan and said, in German, "This is the best America offers? It's a miracle they won the war."

The sound of thick boots in the portico announced the arrival of Pash, whose patience had run out. Epstein met him at the door.

"He's got him," said Pash. "What the hell are we wasting time for?"

Epstein handed Pash a quickly scribbled message. "We need you to authorize an urgent dispatch to Leavenworth."

"Dr. Diebner," Jack said, "would you please take a look at this and tell me what it means?" He unrolled the last page of the lab notes and indicated an equation near the bottom.

"It appears to be a record of an experiment done by my colleague and—and Dr. Weiss. March tenth, 1938. They seem to have produced a sustained chain reaction using enriched uranium in the amount of…it says eighty micrograms."

"So the mighty oak," Jack said, "it's more like an acorn, I guess."

"No. That isn't possible." Puzzled, Kurt looked up at Stefan, his eyelid twitching in disbelief.

"If eighty micrograms produced that result," said Jack, "how much enriched uranium would really be required to destroy London?" He found the metal paperweight, exactly as Hannah had described it, on top of the piano and tossed it to Stefan. "Do you want to tell him or shall I?"

"*Verräter!*" Diebner lunged at Stefan, his face a mask of grief and rage.

Jack suspected that, for Diebner—more egotist than patriot—the gut punch was the realization that he'd been wrong about the science. Duped by a woman. By a Jew.

50

SUBJECT: SITE Y PERSONNEL FINAL REPORT

To: Donovan

From: Delaney

SUMMARY: Agents of this detachment have concluded investigation into Site Y personnel. In agreement with our findings, COL. PASH and GEN. GROVES have signed off on the following: (a) Neither Reich nor Soviet nuclear efforts have proven successful on anything remotely approaching the scale of Manhattan Project; (b) DRS. HANNAH WEISS and STEFAN FREI successfully colluded to cripple Reich nuclear efforts, ensuring U.S. military will remain for some time the only entity in possession of a weapon capable of destruction at this magnitude. PASH holding FREI, DIEBNER, and associates at Farm Hall, England, until tribunal convenes. OPPENHEIMER demanding immediate return of DR. WEISS to Site Y, where her presence is required for final preparations for TRINITY test, anticipated mid-July.

RECOMMENDATION: Give OPPIE what he wants before he bursts a blood vessel in his Adam's apple.

51

Jack watched from the driver's seat of his Buick as thunderheads roiled low over the mesas in Jornada del Muerto, sending down trickles of heat lightning that seemed to connect with the earth just centimeters from the gadget. A crane hoisted the metallic casing, held together with strips of electrical tape, into the air by inches while a uniformed team steered its progress with guide wires. Beneath the tower, exactly where the gadget was expected to fall, Jack noticed a truckload of piled mattresses, which struck him as being almost as useful as cotton batting around a blowtorch. In sharp contrast with his last visit, hundreds of personnel were scrambling to and fro anxiously, setting up spectrograph cameras, ensuring the safety of the viewing platforms.

"What's the status?" Groves called out.

"We may have to postpone," Oppenheimer called back. "The

lightning could set off a premature detonation. Any rain would increase the danger of radiation and fallout."

A bevy of nervous scientists stood by as two GIs steadied the collared sphere that shifted and moaned in the buffeting wind, swinging from a triad of long chains. It was an impressive object, though nowhere near as grand as the bomb core Diebner had envisioned in his presentation to Speer. It had been six weeks since Jack handed Diebner over to Pash, but it still brought a grim smile to Jack's dry lips, the way Diebner's face had fallen as he stared at Stefan and Hannah's equations.

"Ah, Jesus. You again." Groves approached, shading his eyes from a brief flare of the fiery afternoon sun as he gazed up at a white tent being raised high into the air as a shelter for the gadget and the scientists who worked on it.

"Pleasure to see you too, General."

"How was Dooshland?"

"Mixed bag."

Groves honked an ungainly snort of amusement. "You can tell me about it over a bottle of champagne later."

Jack said, "I'm not sure I feel like celebrating."

"Then stay out of my way." Groves scrambled onto the platform, leaving Jack to decide if he wanted to follow him and get a closer look or retreat to the earth-bermed bunker five miles off where Oppenheimer and his team were readying the grand experiment and the state-of-the-art camera equipment that would capture the event and replay it for posterity. Split the difference, he decided, and found an upturned crate where he could sit and smoke as he waited for the sun to go down. Hannah would be at the bunker, and Jack wasn't sure he was ready to face her. Since her release from Leavenworth, he'd observed her through a discreet haze of intelligence chatter and cold dispatches, determined to keep his distance. There were growing rumors of a rocket program, the potential for space travel in the distant future, and Jack had seen Hannah's name on a list of scientists being vetted for recruitment.

Night fell, and Jack drove out across the desert to 10K West, one of the four bunkers placed at the four compass points, each an equal ten thousand feet from ground zero. As he drove, he passed hundreds of servicemen hunkering behind embankments several sandbags high. Their faces, rubbed with zinc oxide, glowed ghostly white, and the absurdity of it all—an increasing sense of futility combined with too much nicotine, hunger, and a hard slug of whiskey from his silver flask—spurred a bitter twinge of heartburn at the bottom of Jack's gullet.

At the bunker, preparations continued through the night. A little after three in the morning, Jack put out his last cigarette and stepped inside. Deep in conversation with Oppie and Reichl, Hannah didn't see him come in. Jack found a shadowed corner from which to observe her checking and rechecking instrumentation and kibitzing with the small band of handpicked witnesses. She wore a pair of khaki pants and a white blouse, its short sleeves rolled up to her shoulders; her hair had grown out and was now a close-cropped thatch of tousled curls. She'd regained some color and substance, but she looked as dog-tired as the rest of her fatigued colleagues. Someone offered her a cup of coffee, and when she turned to accept it, she saw Jack. Emotions flitted in rapid succession across her face—tenderness, gratitude, and maybe something else. Jack was ready to know. She made her way toward him in the crowded space.

"Dr. Weiss."

"Lieutenant Colonel Delaney."

"I'm going by Abramson now."

Hannah hugged him and kissed his cheek. "Oppie tells me you managed to upset General Groves, Wild Bill Donovan, and J. Edgar Hoover all at the same time. Quite a juggling act."

"Meh." Jack mocked a modest shrug. "Actually, they've each asked me to join them. There's a lot of call in government work for someone who's mastered the arts of blackmail and subterfuge."

"So you finally made it to the inner circle."

"Maybe. Although I might find a way to put my skills to better use."

"I don't doubt it." Hannah set her cool hand on the side of Jack's face. "You found a way to protect me. Thank you, Jakob."

Jack covered her hand with his and turned his mouth toward her palm for the length of a heartbeat. "One final question?"

"I love him. I always will," said Hannah. "But in a different time and place, if Hannah had met Jakob…"

"I would have…" Jack's bittersweet smile told her the rest.

"And I would have let you."

Hannah squeezed his hand amid the bustle and excitement of the bunker, and Jack savored it for what it was—their unspoken goodbye—before he turned away from everything he might have had with her. There was no bitterness in it, to his surprise, because the next moment held the realization that he was still capable of feeling something he'd stopped believing in a long, long time ago.

Hannah rejoined Oppenheimer and was immediately and fully reengaged with her work. Shortly before five in the morning, Oppenheimer, Reichl, and the rest of their team slathered on sunscreen. Jack followed suit and found a place to stand out of their way.

On a steel table at the center of the bunker, Otto Frisch opened a metal box, revealing a series of switches. He closed his eyes, and after a deep inhale followed by a slow exhale, he flipped the first switch, arming the device. A red light appeared on the switchbox above it, and a corresponding red light appeared at the perimeter of the tower in the distance. A flare went up from the sandbags. The men moved gas masks over their faces and lay down, one man next to another, nut to butt, stretching across the desert in a seemingly endless row of bodies. The scientists donned specially engineered sunglasses and goggles. The cameramen raised thick sheets of welding glass. Oppenheimer set his goggles in place and moved to the center window slot, silent, taciturn.

There was nothing to see; the night was black as pitch, even though late-evening storm clouds had dissipated on the wind. The clock on the wall ticked toward zero. Jack closed his eyes, remembering the heft of the metallic paperweight in his hand.

The inside of the bunker went brilliant white, then blood orange, then violet, then amber. There was a long, rolling howl— a deafening choir of oncoming fate—and then a wall of wind that slammed into the shuddering bunker. Oppenheimer staggered back, his face distorted by the blast, looking as if an epic struggle of demons and angels raged beneath the surface, threatening to tear the gaunt skin from his skull. It hardly seemed possible that there would be anything left after that moment, but the next moment ticked into being, and the next, and, years later, Jack would hear Oppenheimer describe it to a television camera:

"We knew the world would not be the same. A few people laughed. A few people cried. Most people were silent. I remembered the line from the Hindu scripture, the Bhagavad Gita. Vishnu is trying to persuade the prince that he should do his duty, and to impress him, he takes on his multi-armed form and says, 'Now I am become death, the destroyer of worlds.' I suppose we all thought that, one way or another."

52

The sky over Berlin as it might have been, a city of sterling ideals and unbroken glass. Beneath the copper turrets of Kaiser Wilhelm, lovers carousel around and around the ballroom: Gregor and Annalise, Ulrike and Lotte, Stefan and me. Below our light feet, Einstein's laboratory waits, a silent cocoon from which brilliant blue wings are destined to unfold. In the park, Joshua plays chess with a neighbor who was never required to hate him. On the street, Sabine and her young man distribute leaflets for an art opening.

And then I wake to the world as it is.

The city herself is divided now. "Build a wall," say the bellicose few to the obedient many, so they build a wall and consign their children to spend their lives by it, guarding their fractured country. In the west, we hear stories of how the Stasi control every facet of life in the Soviet-dominated German Democratic Republic to the east, but in the evening, at a covertly arranged time, housewives on one side of the wall and housewives on the other all wash their windows simultaneously, waving white flags that can be seen from the guard towers. This small but meaningful gesture gives me hope that someday Germany will be free and whole again. I suspect it will be a very long time.

Stefan and I returned to Haigerloch 122 days after Hiroshima—and I know this because Hiroshima is the time stamp from which Stefan and I date all events, however significant or insignificant. We found the house battered and looted but basically intact. A shattered gable in the bedroom upstairs had invited in rain, snow, the substantial branches of a toppled pine tree, and all the creatures who lived in it. We carried out the mossy mattress and slept the first night on a bed of dry leaves. It felt like an appropriate form of shivah: an acknowledgment of how loss had humbled us, a bowing-down to the sovereignty of death. We held each other, weeping for the scorched world and for our part in this terrible reckoning. In the morning, we cleared the overgrown ivy from the windows of the solarium lab and let the light in. Standing at the center of the clean-swept floor, I said, "What shall we work on first?"

"A girl," said Stefan. "Or a boy."

I smiled, touched by his hopefulness. "I don't know," I told him, "if I have enough confidence in the world."

As the years went by, neither of us spoke of this possibility again, and I was secretly relieved to feel that door close inside myself. Our life together is centered on the work we have in common along with a mutually respectful tenderness. In the absence of a family, we are without roles, without religion, and this suits us. We forgive and care for each other in a way we're not capable of forgiving or caring for ourselves. We are both consumed by *tikkun olam,* the work of rebuilding the world, which—like the work of rebuilding the house at Haigerloch—is daunting and sometimes requires a strong stomach for self-examination.

West Germany, the Federal Republic of Germany, is a capitalist democracy. East Germany, the German Democratic Republic, is a socialist republic built, in theory, on all the noble notions for which Sabine risked her life. I remember her quoting Karl Marx: "The philosophers have only interpreted the world in various ways. The point, however, is to change it." Stefan is more pragmatic; he quotes Sir Isaac Newton: "I can calculate the motion of heavenly bodies but not the madness of people." It seems to me that these two statements are the sum of all politics, and I'm comforted knowing that these two opposing *Weltanschauungen*—two disparate views of our one world— are espoused by two people I love, each taking a different side, which makes love the common denominator.

I have loved. I love. I will always love. Little else about my life survived Leavenworth. Most of my belongings were disposed of, or so I was told, but one summer morning, 654 days after Hiroshima, I received by messenger a small silver box. It took me a moment to recognize the tarnished receptacle, but when I opened it and saw the jeweled night moths, it was like seeing an old friend at the garden gate. Stefan gathered my hair in his hands and tucked the comb in to secure a French twist above the nape of my neck.

"Back where it belongs," he said. "But what's this?"

Cradled in the velvet beneath the comb lay a small, copper-colored object, the size of something one might find on a charm bracelet; it looked like a stubby stem topped by a splay of delicately curled petals.

"I think it's meant to be a mushroom," I said, weighing the strange item in my hand. "Or maybe a lily."

Stefan held the little totem up to the light and examined it with the innate curiosity of an intelligent child.

"It's a bullet," he said. "One that apparently served its purpose."

53

FIELD NOTE
CONFIDENTIAL

September 27, 1949

SUMMARY: (1) Mossad operative GISELLA PROUST reported via encrypted message to CIA contact: OPERATION EDEL-WEISS has commenced per objectives set forth in initial briefing. (2) PROUST's participation is conditional, pending your personal guarantee of the following: (a) financial and logistical support for transfer of the remains of her father, JOSHUA WEISS to Israel; (b) permanent access to Paris apartment at 29 rue des Rosiers; (c) continued deep-cover status.

RECOMMENDATION: Jack, I figure you'll want to handle this one personally.

AUTHOR'S NOTE

While some of the characters who appear in this book were inspired by historical figures, it is important to stress that this story is fiction and that the portraits of the characters in it are fictional.

There are two compelling questions at the heart of *Hannah's War*. The first one was embedded in the August 7, 1945, issue of the *New York Times*—the day after the United States dropped the atomic bomb on Hiroshima. In the *Times'* summation of the complex and secret history of the Manhattan Project, this sentence leaped from the back pages:

"The key component that allowed the Allies to develop the bomb was brought to the Allies by a female, 'non-Aryan,' physicist."

Who was this woman, I wondered, and why had I never heard of her? So began my years-long quest to shed light on the story of Dr. Lise Meitner, the woman who discovered nuclear fission and has been erased (as so many great women have been) from history. Meitner's story plunged me deeply into research about the development of the atomic bomb and the physics that propelled it.

The second question has remained unanswered for seventy-five years: Why did the Germans never develop an atomic bomb?

It's tempting to assume that the United States, victorious, had succeeded in creating the bomb because of its citizens' tenacity, ingenuity, and moral authority. What I discovered, however, was that the mad, almost desperate engine behind the Manhattan Project was the unthinkable possibility that the Germans would get it first. This weapon of unimaginable destruction would be placed in the hands of Hitler, a man who had no compunction about using it. Yet when the German scientists were captured, they had nothing, not even the most primitive atomic pile. Why? Many have suggested explanations, but the only man who could truly answer that question, Dr. Werner Heisenberg, the head of the German's bomb program, took the information to his grave.

These two mysteries are the poles between which I wove my story.

In writing this novel, I worked to adhere to the chronology and geography of history. I've tried to be accurate in historical details, especially details about real figures like J. Robert Oppenheimer and General Leslie Groves.

I absorbed facts from many exceptional biographies, historical texts, interviews, documentaries, diaries, letters, and archival films. The resources below were touchstones in my research and would be fascinating for anyone wanting to know more about this extraordinary era and its morally compromised, tragic heroes.

Although inspired by two historical characters—Dr. Lise Meitner and Dr. Werner Heisenberg—everything else in *Hannah's War* is the product of my imagination.

AUTHOR'S NOTE

FURTHER EXPLORATION

Bird, Kai, and Martin Sherwin. *American Prometheus: The Triumph and Tragedy of J. Robert Oppenheimer.* New York: Alfred A. Knopf, 2005.

Conant, Jennet. *109 East Palace: Robert Oppenheimer and the Secret City at Los Alamos.* New York: Simon and Schuster, 2005.

Dyson, Freeman. *Disturbing the Universe.* New York: Harper and Row, 1979.

Else, Jon H., dir. *The Day After Trinity.* Documentary. New York: PBS, 1981.

Frank, Charles. *Operation Epsilon: The Farm Hall Transcripts.* Berkeley: University of California Press, 1993.

Frankenberger, Stefan, and Elizabeth Orth, eds. *Yours, Lise: The Physicist Lise Meitner in Exile* (audio CD). Leipzig: Buchfunk Verlag, 2018.

Frayn, Michael. *Copenhagen.* London: Methuen Drama, 1998.

Kelly, Cynthia C., ed. "Voices of the Manhattan Project" (website), April 11, 2018. http://www.atomicheritage.org.

Medawar, Jean, and David Pyke. *Hitler's Gift: The True Story of the Scientists Expelled by the Nazi Regime.* New York: Arcade, 2001.

Norris, Robert A. *Racing for the Bomb: General Leslie R. Groves, the Manhattan Project's Indispensable Man.* South Royalton, VT: Steerforth, 2002.

Powers, Thomas. *Heisenberg's War: The Secret History of the German Bomb.* Cambridge, MA: Da Capo, 2000.

Rhodes, Richard. *The Making of the Atomic Bomb.* New York: Simon and Schuster, 1986.

Sime, Ruth Lewin. *Lise Meitner: A Life in Physics.* Berkeley: University of California Press, 1996.

ACKNOWLEDGMENTS

Hannah's War wouldn't exist if it hadn't been for the woman who discovered nuclear fission, Dr. Lise Meitner. Because she was a Jewish woman in a world dominated by men, her name was erased, even by her scientific partner, who was awarded a Nobel Prize for their collaborative discovery. It was her story, buried in the back pages of the *New York Times,* that inspired me to begin this journey. I hope *Hannah's War* does Dr. Meitner justice and gives her some of the recognition she so richly deserves.

Ruth Lewin Sime, author of *Lise Meitner: A Life in Physics,* offered extraordinary resources and support; she spent hours reading drafts and responding to my work, checking the physics and the historical record. The liberties taken in the novel are mine; the truth of Meitner's life is best found in Ruth's wonderful book.

Studying the plays of Shakespeare, Brecht, Ibsen, and the Greeks provided me with the best possible foundation in story structure; to my colleagues at the Yale Drama School—Ming Cho Lee, Robert Brustein, Andrei Belgrader, Stanley Kauffmann, Ben

Cameron, Frances McDormand, John Madden, Doug Stein, Tony Shalhoub, John Turturro, and Kathie Borowitz—thank you for being exceptional collaborators and teachers.

I'm grateful beyond words to visionary poet and teacher Ellen Bryant Voigt for founding the MFA Program for Writers at Warren Wilson College. My four years working one on one with mentors Charles Baxter, Joan Silber, Antonya Nelson, and Mary Elsie Robertson provided a fellowship devoted to the power of the written word and gave me, when the time came, the patience and confidence to face down the blank page and know that, eventually, the right words would come.

My deep gratitude to my manager, Ava Jamshidi at Industry Entertainment, for seeing the novelist trapped in a director's body and for having the foresight to introduce my work to book agent Adriann Ranta Zurhellen at the Foundry. Few debut authors can possibly be as lucky as I was in having a terrific agent like Adriann convinced that, if I wrote a novel, she could sell it. And, true to her word, she did.

The word *midwife* comes from an old English word meaning "with woman." Since women have been birth attendants throughout history, midwives have existed for as long as babies have been born. In history, midwives ran the risk of being accused of witchcraft. By that definition, Joni Rodgers is the midwife to *Hannah's War*—with a bit of the witch in her as well. She created a magical cocoon by the ocean, the Westport Lighthouse Writers Retreat; it was the ideal place to give birth, and Joni was the midwife I both wanted and needed by my side.

I've cited many of the most important research sources in my

ACKNOWLEDGMENTS

author's note, but there are two people I'd like to single out for special mention: Cynthia C. Kelly, who created the "Voices of the Manhattan Project Archives" for the Atomic Heritage Foundation, and Jerry Hanks, a self-styled Manhattan Project "brat." Jerry shared his memories of growing up on the Los Alamos base while his father, a metallurgical engineer, helped develop the atomic bombs that the B-29 *Enola Gay* dropped on Hiroshima. Jerry not only generously shared his own knowledge but also opened many doors and made countless essential introductions.

Early readers, friends, champions: Deborah Kampmeier; Deborah Stern; Linda Lichter; Rhonda Bloom; Sara Grace; Meghan Scibona; Amy Bloom; Paul Vidich; Martha Hall Kelly; Kate Quinn; Elinor Renfield; Ellen Gesmer; Amy Rosenthal; Maria Geise; Geoff Parkhurst; F. X. Feeney; Eva Aridjis; Catherine Dent; designer Adrian Kinloch; my brother and sister, Peter and Kristin Eliasberg; my mother, Ann Pringle; and my father, Jay Eliasberg, who, although he didn't live to see the book completed, always believed I could do it.

When I finished the manuscript, my wildest dream was that it would be published. That the book would be edited by the peerless Judy Clain and published by Little, Brown was beyond the realm of my imaginings. Every note Judy gave me was wise and insightful and raised the bar, inspiring me to make the book better with each revision. Judy assembled a dream team to usher the novel into the universe; she may have spoiled me for life. Lucy Kim designed a book jacket so stunning I gasped aloud when I saw it, Nicole Dewey and Maggie Southard have been the book's PR geniuses, and Tracy Roe copyedited every sentence, every word, with both passion and care.

From the initial idea, through obsessive research, to final draft, *Hannah's War* took years of my time as well as my heart. If my daughter, Sariel Friedman, ever resented Hannah Weiss for causing me to be preoccupied, cranky, or distant, I never felt it. Sariel was my loudest cheerleader, my first and best reader, my most honest critic, and my fiercest protector. I wrote *Hannah's War* in part to show Sariel and her peers that history is filled with remarkable women of towering achievement and moral integrity; we need only look beyond the authorized texts in order to discover them.

I write to shine a light on those women, and I hope my work will be a beacon for women in my daughter's generation and beyond, helping them to live not only with authenticity and pride, but also with the support and acknowledgment of the wider world.

READING GROUP GUIDE

1. Jan Eliasberg has worked for years as a screenwriter and film director. How do you think her experience in film has influenced *Hannah's War*? Were there particular scenes or locations you were able to visualize distinctly? Who would you cast as Hannah, Stefan, and Jack?

2. Jack Delaney hides his identity for much of the novel. Although he is American, he is concerned that his religious background will negatively affect his career prospects. His colleague Aaron Epstein is open about his Jewish faith. How is Epstein treated differently? How do you think American attitudes toward Judaism have changed since 1940? Are there identities or opinions that you hide in your daily life? What compels you to withhold personal information?

3. When Jack first arrives at Los Alamos, he believes that the Axis informant is a male scientist. After registering that Hannah is a woman, he muses she is "a beautiful woman working in a world of lonely men." How does Hannah's gender influence her research and her presence in various laboratories?

4. What does the behavior of the other working women in the story—Alice Rivers at Los Alamos and Karin Hoenig at the Kaiser Wilhelm Institute in Berlin—say about gender norms in the 1930s and 1940s? How do their beliefs about their roles as women and their behavior shed light on Hannah? Were you at all surprised by the lack of or amount of agency these women were afforded?

5. Were you surprised by the revelation that Ulrike Diebner and Lotte Scheer were romantic partners? Contrary to many beliefs, Weimar Berlin was actually quite progressive; there were lesbian and gay magazines and newspapers as well as lesbian and gay clubs that were well known and well patronized. As the National Socialists took power, they marked homosexuals as "deviant" and lesbians as "amoral." The story of lesbians in Berlin and under the Nazis is one we rarely hear about; do the characters of Ulrike and Lotte intrigue you enough to learn more about that lost history?

6. Stefan Frei is a complex character, and Eliasberg gives us good reason to doubt his loyalty throughout the novel. Did you trust

Stefan to keep Hannah's secrets? German citizens are frequently portrayed negatively in Americans' retelling of World War II stories. What biases did you carry when you first met Stefan? How has your attitude changed since finishing the novel?

7. During her final months in Berlin, Hannah was almost constantly confronted with Nazi imagery and propaganda. In one scene, when Hannah calls Gregor Stern's house, she is forced to repeat "Heil Hitler" to the housekeeper lest she be found out as a Jew. How would you respond in that situation? How might you be complicit in racism in today's sociopolitical climate?

8. Hannah's brilliant research contributes to the atomic bombing of Hiroshima and Nagasaki, devastating events which helped to end World War II but also cost hundreds of thousands of innocent lives. Stefan and Hannah are deeply affected by the bombings and feel responsible for the deaths of many innocent people. How do you think Hannah reconciles those feelings of guilt? How do Americans continue to process this violent history? How does the threat of nuclear attack influence foreign policy in the twenty-first century?

9. Scientist Peter Reichl has organized a petition calling for ethical oversight of how the bomb is going to be used; in fact this

dissent is one of the reasons that Jack is sent to Los Alamos to find a spy. How did you understand the different levels of moral questioning and dissent in the characters of Reichl, Oppenheimer, and General Groves? Have you ever been in a position in which you were working for a cause or organization and came to question the ethics of the group? How did you handle those moral dilemmas?

10. Jack's investigation of Hannah becomes complicated when he begins to develop romantic feelings for her. Do you believe Hannah deliberately seduced Jack, or was she sincerely interested in getting to know him better? Were you surprised by how intimate and familiar their relationship became? Did their ending feel satisfying?

11. Sabine is a rebel, and she distributes controversial anti-fascist political leaflets throughout Berlin. She taunts Hannah's commitment to the resistance by saying, "It's hard to fight with your eyes closed." Did you sympathize with Sabine's radical activism? How would you fight oppression if you were in her position?

12. One of Eliasberg's goals in writing *Hannah's War* was to shed light on the story of Lise Meitner, the Austrian physicist who discovered nuclear fission. Although denied her share of the Nobel Prize (which was her due), she was an important pioneer for women in science. There has been a huge push for

more female scientists in recent years as the technology industry continues to blossom. Why do you think women are discouraged from pursuing STEM positions, and what can we do to inspire more young girls to join the fields?

13. Do you think that Hannah, as a woman, brings a different perspective to her research than the men in her field?

14. There are a number of instances in *Hannah's War* in which the United States makes morally questionable decisions: the Americans chose not to bomb the train tracks leading into Auschwitz (although they'd located them on aerial maps); they turned away the SS *St. Louis,* carrying hundreds of Jewish refugees; and, finally, the American military deliberately left Hiroshima and Nagasaki untouched so they could be used as civilian targets for the atomic bomb. How do you feel about this morally ambiguous view of America? How does that square with the accounts you studied in your history books?

15. *Hannah's War* ends in 1949, and we learn that Hannah and Stefan have decided not to have children. Where do you imagine their story is headed? What might Hannah think of the world today?

16. In the last field note—the book's very last chapter—it's revealed that Sabine, now called by her assumed name Gisella

Proust, is not only alive but has also been working with the Mossad. How do you think the character you knew as Sabine became an Israeli spy? Do you think Hannah would approve of the way her cousin developed and grew? Are you interested in that story?